Three men wanted her . . .

. . . *And why should they not? A dazzling young widow with an Austrian title, a Viennese fortune, a Paris wardrobe, and a beauty Venus herself might envy, Anthea was the toast of the London season.*

Phillip Montville offered her a home in her native land such as she had not known since her father's bitter quarrel with his family sent him and his young daughter off to the Peninsular wars . . .

Karl von Westendorf offered her an ancient lineage and the puff-pastry life of the Viennese waltz . . .

Lord Lyndock offered her his wit, charm, and the worst reputation in London. It was not a difficult choice for a sensible woman to make—but love has a mind of its own!

Also by Diana Delmore

Dorinda
*Leonie**
*Cassandra**

Published by
WARNER BOOKS

*forthcoming

Diana Delmore

WARNER BOOKS

A Warner Communications Company

All the characters and events portrayed in this story are fictitious.

WARNER BOOKS EDITION

This Warner Books Edition is published by arrangement with
Walker Publishing Company, Inc.,
720 Fifth Avenue, New York, New York 10019.

Warner Books, Inc.
666 Fifth Avenue
New York, N.Y. 10103

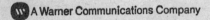 A Warner Communications Company

Printed in the United States of America

First Warner Books Printing: November, 1985

10 9 8 7 6 5 4 3 2 1

=1=

VAINLY ATTEMPTING TO peer through the blinding torrents of rain outside the carriage window, Anthea flinched as an earthshaking roll of thunder struck her ears. The accompanying wild flash of lightning illuminated the landscape, turning the autumn twilight into the brightness of midday. Anthea gasped as she caught a split-second glimpse of the chasm yawning at the side of the road, mere inches separating the wheels from a steep plunge to destruction far below.

The carriage shuddered to a sudden stop, and the thin, elderly lady sitting beside Anthea—huddled in the voluminous folds of her cloak—roused herself from a nap. "What is it? Why have we stopped?" she asked.

The carriage door opened and two faces, streaming with rain, peered inside. John Potter, Anthea's sturdy, middle-aged head groom, touched his finger to his sodden cap. "Tree down across the road, Miss Anthea. Don't rightly know if Luigi here"—he motioned to the anxious-faced Italian guide, the *veturino*, who had been driving the heavy berlin and making all the travel arrangements for Anthea's tour of Italy—"don't know if Luigi and I and Josef between us can move it out of the way. It's a proper huge tree."

"Oh," said Anthea blankly. "What can we do if the tree can't be moved? Surely there's no room to turn around on this narrow road."

"Well, now, there's a very small clearing just short of the fallen tree, but I dunno if even Luigi can manage a turnaround there.

Best thing to do, I'd guess, if we can't move the tree, is for Luigi and me to walk back to that little inn that we passed a bit ago and get help. You and Hannah will be all right, with Josef staying to watch over you . . ." He paused, turning his head to listen intently to the sudden sound of confused shouting and the sharp crack of gunfire. "What the devil . . ." he muttered. "Come along, Luigi, we'd best see what's amiss."

Moments after John's departure, over the noise of the rain pounding on the carriage roof, Anthea heard a scream of pain, followed by a burst of raucous laughter. Clutching at Anthea's arm, Hannah whispered fearfully, "What could it be, Miss Anthea?"

"I don't know, Hannah, but I'm certainly going to try to find out," declared Anthea with sudden resolution. She reached for her reticule on the seat beside her, plunging her hand inside it to retrieve the tiny pistol that she always carried with her on her journeys.

"You're never going to use that nasty thing!" squealed Hannah, grabbing at her mistress's arm.

"I am," replied Anthea, far more calmly than she really felt. "I'll not sit here while John and Luigi and Josef are in danger." Pulling free of the elderly abigail's hands, she opened the carriage door and prepared to climb out.

"Miss Anthea, don't go out there," wailed Hannah. "You could be killed or kidnapped—"

"Nonsense, I could be killed just as easily in the carriage," snapped Anthea, her exasperation momentarily overcoming the fear that she shared with Hannah. She stepped down into the roadway, wincing as the raw wind blasted furiously against her face. She kept her eyes carefully averted from the chasm opening to her left as she edged her body along the side of the carriage and past the nervously pawing team. She was obliged to pull strongly with each step to free her feet from the claylike mud of the road.

Emerging into the roadway in front of the horses and the carriage, she stood transfixed, staring at the scene in the little clearing. For a fleeting moment she had the sensation of observing a static tableau: In the light of the flaring torch held high by an unshaven, roughly-clad man, she could see the crumpled body of her young groom, Josef. Nearby, another bandit—so she assumed he was—had just planted a kick into a prostrate and quivering Luigi. Still another man had seized John Potter, holding him immobile by twisting his arm behind his back. Anthea's curiously dreamlike sensation that time was standing still was shattered abruptly when a pair of arms pinioned her from behind, holding her so tightly that her breath was roughly expelled from her lungs.

A tall man materialized before her—bearded and dressed in shabby, dirty clothes—and now Anthea could see that the bandits numbered at least five, including the man who was holding her.

"*Ebbene*, what have we got here?" the man said in Italian, which Anthea understood well. He leered, the smile revealing rotting teeth. "Something extra for us this time, comrades. The last lady that we stopped was at least sixty years old and shaped like a butter vat." He plucked the little pistol from her fingers, examining it with a chuckle before dropping it into his pocket, and reached out a hand to grasp her chin. Anthea tried desperately to turn her head away from him, shuddering as she caught the stench of old perspiration and the powerful smell of garlic. She had learned his language during her stays on her late husband's estates in the Tyrol. But even if she had had no knowledge of Italian, the man's calculating eyes and avid mouth would have made his intentions unmistakable.

"There's no need for this fellow to keep his filthy hands on me," she said coldly, keeping her voice level by the greatest effort of self-control. "No need, either, to maltreat my servants. You'll find my money in my reticule inside the carriage. Take it and allow us to continue our journey."

"So you've got more than a beautiful face and a gorgeous body," the man exclaimed with a coarse laugh as he tore open Anthea's hooded pelisse. "You've got spirit too. I'll wager that you really would have tried to shoot me with your little popgun. I like that. It will make our little encounter so much more interesting."

The rain was coming down with renewed force, beating against Anthea's face and rapidly drenching the front of her thin gown so that it clung revealingly to her body. "I repeat," she said steadily, despite the man's scorching gaze raking her from neck to knee, "take my purse and leave us to go about our affairs."

The man laughed again. "*Grazie, signorina.* That will do to begin with. Paolo"—he motioned to one of his men—"go get the lady's purse from the carriage." He turned back to Anthea. "And we'll just take this too," he grinned, wrenching the gold and diamond necklace from Anthea's throat and leaving her gasping for the moment from the sudden pain of it. He peered at the necklace, squinting his eyes from the driving rain, before stuffing it, too, into a pocket. "Very pretty, *la mia bella signorina.* Where's the rest of it?"

"I don't know what you mean," said Anthea, shivering from the cold and tossing her head in an attempt to keep the hood of her pelisse from flopping over her eyes.

The man who had been sent to fetch her reticule returned now from the carriage, handing the purse to his leader. "There's an old lady in the carriage, too," the man chuckled; "she took one look at me and fainted dead away from fright."

After running a practised hand through the heavy coins in Anthea's reticule, the bandit leader added them to the rest of Anthea's possessions in his pocket. "*Bene.* But as I was saying, *signorina,* where's the rest of it? And don't play the innocent. You know very well what I mean. You did not start on a journey across Italy with nothing more than a handful of coins to pay your way."

"There's a letter of credit in my trunk," retorted Anthea, "but it will scarcely be of any use to you. You can't imagine that I would be so stupid as to travel with large sums of money in a country where I might frequently encounter thieving villains like yourself!"

The bandit leader showed his dreadful teeth in a thin smile. "Thieves and villains we are, *signorina*, and we know how to get what we want. Now, I could take you aside—your carriage might be a good place—and eventually you'd tell me where the rest of your money is. But with your spirit that might take a little time, and my men are cold and wet and want to get under shelter. So we'll take a shortcut. Paolo," he shouted, "put a rope around the old man's neck and string him up to a tree."

Even as she had spoken, Anthea had realized that she was being both foolish and foolhardy: sewn carefully into the lining of her heavy pelisse was an ample supply of gold coins, a precaution, during her travels, against the tardy arrival of a bill of exchange, or an emergency requiring funds in towns where she had not arranged for a letter of credit. Her instinctive first thought had been to deny these scruffy bandits any further profits beyond the contents of her reticule and her diamond necklace, but she knew that this was sheer madness on her part. Even the loss of a small fortune in gold meant nothing compared to her safety and that of her servants. She glanced at the face of her elderly groom, slack-jawed with terror, his skin paper white in the dim light of the torch, as the bandit Paolo placed a noose around his neck. "Wait," she exclaimed. "Don't hurt my groom. I'll tell you where the money is."

"I'm sure that you will, *signorina*. But we'll just make sure that you don't change your mind, or try to hold back a few coins or a favorite bit of jewelry. Paolo, that oak tree over there has a nice handy branch—hoist the old fellow up."

"No, no, I beg you, don't hang him," cried Anthea frantically. "I swear, I won't hold anything back, I'll gladly give you everything I have—see, my money is all sewn into the lining of my pelisse here."

Later, Anthea would never be certain whether the bandit leader had actually planned to hang John Potter; perhaps he was only indulging in the savage pleasure of observing the groom's fear and Anthea's anguish, prolonging the cruel suspense until the last moment, when he might have intended to let Potter go free. But even as Paolo, having dragged the gibbering groom over to the oak tree, threw the rope over a branch and tugged on it just enough to lift Potter's heels from the ground, the sound of a shot cracked sharply in the air and Paolo collapsed without even a moan.

Before Paolo's startled companions could raise their weapons, a second shot downed the man holding Anthea, and a voice rang, clearly over the noise of wind and rain, calling out in heavily accented Italian, "We have you surrounded—throw down your guns and put your hands in the air or we'll shoot the lot of you."

Making an involuntary move toward the pistol in his belt, the bandit leader froze as a third shot lifted the battered hat off his head. With a muttered curse he threw up his arms. His unwounded men had already dropped their weapons. Moments later a tall man wearing a beaver hat and a long, many-caped greatcoat strode into the clearing, a large pistol in either hand. Casting a swift glance around him, he called to Anthea in Italian, "Are you all right, *signorina*?"

"Yes, oh, yes—but my servants . . ."

"We'll see to them as soon as may be. Meanwhile, do you think you could collect the weapons that these nasty thugs have scattered about? Begin with the pistol in the belt of the ugly fellow next to you."

Feeling curiously light-headed, Anthea found herself obeying the stranger's orders almost without conscious thought. She jerked the gun away from the bandit leader, drawing away hastily as she glimpsed the naked savagery in his eyes, and darted about the clearing, picking up the guns that the other bandits had thrown down. As she bent to grasp the pistol next to the lifeless hand of Paolo, she noted with a shudder that there was a gaping wound in his temple. Rising, she reached out a comforting hand to John Potter, who was shakily loosening the heavy noose from about his throat.

"Don't worry, Miss Anthea, I'll be fine," said the groom, attempting a smile.

Using her sodden skirt as a receptacle, Anthea carried her cache of guns over to her rescuer, who had stood with both pistols at the ready, his alert eyes raking the clearing, until she had completed her task.

"*Grazie, signorina*. Just put the guns down behind me. Now, you misbegotten villains," he said in his execrable Italian, motioning to the bandits, "I'll give you five seconds to get out of here before I start shooting again."

"But . . ." stammered Anthea, breaking into English without thinking as she watched the three remaining bandits scurry for their lives up the precipitous wooded slopes of the little clearing, "I don't understand. Why are you letting them go? Why don't you bring your men in here, tie up the bandits and hold them for the police?"

"For a very good reason, ma'am," retorted the man, switching to incisive English. "I *have* no men, and I think that it would be damned awkward to attempt to hold prisoners without sufficient guard in this weather and in this terrain."

"You're alone?" gasped Anthea.

"Practically so, ma'am. My groom is back there with our horses. We came upon your carriage blocking the road, or so we thought, and we were considering how we might make our way around it when we noticed that you appeared to be in some difficulty." A sudden wild gust of wind whipped the capes of his greatcoat over his hat and he said contritely, "I'm not using the few wits that God gave me. You're soaked through and dying from the cold. Pray allow me to help you into your carriage."

Acutely conscious of her drenched garments and a bone-deep shivering that was wracking her body, Anthea allowed herself to be drawn toward the berlin. "You'll see to my servants? John seems all right, but Josef and Luigi . . ."

"I'll take care of them, ma'am, but right now we must get you under shelter. I'll be back to report to you as soon as possible."

Inside the traveling coach Anthea found a dazed Hannah, evidently just recovering from the deep swoon into which she had been thrown by the frightening apparition of the bandit Paolo. "Miss Anthea," she exclaimed as she gazed in horror at her

11

mistress's disheveled condition. "What's happened to you? Who was that dreadful man who stole your reticule?"

"We were attacked by bandits, Hannah, but they've all gone now. For the love of heaven, get me out of this wet pelisse and toss me that lap robe before I die of cold."

Anthea was fully engaged for the next few minutes, blotting her wet gown with Hannah's shawl, then enveloping herself in the warm carriage rug while she attempted to answer the abigail's excited questions. Before she could begin to worry again about Josef and Luigi the carriage door opened, and she looked up into a pair of intensely brown eyes in a handsome, strong-boned face topped by curling chestnut hair. In the flickering light cast by the carriage lamp she was seeing her rescuer clearly for the first time.

"Your servants will survive handily, ma'am," he said in reply to her questioning gaze. "The younger groom—Josef, is that his name?—has a flesh wound in his arm, and the older fellow will have a sore throat for some days, that's all. The veturino is suffering more from fright than anything else."

Anthea breathed a deep sigh of relief. "Thank God. I thought for a time that all of us would surely be murdered. And my thanks to you, too, sir, for rescuing us. It's a near miracle that you came upon us at all—we've seen no other travellers for several hours, not since we took the turning for Pavia. You'd think that there would be more traffic on the main Genoa to Milan road, but—" She paused in some confusion, fearing that the mild relief occasioned by the ending of her ordeal with the bandits was causing her to speak incoherently. She noticed suddenly that the rain was pouring like a miniature waterfall down her rescuer's neck from the curling brim of his beaver hat, and she said hastily, "Please do excuse me for chattering on so while you stand outside in this dreadfully inclement weather. Won't you sit inside with us while we talk?"

"Well, I won't deny, ma'am, that it would be pleasant to take shelter for a spell." He climbed into the berlin, making the space inside seem even more confined, and Anthea realized that he was an extremely large and powerful man. "As to this being the main

12

Genoa to Milan road," he resumed, "I've been thinking about that. Even granting that Italian roads are the worst in the civilised world, still, it's hard to believe that this miserable cart track can be the main road to Milan. No, I fancy that we'll discover that the road signs were switched at the Pavia turn-off. Very likely the bandits who attacked you have waylaid many another traveller at this particular spot."

"You may be right," agreed Anthea thoughtfully. "Luigi—my veturino—has never guided a tour to this part of Italy before, and in this dreadful weather it would have been very easy for him not to recognise that the sign had been changed."

"Exactly so. I took the turning myself without the slightest feeling of uncertainty." He broke into laughter, his dark eyes dancing with golden lights. "Pray accept my apologies, ma'am," he begged with a smile of incandescent charm, as he observed Anthea's look of offended surprise. "It just struck me as so strange —ludicrous, really—for two complete strangers, only moments before in imminent danger of injury or death, to be calmly discussing the state of Italian roads."

Anthea's own smile was somewhat strained, but she replied readily, "There's no need to apologise, sir. I'm much too grateful for your timely help. As to our being strangers, we can certainly remedy that. I am"—despite herself, she hesitated for a fraction of a second—"I am Frau Steinach, and this is my abigail, Hannah Simms."

"Frau Steinach," he repeated. Was there an almost imperceptible lift of one eyebrow? "Somehow I assumed—but no matter. Allow me to introduce myself. Geoffrey Stretton, at your service. Now, ma'am, I've intruded myself on you not merely to inform you that your attackers have fled but to discuss with you what steps we should take to extricate ourselves from our predicament."

"But I had thought—now that there are at least five of you, can't you lift the fallen tree from the road? John even suggested that Luigi might be able to turn the team in the clearing."

Stretton shook his head. "Even if your horses had wings, your veturino couldn't turn them in that space. As to lifting the

13

tree—none of your three servants is feeling very stout. Even if they were healthier I doubt that we could move the tree. It will take several mules with strong ropes to do that. I'd like to suggest that we leave your carriage here and take rooms for the night in that small inn that we passed several miles back. By morning the storm should be over and it will be much easier to organise a relief expedition."

Quailing inwardly at the thought of traversing the treacherously narrow mountain road on horseback, in rapidly falling darkness and buffeted by flailing wind and rain, Anthea could only say with as much calm as she could muster, "That sounds like the most sensible thing that we could do, Mr. Stretton. Let us leave immediately. I'm anxious to get my servants under shelter as soon as possible."

The greasy-looking proprietor gaped in amazement as the travel-worn, completely drenched procession filed forlornly into the public room of his tiny inn some two hours later. As Luigi, gesticulating widely, discussed their requirements with the proprietor, Geoffrey Stretton murmured to Anthea, "I have a strong suspicion that the innkeeper is a confederate of the bandits who attacked us—or, at the very least, is fully aware of their activities. We'd best keep our eyes open tonight. My man has a pistol, and so, I've observed, does your head groom." He paused abruptly, eying Anthea with a rueful smile. "My apologies, ma'am. I was speaking without thinking. I've no wish to cause you anxiety. Doubtless the bandits are far too demoralised to mount another attack tonight."

Shrugging, Anthea said carelessly, "Thank you, Mr. Stretton, but I'm not at all concerned. I do wish, however," she added, "that that dreadful man—the bandit leader, I mean—hadn't escaped with my own pistol as well as my reticule and necklace."

"I'm sorry—I should have searched the ruffian before I chased him off."

"No, no, I don't begrudge the money or the necklace, they're easily replaced But the pistol had—how shall I put it? Sentimental value, perhaps? My father gave it to me and instructed me in its use, many years ago, during his service in the Peninsula."

A quick smile crinkled the corners of Stretton's expressive brown eyes. "I see that you're a lady of many parts, Frau Steinach. I begin to think that you might have foiled the bandit attack without any assistance from me."

"Now that, Mr. Stretton, is pure nonsense," smiled Anthea, turning to speak to the veturino, who had just come up to her wearing a deeply worried expression.

"Miladi, I must tell you that this is not the sort of establishment to which you are accustomed," he said, wringing his hands. "There are two bedchambers and a small private parlour, but one can only guess as to their condition. However, judging by the common room here"—he glanced meaningfully over the dirty, refuse-strewn floor, the primitive wooden furniture and the puffs of throat-irritating smoke emanating from the poorly laid fire in the great stone fireplace—"I do not think that we can hope for much in the way of comfort. And the innkeeper tells me that he does not have a cook; he prepares the food himself, such as it is." He stared resentfully at the proprietor, who looked, Anthea thought resignedly, little more savoury than his premises.

She hastened to soothe the guide's ruffled sensibilities. "No one could possibly blame you for the inn's deficiencies, Luigi. Up until now you've provided me with superior accommodations and service, all the way across Italy. And if it hadn't been for the bandit attack, I'm sure that I would now be snugly retired for the night at the inn that you chose for me at Novi."

Considerably mollified, the veturino returned to his assault on the harassed landlord, insisting that the two unfortunate local patrons, drinking wine at a table in the corner, be forced out into the inhospitable night so that the common room could be reserved for the exclusive use of the foreign visitors' servants.

"Pray enlighten me, ma'am," observed Stretton, as he and Anthea, with Hannah, followed a slatternly serving girl up the rickety staircase, "as to your great success in finding superior hotels in Italy. My own experiences have been almost uniformly bad, beginning with an inn—if one can call it that—in the Col di Tenda, where the sheets were apparently never changed from one year to another, and the innkeeper informed me angrily, when I complained about the bedbugs, that I must have brought the creatures with me in my luggage.''

Anthea laughed. ''Oh, I had to say something to keep up poor Luigi's spirits. He really has tried to do his best, but I must admit that, except for a few hotels in some of the larger cities, the inns in Italy are very nearly as bad as the roads.''

As she surveyed the bedchamber that had been allotted to her, Anthea thought with a sinking heart that Luigi's fears had been more than justified. The small, grimy room, equipped only with a sagging bed and one battered chair, showed practically no sign of proper housekeeping. There were no shutters on the single ill-fitting window and the rain was beating against its cracked panes with ever increasing fury, sending in gusts of chill wind that threatened to extinguish the meagre flames of the tiny fire.

''I don't expect that anybody has put a broom to this place in donkey's years, Miss Anthea,'' said Hannah grimly, pointing to the spiderwebs that festooned the ceiling, plainly visible despite the dimness of the light cast by the tallow candle that had been left by the serving maid as their only source of illumination.

''I'm afraid that we must put up with it, Hannah. It isn't as though we had any choice of accommodation. Help me into dry clothes as quickly as possible, so that we won't be obliged to spend any more time in here than we must.''

Anthea's teeth ceased to chatter from the cold as Hannah dressed her in a warm long-sleeved gown of fine dark red merino, taken from the small portmanteau that contained everything necessary to her comfort on brief overnight stops. There was no mirror in the room, but as she held up her small hand glass Anthea could see that Hannah had done her usual skillful job in arranging the jet-black masses of curls that framed her deeply blue eyes, dazzlingly fair skin and the features that admirers had often assured her were classically regular. She had always accepted the compliments with laughing thanks, for she was without great personal vanity. Tonight, however, she suddenly realised that she was examining her reflection more closely than usual, and she slammed down the hand mirror, her cheeks warm with colour. It had been far too long, she decided, since she had mingled in polite society; otherwise, the prospect of spending some time in the company of a charming and handsome gentleman would never have prompted her to take special pains with her toilet.

Hannah had noticed her lingering gaze at her mirrored reflection. "Are you really going to have supper alone with the English gentleman?" she asked suspiciously.

Anthea eyed her calmly. "I certainly am. I must eat, after all, and there is only one private parlour. Would you have me banish poor Mr. Stretton to the common room to eat with his own servants? I'm surprised at your lack of charity, Hannah. Especially since, if Mr. Stretton hadn't rescued us from the bandits, we probably wouldn't be having any supper at all. We might all be dead."

Hannah continued to grumble. "That's as may be, Miss Anthea, but it just doesn't look right, dining with a complete stranger. Now, if you'd only taken my advice and brought a chaperone along with you on this journey, there'd have been no problem."

Anthea rose, shaking out her skirts. "I'm tired of hearing about chaperones. I'm perfectly capable of taking care of myself, as I've told you often enough. Come, let's get out of this horrible room and go downstairs. I'm famished."

Geoffrey Stretton was just emerging from his bedchamber as she stepped outside her door. "I trust that your accommodations are superior to mine," he said, raising an eyebrow. "They could hardly be worse. The bedstead in my room is actually broken."

Anthea smiled wryly. "My bedstead seems reasonably intact, but my maid informs me that the mattress has a distinctly unpleasant odour. She thinks that it must be stuffed with damp leaves."

"That settles it," replied Stretton with an air of determination.

17

"These bedchambers are uninhabitable. I suggest that we join forces and while away the night as best we may in armchairs before a fire in the private parlour."

After inspecting her uninviting bed and mattress, Anthea had already reconciled herself to spending the night in a sitting position, but now she glanced at Stretton with a faint stirring of unease. There was a flirtatious glint in his eyes, an edge of familiarity in his voice; perhaps he had assumed, since she was travelling unconventionally without a chaperone and with only servants for escorts, that she was a member of the demimonde.

She said nothing, however, as she descended the staircase and entered the small private parlour. As she inspected the room, she had to admit to herself that Stretton's suggestion had merit: This room, while only slightly cleaner than the bedchamber she had just left, did possess several quite comfortable-looking armchairs, and in the large stone fireplace a roaring fire was fast dissipating the raw chill of the autumn night.

Entering the parlour on their heels came Anthea's head groom, John Potter, his throat marked by an ugly rope burn, to inform her that the horses had been taken care of; behind him came the veturino with the innkeeper to take their orders for refreshment.

"This is a very tolerable claret, surprisingly enough," said Stetton, taking a preliminary sip of the wine that appeared promptly. He poured a glass for Anthea and took it to her as she sat in a chair before the fireplace. He lifted his own glass, grinning cheerfully. "To a wonderful evening, ma'am. Frankly, I never hoped for such a lovely ending to such a dismal day: dining with a beautiful, intriguing, mysterious lady. I look forward to learning all about you: who you really are—so obviously English despite that ugly German name—all the secrets of your past and, most important of all, your plans for the future."

Stiffening, Anthea rose, backing away from him until they were separated by the length of the fireplace. "I fear that you're labouring under a delusion, Mr. Stretton. I'm travelling alone because I choose to, not—as you seem to have assumed—because I'm between protectors. I have never had a protector, incidentally, nor do

I require one. And what name I choose to use, I must point out, is entirely my own affair."

The smile faded from Stretton's lips and the expressive dark eyes sharpened. But after a short pause he said easily and with no trace of embarrassment, "If I've made the slightest false assumption about you, Frau Steinach, please accept my most profound apologies. I hope that you won't change your mind about joining me for dinner and an evening of pleasant conversation."

Anthea hesitated. At last she said, "I would like to dine with you, but only if it's understood that it will be merely a friendly social occasion."

"But of course. Two ships passing in the night, exchanging polite signals." His bland reply brought a faint flush to Anthea's cheek and a nettled feeling that she had been caught off balance.

Hannah now entered the parlour with a large tray of steaming food. To Anthea's puzzled gaze she replied grimly, "Heaven knows what that kitchen of his is like, but I wasn't going to let the innkeeper serve this food. His dirty thumb would be in the soup as soon as Bob's your uncle." She arranged the food and the dishes on a small table that she drew up between the two armchairs, but even after she had served her mistress and Stretton she continued to hover around them until Anthea ordered her gently away to have some supper herself. Very reluctantly Hannah left the room, turning several times to fix Anthea with a worried frown. She bobbed a deep curtsey at the door, saying in quite unnecessarily loud tones, "If you should want anything, Miss Anthea, anything at all, I'll be right outside."

After she had left the room, Stretton raised a quizzical eyebrow. "It seems that you have a watchdog. I don't think that your maid approves of me."

"It's not you, precisely, Mr. Stretton. She doesn't think it proper for me to dine alone with a stranger. She cares much more for the conventions than I do. Before I was married, you see, I lived for a time with my father in Portugal, where life was much more informal. I learned to like it that way."

The eyebrow raised still higher. "Portugal? Informal? I had the impression . . ." His voice trailed away as he lifted his quizzing glass to peer at the food in front of him. "Now, what have we here? This looks like a dish of boiled giblets, but I don't recognize the white stringy substance."

"It's egg white, I fancy."

"Really? Well, it seems to be identifiable, at any rate. But this ragout—I grant you that it smells appetizing enough, but what is it made of? Some kind of fowl, perhaps, but *what* kind?"

Anthea burst out laughing. "Better not ask. It *could* be chicken, but then again it might be kite, or jackdaw, or magpie —I've had all three during my stay in Italy." She laughed still harder at his appalled reaction. "Do cheer up, sir. We might have been served boiled snails or fried frogs. Those were on the menu at an inn near Siena where I once stayed; Hannah almost went into hysterics at the sight of them."

"Spare me the details, I beg of you. Fried frogs are beyond the pale, but I'm famished enough to begin to believe that these odd-looking giblets and this mysterious ragout are food for the gods."

And indeed, though the soup was watery and the table wine on the sour side, Anthea and Stretton found the meal palatable enough.

"You're travelling for pleasure, Frau Steinach?" Stretton asked after a moment.

"Yes, I'm a recent widow and I've been travelling in Italy since shortly after my husband's death. You, too?"

"Indeed, yes. My generation was denied the Grand Tour of the Continent by the war, of course, so immediately after the Battle of Waterloo I resigned my commission in the army in order to visit Italy. Have you had a pleasant journey?"

"Very much so. I'm a very common kind of tourist. I've been visiting all the famous sights that I dreamed of as a child. The Uffizi gallery in Florence. The ruins of Theodoric's palace in Ravenna. The Colosseum in Rome. The Palazzo Simonetta near Milan. St. Mark's in Venice. My tour would have been a complete delight save for the fact that Italy must place more difficulties in the way of the traveller than any other country in the world. One must procure a separate passport for each tiny Italian state, change one's money and submit to customs inspection at each frontier—and more often than not bribe the customs inspector not to open the bags at all so as to prevent one's belongings from being looted. The roads range from terrible to nonexistent and are ridden with bandits, the hotels and inns are dirty and inefficient and almost none of them has door locks, so that you must carry your own with you." Anthea paused, breathless. "And yet, in spite of it all," she chuckled, "I've quite fallen in love with Italy."

Stretton laughed. "I agree with you, the beauties of Italy make up for all the ghastly difficulties one must endure to see them. But," he added feelingly, "I'm still a trifle flabbergasted when I remember an experience that I had at an inn south of Naples: I questioned the landlord about the size of the bill, only to be faced with a cocked pistol and the admonition to pay up, or else. All the bandits of Italy are not on the roads, I assure you! And then, of course, there was the time that I asked another innkeeper the location of the privy and I was told that it was in the courtyard—*any* place in the courtyard . . ." He stopped abruptly. "I do beg your pardon, Frau Steinach. I was forgetting my company."

"Ah well, Mr. Stretton, I'm not exactly a pea-green girl, you know," Anthea replied, shrugging. Changing the subject, she asked, "You mentioned that you fought at Waterloo. What was your regiment?"

"The Royal Horse Guards."

"Oh, the 'Blues,' " she exclaimed delightedly, thinking how impressive he must have looked in the blue tunic with red and gold collar and cuffs and the polished steel breastplate for ceremonial occasions, topped by a black-japanned and gilt helmet with nodding red and white plumes. "Papa was used to call you the 'Hyde Park soldiers,' " she said with a reminiscent smile.

"You're giving yourself away," teased Stretton. "Unless you take me for a Johnny Raw, you can't deny that Papa was an army man."

Anthea bit her lip. "You're right," she said after a pause. "Papa was in the Ninety-fifth Rifles."

"The famous Light Division! I finally got a glimpse of them in action when, Hyde Park soldiers or no, the Blues arrived in the Peninsula for the Battle of Vittoria. Is your father still serving?"

"No," she said briefly. "He left the army after Salamanca in 1812. He's dead now." Her thoughts wandered as she remembered Major John Blanchard, so charming—at times utterly beguiling—so handsome and lighthearted. Very much like her present companion, she thought suddenly.

She was recalled to the present when she realized that Stretton had been talking to her for some time. "I'm sorry. What did you say?"

"At the risk of seeming to pry, I was observing that I understand you much better, now that I know that you were with your father in the Peninsula."

"Really?" A chilly note crept into Anthea's voice.

"Why, yes," replied Stretton easily. "I was puzzled when you said that you had learned to like informality in Portugal—it's been my experience that the Spanish and Portuguese insist on an ironclad etiquette that makes London society look positively decadent. And then I did wonder, you know, why your father chose to instruct you how to use a pistol—it's not your average young lady's accomplishment."

Anthea's lips relaxed in a smile. "You're very observant, sir. My mother died many years ago, so I always accompanied my father wherever his orders took him. Which meant, of course, that I did not live the sheltered life typical of most girls my age. Knowing how to use a pistol was a necessity. More than once Hannah and I were forced to ride out of some little Portuguese town with a squadron of French cavalry on our heels."

"To think that if I had only been fortunate enough to be posted to the Peninsula a little earlier, I might actually have met you there," lamented Stretton. "Oh, well, no use crying over lost opportunities. May I ask if you're going to Milan? I have acquaintances there; perhaps we might see something of each other if you plan to stay there."

Steeling herself against the magnetism of his smile, Anthea answered, "No, I'll be staying just a night or two in Milan, as a stopover on my way to Vienna. Yes," she added, as he opened his mouth to ask the obvious question, "I live in Vienna."

He stretched out in his chair, his eyes narrowing speculatively as he said lazily, "My travel plans are very far from being cut and dried, Frau Steinach. If I were to make a detour to Vienna, would you allow me to call upon you?"

"I think not, Mr. Stretton. I don't wish to appear rude, but I see very little point in our meeting again. Would you mind very much if we just considered this pleasant evening that we've spent together as a one-of-a-kind experience?"

"Ah, but I would mind very much. I simply cannot believe that a lady bearing the lovely name of Anthea—your abigail did call you that, did she not?—I cannot believe that a lady named Anthea could be so utterly unromantic."

"That *is* my name, Mr. Stretton. I fail to see why it should have any connection with romance," said Anthea frostily.

"Then your education has been sadly neglected," retorted Stretton with an impish grin. "Do you mean to say that you have never read Robert Herrick's poems? Herrick was one of the Cavalier poets," he added kindly. "In my salad days I was much given to romantic, lovesick poetry, and I well remember mooning over Herrick's lines in "To Anthea":

> . . . *bid me love and I will give*
> *A loving heart to thee.*
> *Bid me to weep, and I will weep,*
> *While I have eyes to see:*
> *And having none, yet I will keep*
> *A heart to weep for thee.*
> *Thou art my life, my love, my heart,*
> *The very eyes of me:*
> *And hast command of every part,*
> *To live and die for thee.*

"Thank you, Mr. Stretton. You recite very well. And now, if you'll excuse me, I'll ring for Hannah. She'll bring me a lap rug and then I would really like to make myself as comfortable as possible in this chair and get a little rest. It's been a very strenuous day."

In a quick, lithe movement he rose, grasping her hands to pull her to her feet in front of him. "Your lips are lying," he murmured, his face very close to hers, "but those achingly beautiful eyes of yours are telling the truth: you're no ice maiden, my lovely Anthea. Come, confess it, you want me to kiss you, to hold you close, just as much as I want to do it. Like this." He slid his arms around her, tightening his grasp, while his lips gently traced a path from her temples down to her cheeks.

Anthea's heart was pounding, her breath coming so quickly that she felt close to suffocation. This fiery tumult in her body was new to her, half threatening, half darkly enticing. Physical love with her elderly husband had been for her purely mechanical, a duty to be fulfilled. Never before had she felt with anyone this sensation of being swept along on a torrent of burning desire. As Stretton's mouth crushed down on hers in a scorching kiss, she went limp, wanting nothing more than to surrender her body to his. But that bright intelligence, that strong will that had always carried her unscathed through her short life, soon asserted themselves and she pushed Stretton away with such force that he staggered back against the table.

"I've never moved in London society, Mr. Stretton," she said coldly, "but I had always assumed that it had a certain amount of *ton*. I would have thought, for example, that an English gentleman would not press his attentions on a lady unless he received some encouragement to do so."

Stretton's face flamed crimson. "Your pardon if I've misunderstood your circumstances," he flashed hotly, "but, in my social circles, ladies—or those who wish to be thought ladies—do not roam the public highways without chaperones, attended only by a pair of grooms and an abigail."

Anthea drew herself up, her eyes kindling with angry resentment. "Let me understand you. If I were a demirep—oh, yes, I do know the term and I'm unladylike enough to use it!—if I were a demirep, it would be quite all right for you to foist yourself upon me, is that correct?''

"Now, just a moment," said Stretton, his color still high, "you're putting words in my mouth."

"Am I? I'll wager that I'm not far off the mark as to your thoughts, however! Well, Mr. Stretton, I'm not one of your fair Cyprians, your 'Fashionable Impures,' but even if I were I would certainly reject your overtures. You see, when a man tries to seduce me—there's my unladylike side coming out again!—I like him to have a certain amount of address, of polish, in both of which qualities you are lamentably lacking. And now, sir, you will oblige me by finding another room in which to spend the night.''

=2=

ANTHEA OPENED A drowsy eye as Hannah pulled back the draperies at the windows. She sat up, feeling her usual sense of fleeting disbelief as she gazed around the walls of the bed-chamber, with their elaborately carved panels and gilded and polychrome *boiseries*. Even after more than two years, she occasionally had to remind herself that she was now the Furstin von Hellenberg, mistress of a baroque Viennese palace in the Herrengasse near the Hofburg, the Imperial Court Palace. Not to mention her hunting castle in the Marchfeld, the fertile plain east of Vienna, an estate in the Weinviertel on the Danube and extensive lands in Burgenland (in western Hungary) and in Italy.

"You're a real slugabed this morning," said Hannah, helping her into a silken dressing gown. "The coffee is what they call 'Brauner,' " she added disparagingly, as Anthea sat down to her breakfast at a dainty rosewood table delicately inlaid with tulip-wood. "I can't seem to make the cook realise that you want more milk in your coffee."

"It might help, Hannah, if you would try to learn a little German. Just ask for 'Milch Gespritzt,' and my coffee will arrive exactly as I like it."

Hannah sniffed. "I've got no use for German, or for Vienna, either. Being English born is good enough for me. And you know, Miss Anthea, even though you're a Serene Highness now—or *Durchlaucht*, as I guess they say here—living in all this luxury" —she pointed around the room—"I often think that we were

26

much happier and more comfortable back when the major was still alive and you were plain Miss Blanchard.''

"Don't talk nonsense," said Anthea sharply. "You've forgotten what it was like to have all those unpaid bills, with tradesmen dunning us around the clock. And those dreadful lodgings in Geneva, right over a fishmonger's shop—I thought that I would never get the smell out of my hair and my clothes. Now we have a rather nice roof over our heads and our only worry seems to be whether my coffee is white enough.''

Catching sight of Hannah's rather stricken expression, Anthea broke off. "I got so many compliments on my gown last night at Count Edeleny's ball," she went on in softer tones. "And the countess gave me fair warning that she would try to steal you away from me. Nobody in all Vienna, she said, dresses hair as beautifully as you do.''

At once Hannah brightened. While Anthea finished her breakfast, the abigail went to the wardrobe and began to lay out her mistress's clothing for the day. "You came in very late last night," she grumbled with the license of an old family servant. "Past three it was. And it's been the same since we returned from Italy. Balls and parties and routs and court functions almost every night. You'll wear yourself out if you don't watch yourself.''

Anthea listened forbearingly. She thought, as she so often did, that she was fortunate to have Hannah with her, though the older woman was becoming increasingly irascible and overly protective, finding it hard to accept that her charge was now a grown woman. Hannah was, however, a link to the past, someone who loved her dearly for her own sake and who remembered what life used to be like. She had cared for Anthea almost from the moment of her birth. She had come to the Blanchard family when Anthea was only a few days old.

John Blanchard, Anthea's father, had been a member of a distinguished Gloucestershire family. As a younger son of the Earl of Repton, he had been expected to marry well. Instead, on a holiday trip to Ireland, he had met and fallen in love with the lovely daughter of an impoverished country solicitor. His marriage to his

Irish sweetheart had been a happy one, though brief—his wife died when Anthea was very young—but it had meant severing all ties with his family. His father had refused to acknowledge in any way his son's imprudent marriage.

Anthea had loved her father dearly. He was a man of infinite charm, his eyes constantly alight with ready laughter, a jest or a quip or a graceful compliment always on his lips. He could hold an audience spellbound with a story and he possessed a personal magnetism that drew people of all ages to him. In his own way he had been a good parent, taking his little daughter along with him on his campaigns, with the faithful Hannah to care for her physical wants and a governess, whenever he could afford to hire one, to train her mind. But he was also a feckless, improvident man of no great depth of character, who was never able to live on his military pay, though as an inveterate gambler he had frequent periods of prosperity. Toward the end, he became a heavy drinker and his erratic luck turned against him so that he lost far more often at the tables than he won. Finally, after the Battle of Salamanca, his drinking and gambling problems worsening, he was asked to leave his regiment. He and Anthea drifted to Switzerland, where he continued his unavailing assault on the gaming tables. His affairs reached their nadir when he was caught cheating at an exclusive Geneva club.

Even now, years after the event, Anthea could feel a fresh stab of pain when she remembered her father's final disgrace. Loyally she clung to the belief that he would not have descended to cheating if he had not already been suffering from a deteriorating liver disease and a mental state bordering on insanity. But ill or not, mentally disturbed or not, John Blanchard had certainly been headed for debtors' prison until the intervention of Prince Ferdinand von Hellenberg, an elderly Austrian aristocrat whom he had met in the salons and clubs of Geneva. The prince had offered to pay off all her father's debts and to grant him a lifetime allowance in return for the one asset that John Blanchard still possessed, his daughter's hand in marriage.

Though the prince was so much older than herself, and she felt nothing more personal for him than a mildly affectionate gratitude, Anthea's marriage had not been unduly unhappy. Prince Ferdinand was not, first of all, an especially demanding husband. He was, however, a fastidious, cultured, distinguished-looking man who had introduced her to the world of the arts, music and fashion, a world to which she had never been exposed in her years of military life. When he died, after little more than a year of marriage, she was grateful to him for settling her into a gracious, luxurious way of life and for easing her father's last days—John Blanchard died only a few months after her wedding—but she had never had the least romantic love for the prince, and now that he was gone she felt nothing but relief, a sense of freedom that she was her own person again. Her sense of relief was so great, in fact, that within days of her husband's funeral she had made a vow to herself never to marry again, never to surrender her independence to another man. In this she was considerably helped by the fact that Prince Ferdinand had been a childless widower, the last of his long line, and she had inherited, with no strings attached, his vast wealth and endless estates.

Anthea was just finishing her coffee when Hannah answered a knock at the bedchamber door. "Herr von Westendorf is downstairs and wishes to see you," the abigail told her.

"Karl? How nice. Show him up to my boudoir."

Hannah looked disapproving. "It doesn't seem right, inviting a gentleman practically into your bedchamber and you not even dressed properly. I can't imagine what the ladies of the regiment would think."

Anthea stood up, glancing down at her dressing gown. "I'm far more completely clothed than I was last night in that skimpy ball gown," she said impatiently. "Really, Hannah, I wish that you would remember that we're no longer living in some stuffy provincial backwater in Portugal. This is Vienna, thank God, where we're much more cosmopolitan about dressing gowns and boudoirs. Please have Graf von Westendorf come up immediately." She walked into the boudoir, a delightful little room with a gilded ceiling and damask silk wall panels.

Shortly afterwards, Hannah ushered Karl von Westendorf into the room. He was a slight, dark-haired young man of middle height, with bright blue eyes and attractive if irregular features. He stopped on the threshold, clicking his heels in a deep bow, greeting her with the formal "Durchlaucht." With Hannah's departure, however, his formality dissolved. He rushed over to Anthea, kissing the hand that she extended to him, murmuring, "Chérie, you're looking even more ravishingly beautiful than ever—I don't quite see how I've endured this long separation from you." He spoke in French, as did so many of the Austrian upper class, which was agreeable to Anthea, since her French was more fluent than her still rather halting German.

"I've been back in Vienna for almost four months, Karl, and it did seem strange not to see you before now," laughed Anthea, removing the hand that Karl showed no signs of releasing. "Somebody—I forget who—told me that he thought you were in Hungary."

Karl grimaced. "All too true. My revered papa decided that I needed another long restful stay on our country estate in Hungary, as far away as possible from Vienna. I returned only yesterday. But let's talk about something more interesting. Did you miss me while you were gone?"

Anthea gazed at him, unable to resist returning his engaging grin. She was fond of Karl and believed that he was genuinely fond of her, even though she suspected that part of the reason that he had been courting her so persistently since the end of her mourning period was that she was the sole heiress to the vast Hellenberg fortune and estates. He himself came from a titled and wealthy family, but he was a younger son with extravagant tastes and a liking for gambling that approached the intensity of John Blanchard's obsession with the tables. Chronically deep in debt, he was periodically banished to the country by his long-suffering parent, in the hope that exile from frivolous society would cause him to search his soul and mend his ways. None of his enforced stays in the country had ever made the slightest change in Karl's life-style, however, and it was generally accepted that only marriage to an heiress would provide him with a stable future.

"I can't begin to tell you how dull life has been without you," he said now. "Please tell me that you've no plans for another sightseeing journey."

"Not for the immediate future. But I'm an independent woman now, you know, and there's a great deal of the world that I haven't seen yet."

Seating himself beside her on the gilded and brocaded settee, Karl took Anthea's hand again, stroking it as he eyed her quizzically. "There's a rumour afoot that you travelled very lightly indeed while you were in Italy—you had with you just your abigail and several grooms, all of them old and trusted—not to say closemouthed—servants. Some people are wondering why you had such a modest entourage. In fact, I've heard speculation that you travelled so modestly to avoid calling attention to yourself; that you were, perhaps, meeting a lover in secret."

Anthea snatched her hand away, more amused, however, than angry with Karl's gossip. "Really, you Viennese have the filthiest minds. I suppose that all the time that I've been away some of my dearest friends and all my worst enemies have been imagining me in the arms of a *cicisbeo*, or a whole procession of them, I don't doubt."

"You wrong me," protested Karl. "I *know* that you had neither official lovers nor secret admirers in Italy. You're much too cold for any such romantic dallying," he went on mock-reproachfully, once again edging himself closer to her on the settee. "Otherwise, my love, you'd long ago have given a bit of encouragement to someone who has loved you fervently and faithfully—no, distractedly—all these years." He put his arm around her shoulders, pressing his face into the mass of curls above her ear.

Pushing him away, Anthea jumped up from the settee. "It's not that you aren't almost irresistible," she assured him, "but, as I've told you before, I simply have no intention of marrying again.

So, if just being my very good friend isn't enough for you, why, then, perhaps we should agree not to see each other any more."

Karl raised his hands in surrender. "Of course being your friend is enough—for now." He raised her hand to his lips. "But I won't promise to stop hoping that one day I can persuade you to become the Gräfin von Westendorf. Because of all the women that I have ever met, Anthea, you were meant to surrender yourself to passion, to give yourself completely to some man who could break down your defenses—All right, all right," he added hurriedly, as Anthea walked to the door, throwing it open and motioning him outside. "I won't say another word. Are you planning to attend Baron von Altenburg's rout this evening? I would be happy, *enchanted*, to escort you."

Karl stayed for a while longer, enjoying with a kind of malicious amusement the latest tidbits of gossip with which Anthea brought him up to date on the events that had occurred during his current exile. When he had gone she returned to her bedchamber, where Hannah was waiting to dress her in a morning gown of pale green jaconet muslin with deep flounces of French work. She gave a satisfied look at herself in the cheval glass, glad that she was at last out of the sober grays and lavenders of second mourning.

Going downstairs to the small salon on the ground floor that she used as a study, she sat down at her desk to look over her correspondence and to make her plans for the day. As she reached for her letters, her eyes fell on a small worn book in faded red leather. She had found it in a little shop near St. Stephen's Cathedral that specialised in foreign language books for the many expatriates of Vienna. It was an old edition of the Cavalier poets, printed with the quaint spelling and in the old-fashioned lettering of the late 17th century. She picked it up, the book falling open at the section devoted to Robert Herrick's poems.

Anthea had tried to tell herself, prompted by some obscure need to explain her reason for acquiring the book, that she had sought for it purely out of curiosity, or perhaps the desire to reacquaint herself with her English literary heritage. And, indeed, she had conscientiously worked her way through the poems of

Thomas Carew, the Duke of Buckingham and Richard Lovelace. But invariably, as she was doing now, she would seek out the lines of "To Anthea"—the full title, she learned, was "To Anthea, Who May Command Him Any Thing"—and then her thoughts would rush back to that evening a few short months ago in the Ligurian Alps—the most exciting and dramatic evening of her life—when she had been rescued from the bandits by Geoffrey Stretton.

Her cheeks burned as the words "Thou art my life, my love, my heart" recalled vividly those tumultuous moments when she had been locked in the arms of the young English officer. She was an honest person, and she did not attempt to deny that she had felt an elemental response to Stretton's caresses. She was glad, however, that there had been only the one brief searing moment when she had been tempted to surrender to his hard embrace. Then, in the next instant, almost instinctively, she had raised her defenses against that practiced, confident charm of his. She smiled to herself now, recalling the dazed bewilderment of Stretton's expression when she had ordered him out of the inn parlour that evening. Was it, perhaps, the first time that he had ever been repulsed? And the next morning, she had been hard put to smother a laugh as she observed his repeated attempts to apologise to her, only to be foiled each time by her manoeuvre to keep herself from being alone in his company. She thought with considerable satisfaction that the incident must have been among the most frustrating of young Mr. Stretton's life.

She turned her attention back to her correspondence. Midway through the pile of invitations and bills she came upon a letter in a small, precise handwriting, franked in a heavy hand by a Sir Phillip Montville. She held it in her hand for a moment, not recognising the English name. When she opened it, her eyes flew down the spidery crossed lines to the signature, Harriet Montville; she was no further enlightened. Perplexed, she read the letter quickly, learning, with a little shock of surprise, that the writer was her father's younger sister.

Anthea had practically no knowledge of her father's family.

There had been no communication, no contact of any kind, between John Blanchard and any of his relatives since the announcement of his marriage to Moira O'Driscoll in 1793. Or so Anthea had thought, until, shortly before his death, John had revealed during an evening of tearily drunken reminiscence that one of his younger sisters had written him a note of sympathy following his rupture with his father. But it had been too much to expect that the sister, very young at the time, would continue to brave her father's wrath by writing to him. At any rate, there were no more letters, and Anthea had even forgotten the sister's name, which presumably was Harriet. So far removed from Anthea's consciousness was the Blanchard family that she had not even thought to send either the notice of her marriage or of her father's death to the *Times* or the *Morning Post* in London.

"My dear niece," the letter began. "I've dithered for months about writing this letter. I wasn't at all sure, you see, that you would be happy to hear from me. I have had a guilty conscience for years now about losing contact so completely with my brother Jack. At first, of course, while I was still living at home, there was really no way that I could write without Papa's knowing about it. Though I did send Jack one letter—I've often wondered if he received it—by an old friend of his, visiting the house at the time, who promised to frank it for me. But since then, and especially when I was first married and the children started to come, I must confess that I rarely even thought of Jack. I did hear, once or twice, that he was serving in the Peninsula. Then, about a year ago, purely by chance, I happened to be seated at a dinner party next to a gentleman, a bare acquaintance, who had just returned from service in our embassy at Vienna. He told me about the recent death of your husband, Prince von Hellenberg, and about Jack's death some time before that in Switzerland. The old memories came welling back, and I felt such grief that Jack and I had never known each other as adults. I did not even know that I had a niece! And now, after fretting over it for so long, I have decided to risk a rebuff and invite you to come visit me in England. I would like so much to know you and to have you know England. I married Sir

Josiah Montville in 1797—Josiah died five years ago—and I have five children: Edmund, who has just received his army commission, Fanny, who will come out this spring, Julian, who is at Harrow, and Emma and Louise, both still in the classroom. Josiah was a widower when we married; my stepson Phillip is as yet unmarried and the children and I at present make our home with him. My dear Anthea, I will be waiting with the greatest of expectations to receive your reply to my letter; I pray that you will allow me to know and to love Jack's daughter.''

Anthea read the letter a second time, touched more than she would have believed to hear from a member of the Blanchard family, whom she had schooled herself over the years to regard as unjust and hardhearted. The letter touched off a train of speculation in her thoughts; from wondering about what sort of life she might have had if the Blanchard family had been loving and accepting of Moira O'Driscoll, she began to think about the existence that she was now leading. For some time now, she realised, she had been growing increasingly dissatisfied with the emptiness of her daily routine, a constant round of parties, balls, teas, promenades, court functions, house parties, in the company of a group of people for whom she felt no real closeness. Leaning back in her chair, her hand half covering her eyes, Anthea admitted to herself a longing for roots, a yearning for a settled, normal family relationship—feelings that she had never allowed herself to entertain during those lonely, gypsy years with her father's regiment.

She thought of her oft-repeated pronouncement that she would never marry again: Was a second marriage so impossible? She had been soured, of course, by her experiences with a much older husband whom she had never loved, and she knew with all the wisdom of her being that she did not want a husband like her amiably selfish father, or like Karl, who shared so many of John Blanchard's characteristics; they were men who traded on their charm, refusing personal responsibility, allowing family and friends to support them and to manage their lives. Or like—here her memory unwillingly reverted to Italy and Geoffrey Stretton, and she knew that she had instinctively shied away from any closer contact with him because the young English officer was the epitome of all the charm that she had come to distrust in her father and in Karl.

Drawing a sudden quick breath, Anthea moved her chair closer to her desk and took up her pen resolutely. She would, she decided, go to England to visit her Aunt Harriet. There she might hope to find a family stability, or even, possibly, a chance for the romantic love that she had never known as yet.

=3=

WHILE JOHN POTTER and his assistant groom, Josef, were strapping her luggage onto the top of the heavy travelling berlin, Anthea stood outside the King's Head Inn in Dover, breathing in the soft May air scented with the thyme that grew on the towering high cliffs above the harbour, taking one last glance around the town, dominated by its great castle, before she started on her drive to London. She had begun her journey across Europe only a few days after she had decided to return to England, and her trip had been easy and uncomplicated. The abysmally inclement weather that had plagued the Continent during the early spring had changed to bright, balmy days as she travelled across France, stopping in Paris to replenish her wardrobe. She was wearing several of her new purchases now: a high crowned straw bonnet trimmed with a profusion of roses, a pelisse in white cambric striped in a soft dove colour, worn over a light muslin dress sprigged in primrose.

She had, she mused, been extremely fortunate during her Channel crossing from Calais. The weather had been perfect, with a fair wind pushing the ship across to Dover in only three hours. From other well-travelled fellow passengers she had learned that the crossing often took five or six hours, frequently in such foul weather that most passengers took deathly sick. Nor had she been obliged to wait a week or more for her ship because of bad weather or adverse winds. The only unpleasant note to mar her arrival in her native land had been the excessive strictness of the Dover customs officials; they went through her belongings so thoroughly and so minutely that she wondered briefly if they suspected her of smuggling contraband into the country. But no, a returning fellow Briton had told her sourly, English customs were notorious for being the strictest in Europe; his own father, he said, had been wearing, while going through customs, the breeches and waistcoat of a new suit he had bought in France; the coat to the suit, unfortunately, was in his luggage and was confiscated.

As she drove over the Kentish downs toward Canterbury, the towers of the majestic cathedral becoming dimly visible over the city walls, she began to marvel at the sheer beauty of the countryside. She had been so young, only three years of age, when she left England to follow her father on his campaigns, that she had no recollection of her native country. Now she admired the softly luminous green of the rolling fields, the orchards of apple, cherry, pears and hops, the luxuriant hedgerows and woods of oak and beech, the snug villages with their trim thatched cottages, covered with roses and honeysuckle and clustered around the village green, the bustling prosperous market towns. She was much impressed with the neatness and cleanliness of the towns and villages, and with the clean, well-fed, neatly dressed people: field labourers in round smocks of blue or tawny or olive green, yeomen in fustian coats and corduroy breeches, market women in scarlet cloaks and black silk bonnets, cottage women in gray stuff gowns and checked aprons—all in vivid contrast to the often wretched living conditions of the peasantry that she had seen during her travels on the Continent, even on her husband's—no, her own—estates, she thought with considerable unease.

Driving through Rochester with its soaring cathedral and massive Norman keep, Anthea's party crossed the Medway and went on to Shooter's Hill, where they made the last of their five changes of horses at the Bull Inn, having passed by Gad's Hill, where in former times, the postilions informed John Potter with relish, highwaymen were active and one could often see their corpses rotting in irons on the gibbet.

It was now midafternoon, and soon the berlin crossed an area of marshy meadows, strewn with masses of mean dwellings and grimy factory buildings, with the skyline of London coming into view. As they passed over the high balustraded Westminster Bridge, with its curious hooped lamp posts, Anthea looked downstream, catching a glimpse of a vast building, rising like a Venetian palace from the waterfront, and beyond it the luminous floating dome of a large church; farther downstream she spotted the dark humped outline of another great bridge—London Bridge, she later learned—surrounded by wharves and factories, with the river beyond it crowded with a vast mass of shipping.

A short drive from Westminster Bridge brought the party to the famous Golden Cross Inn, at the juncture of the Strand with Charing Cross, across the street from the impressive facade of Northumberland House. As they clattered to a halt on the cobblestones of the courtyard a small army of hostlers, grooms, porters and maidservants bustled out to greet them. Soon Anthea was settled into a comfortable suite of rooms, where she ordered dinner and decided to retire early after the fatigues of the long journey. Next morning after breakfast she sent one of the inn servants to her aunt's house in Grosvenor Square with a note saying that she had arrived in London the previous day. Within the hour, much to her surprise, Hannah brought her Sir Phillip Montville's card with a scribbled message telling her that he was waiting below.

"Show Sir Phillip up immediately, Hannah," she said, giving a hurried glance at her hair in the cheval glass and wondering at her cousin's extreme promptness in calling upon her; she had rather expected to receive a note from her aunt, inviting her to Grosvenor Square that day or the next. Not that Sir Phillip was really her cousin, she corrected herself; he was Aunt Harriet's stepson by her husband's first marriage, and thus his courtesy in visiting her the moment that he heard of her arrival was even more surprising.

When Phillip Montville was shown into the sitting room Anthea had a few moments to study his appearance while Hannah took his glossy black top hat and stick. He was a tall, well-built man, brown haired and blue eyed, with open, regular features and an expression of great seriousness and reserve, which could dissolve, Anthea soon discovered, into a smile of considerable warmth. He was well dressed, in a coat of blue superfine, light coloured pantaloons and highly polished Hessians, but he was obviously not a member of the Dandy set; not for him the carelessly tied spotted Belcher handkerchief worn instead of a cravat, or a gigantic bunch of seals dangling from his fob, and he certainly had no need for the corset known as the "Apollo."

"I must thank you, Sir Phillip, for responding so promptly to my note in person," Anthea smiled, after she had asked her cousin to be seated and had sent Hannah for Madeira and biscuits.

"I'm surprised, Your Serene Highness—thank you, I should like to call you Cousin Anthea—I'm surprised, Cousin, that you could think that we would act otherwise," replied Phillip earnestly, fixing on her a direct unwavering gaze that Anthea soon learned was characteristic of him; Phillip Montville always concentrated fully on the person or thing that engaged his attention. "You are, after all, a very close relative, on her first visit to England after many years. But I must tell you, Your Highness —Cousin Anthea—that my stepmother and I are very distressed that you should have taken rooms in a hotel instead of coming straight to us. I'm here to take you to your aunt at once; your servants can bring on your belongings and your carriage later."

"I couldn't possibly impose on your hospitality," demurred Anthea. "I have with me my own staff, my own carriage and horses. I can't ask you and my aunt to take on those responsibilities, especially since I may be staying here in London for some time. I had thought of taking a house." As she spoke, Anthea realised with a little quiver of inward amusement that it was partly her newly found independence that was speaking: after being the sole mistress of her great house in Vienna, accountable to no one for her actions, she was reluctant to risk losing any of that independence by being a long-term guest at the Montville residence.

"I couldn't possibly allow you to take a house," said Phillip firmly, and then, as Anthea lifted her eyebrow, he hastened to add, "I think that it would break my stepmother's heart if you were to stay anywhere other than Grosvenor Square. And then, consider, what would our friends, what would society, think if you chose not to live with us during your stay in London?'' He looked as though he were mustering even further arguments when Anthea threw up her hands and said with a laugh, ''You've convinced me, Cousin. I would be happy to accept your invitation.''

As she drove out of the centre of the city in Phillip's curricle —drawn, she noted, by a fine team of well-matched grays— Anthea was getting her first real look at residential London. There were no palaces, she saw, indeed very few large buildings at all, unlike other major European capitals that she had visited. Instead there was street after street of unpretentious but finely proportioned houses of gray or brown brick, three or four storied, with white pillars on either side of pedimented doors and neat wrought iron railings fronting on pavements made of broad flagstones. This was, Phillip informed her, Mayfair, the most elegant quarter of London, the site of all the best shops and the most exclusive clubs.

The end of the drive brought them to Grosvenor Square, a huge area lined on all four sides with more or less uniform houses of brown brick; in the middle of the square was a large formal circular garden surrounded by an iron fence, planted with trees and intersected by walks leading to a tall gilded equestrian statue in the centre. On the north side of the square were several very large houses in the ornate Palladian style, and it was in front of one of these that Phillip stopped the curricle. Handing Anthea down from the vehicle, Phillip escorted her up the steps of the house, through a large entry hall and up a great staircase to the first floor and a small sitting room.

''Anthea! My darling girl!'' cried Harriet Montville, jumping up from her chair and rushing to throw her arms about her niece. ''I've been counting the days ever since we received your letter saying that you were coming to England,'' she said after the first embrace. ''But we certainly expected you to come here, not to some horrid hotel,'' she added reproachfully. ''Of course, it was understood that you would be staying with us.''

Harriet was a fine-looking woman in her early 40s, with gray eyes and light brown hair untouched by gray, tucked under a becoming Cornette cap of cambric frilled with lace. She looked,

Anthea thought with a pang, very much as John Blanchard had looked before alcohol and dissipation took its toll, with the same sparkling eyes and the same warm smile.

"Cousin Anthea and I have settled the matter of the hotel, Mama," intervened Phillip. "No need to vex yourself or her with any further mention of it."

"Oh, very well, Phillip, I'm sure that you're exactly right," replied Harriet instantly. It was Anthea's first intimation that Phillip was the undoubted master of the house.

"I'll leave you to get better acquainted with our new cousin, Mama," he said now. "I look forward to seeing you later with the rest of the family, Cousin Anthea."

After Phillip had gone Harriet drew Anthea to a place beside her on a little settee with rolled ends and claw feet. Glancing about the room, Anthea thought to herself that the Montvilles must be very prosperous indeed, with their fine large house in the most fashionable part of London, furnished, judging by this room, with no sparing of expense.

She turned her eyes back to Harriet, to find her aunt gazing at her closely. "My dear, you must have the look of your mother," Harriet said, "for you don't resemble the Blanchards at all." She paused, sighing. "I've always been so sorry that I didn't know your dear mother. I think that my father was most unfair when he refused to receive Jack's wife. But he was a domestic tyrant, I'm sorry to say, and he was seriously strapped for funds. When he inherited the title he fell victim to a building mania, like so many young men of his generation when they returned from the Grand Tour. He completely redid the park at Barstead Abbey and made great additions to the house—would you believe it, my dear, he put in a new dining room fifty-three feet long! So, with the family fortune gone, he insisted that his children must marry well. My elder brother Henry did so; his wife was an impressive heiress, but it hasn't been a very happy marriage and there are no children, so the title will go to a distant cousin. Then Jack married for love, and not only did your mother have no dowry at all, but she represented, to my father's thinking, a complete mésalliance . . ."

She broke off with a blush. "Please forgive me. I do rattle on so."

"I'm not at all offended," Anthea reassured her. "In fact, I'm very interested in your talk of the family. You see, Papa never wanted to talk about Mama or the Blanchards. I think that he was so unhappy when Mama died, and so distressed about the treatment he had received from his father, that he just wanted to put it all out of his mind, pretend, perhaps, that it never happened. You'll find it hard to believe, but I've never even seen a portrait of Mama."

"My dear!" exclaimed Harriet with quick sympathy. "How alone, how rootless you must have felt as a child."

"Rootless, yes. That explains it exactly. That's why I'm so anxious to find out all about Papa's family now. Did my grandfather—the Earl of Repton—insist that you marry a wealthy heir, too, Aunt?"

"He did, indeed. Oh, he would have preferred both money and a title in a son-in-law, and he undoubtedly had to swallow his pride a little when he gave my hand to Josiah Montville, but the money was certainly there. Josiah's father, I must tell you, was a simple yeoman farmer who began his career by producing cotton goods in his own house and ended by owning a small mill; Josiah expanded the family business a thousandfold, bought a large estate in Rutland, became a member of Parliament and was knighted, just before he died, for financial help rendered the government during the war. He was a widower when we married, and considerably older than I was, but we rubbed along together quite happily. And the children! I need hardly tell you that Edmund is the handsomest officer in the Seventh Hussars, that Fanny will surely break all hearts by the end of her first season and that Julian is going to be a great scholar. And I expect that Emma and Louise will be just as sought after as Fanny, once they leave the schoolroom."

Here Harriet broke off, her eyes twinkling. "But that's enough. I *never* have to be persuaded to talk about my remarkable family. But what about yourself, my dear? I was so shocked to hear that your husband had died, so soon after you were married, and so soon, too, after Jack passed away. You made a long journey to Italy, I suppose, to distract yourself from your sorrows. I always think that a change of scenery, meeting new people, is so helpful in getting over a great personal loss.''

"I won't deceive you, Aunt. I felt no great sorrow when the prince died. It was a marriage of convenience only, to rescue Papa from a debtors' prison or worse. I'm glad that you didn't see Papa at the end. He wasn't the same man that you knew.''

Harriet looked distressed but not entirely surprised. "I had heard—rumours," she admitted. "But all that's behind you now. We're going to make you so happy here that you'll stay on in England permanently—or at least for a very long while! I'm bringing out my daughter Fanny this spring, as I wrote to you, and there will be parties and balls and entertainments every day from now on until late in June, so that by the end of the season you'll have been thoroughly introduced to London society. Though I assure you that I will need to make very little effort; the news of your beauty and title and fortune will spread like wildfire and everyone will be begging for invitations to meet you.''

"You're exaggerating my charms, Aunt," laughed Anthea. "But I do look forward to learning to know you better, and to meeting all my cousins and to making my way in London society.''

=== 4 ===

"WHAT A SQUEEZE," said Julian discontentedly. "I daresay that Almack's is all the crack, but I'd as lief be almost anywhere else." The tall, loose limbed, rather coltish lad, with the Blanchard gray eyes and light brown hair, was standing behind Anthea's chair. She was sitting out this dance because Julian, at the last moment, had had an attack of stage fright at the prospect of leading her out for the country dance.

"That will be quite enough, Julian," said his mother with considerable asperity. Resplendent in purple satin and a plumed turban, Harriet was seated beside Anthea. "You don't seem to realise how fortunate you are to be here at Almack's, or how nearly impossible it is to obtain vouchers of admission unless one possesses the very highest of social credentials. Of course, my dear boy, if you hadn't been dismissed from Harrow for that dreadful escapade with the farmer's bull . . ."

Julian looked mulish rather than repentant. Since his departure from Harrow he had been living with the family in Grosvenor Square, studying with a tutor to prepare himself for Cambridge in the fall. Phillip had indicated that he preferred to have Julian in London, rather than in the country, so that he could keep an eye on the boy and make sure that he was actually studying. Anthea had perceived this as one more indication that Phillip was in complete charge of his stepmother's young family. But he seemed to be on excellent terms with Harriet, and it was obvious that her aunt felt only gratitude for her stepson's efforts.

As she gazed around the crowded rooms Anthea found herself

agreeing with Julian's opinion of Almack's Assembly Rooms, where, for a fee of ten guineas, guests could dance every Wednesday evening for the 12 weeks of the season. The place was ruled dictatorially by a committee of patronesses, headed by the famous Lady Jersey, who enforced the most rigid of standards: Gentlemen were obliged to wear breeches and white cravats, no one was admitted after the stroke of 11 P.M. and vouchers were handed out to only a fraction of the eager folk who craved admission. The Duke of Wellington himself had twice been excluded, once for wearing trousers, once for appearing at a few minutes after 11. Anthea, of course, had had no difficulty in obtaining a voucher, not only because Harriet had sponsored her, but because she had known the family of Princess Esterhazy, one of the patronesses, in Vienna. Anthea suspected that the greatest reason for Almack's popularity was its sheer exclusiveness; the real pleasure in going there was simply the opportunity to be seen mingling with the influential and the fashionable.

"Really, Mama, I can't think why you and Fanny delight so in coming here," Julian continued to grumble. "I thought, when I was obliged to come up to London, that I would at least see some of the sights, but instead I've had to keep my nose deep in my books, or go out paying calls with you and Fanny and Cousin Anthea . . ." At his mother's exasperated look he broke off with a sheepish grin. "Your pardon, Mama—it's this confounded shirt point, it's digging into my chin." And indeed, if Julian's shirt points had been a fraction of an inch higher he would have been unable to move his head. "There's one thing, anyway," he added, brightening, "I can always enjoy my morning rides with Cousin Anthea. You will be riding tomorrow, Cousin? You won't be too tired after an evening at Almack's?"

"No, not at all," Anthea smiled, hastening to reassure him. "I told you how much I rode when I lived with my father in Portugal. There's a real void in my life if I go for long without a fast daily gallop."

She had become fond of Julian during her brief stay in Grosvenor Square, and she was pleased that he seemed to enjoy her company. Raised as an only child by a single parent, she was beginning to see how much she had missed the closeness of family life, and marvelled at how quickly and completely she had been accepted by the entire Blanchard family. The two younger girls, Emma and Louise, were seldom in evidence; like most schoolgirls, they would remain virtual nonpersons until their debuts. They were obliged to maintain a normal classroom routine with their governess during their London stay, but they treasured the few moments that they could snatch with Anthea: They were enormously intrigued by the thought that she was a real princess, despite her constant disavowals. She was only a serene highness, she told them, more like an English duchess. The older boy, Edmund, was off with his regiment, so she had not met him as yet, but she had grown close to Fanny, a beguilingly pretty girl of elfin charm, closely resembling both her mother and Julian, who had taken to Anthea like an affectionate younger sister.

Anthea spotted Fanny now, dressed in sheer white muslin with lilies of the valley in her hair, coming off the floor after the country dance. "How lovely Fanny looks tonight," she remarked.

"Thank you, my dear. But then—and I really don't think that I'm prejudiced, do you?—Fanny always looks lovely." Harriet looked pensive. "I daresay that she will be married and settled down by the end of the year. Did I tell you that Phillip has already received several offers for her? Though I must say, Anthea," she added with an affectionate glance at her niece, "if Fanny looked as striking as you do tonight, Phillip would be fighting off her suitors with both hands! You must be the only woman in these rooms who could wear such a gown."

Anthea looked down at her dress, a white net frock over a slip of brilliant green satin, cut very low at the bodice and trimmed with a bottom flounce of rich blond lace, intermingled with tiny knots of yellow roses; on her head she wore a Kent-type turban of green Parisian gauze embroidered with yellow roses. It was, as Harriet had said, a striking ensemble, in which most women without her colouring and figure would have looked faintly ridiculous.

Anthea looked up with a smile as Phillip came up to her. "I'm here to claim my dance before one of my rivals pirates you away," he said pleasantly as he led her out for the quadrille then forming. "No need to ask you if you are enjoying yourself. That lovely glow in your cheeks makes you look more beautiful than ever."

With a murmured thanks Anthea took her place beside him in the set, her mind only partly concentrating on the first of the five consecutive figures of the quadrille, wondering rather uneasily if Phillip, usually so serious minded, so reserved, was becoming fond of her. It seemed out of character for him to bestow such warm personal compliments, and certainly his eyes, as they rested on her figure in the outrageous Parisian gown, had betrayed more than a cousinly affection. Would it be such a bad idea, she thought fleetingly, a match between herself and Phillip? She was becoming ever more fond of him and of his family, and he possessed none of the raffish irresponsibility that she had so disliked in her father and Karl von Westendorf; indeed, from what she had observed to date, Phillip had taken upon himself the stewardship of his step-mother and younger brothers and sisters. Then, another factor that must weigh with her if she were ever to break her resolve not to marry again, Phillip was well-to-do in his own right; her fortune, though doubtless it would not come amiss, was not necessary for him to maintain his station in life.

Musing over this somewhat disturbing new idea, Anthea moved absentmindedly through the figures of the quadrille, saved from making a mistake by Phillip's competence. He danced, as he seemed to do most things, extremely well. Afterwards, sitting beside Harriet, with Phillip remaining beside her to chat, Anthea was rather surprised to glimpse Lady Jersey, the doyen of the patronesses, bearing down on her. Lady Jersey, beautiful and haughty and so conscious of her great position that she was often downright rude, had been only offhandedly polite when she had met Anthea earlier in the evening, but now she was wreathed in smiles. "Your Serene Highness, here is a friend of mine who would particularly like to be made known to you. Madame von Hellenberg, may I present Lord Lyndock?"

Anthea barely restrained a gasp as her eye shifted to the man standing beside Lady Jersey. He was tall and superbly built, with laughing brown eyes in a handsome face framed by chestnut curls; he wore a dress coat of black superfine and breeches of black Florentine silk, moulded to his broad shoulders and powerful thighs like a second skin; his marvellously arranged cravat made the neckwear of every other gentleman in the room look slightly out of style. He looked supremely at ease in this, the top bastion of London society, just as, very recently, he had seemed quite in his element chasing away bandits in the Ligurian Alps.

Clicking his heels, Lyndock murmured "Durchlaucht," lifted Anthea's hand in a formal kiss, bowed politely to Harriet and nodded to Phillip with a careless "Glad to see you again, Montville." To Anthea he said coolly, "May I have the pleasure of this waltz, Madame?"

"I'm sure that Her Highness will delight to waltz, coming as she does from the city that is the very cradle of the waltz," smiled Lady Jersey with a touch of her familiar spite, and Anthea wondered, as she walked with Lord Lyndock to the dance floor, if he were one of the patroness's many flirts.

As Lyndock slipped his arm around her waist, he said, with a formality belied by the dancing lights in his eyes, "I wonder, Your Serene Highness, if you realize how very risqué you and I would have appeared only a few short months ago in daring to dance the waltz?"

"Daring, Lord Lyndock?" replied Anthea in a tone of polite interest.

"Why, yes. You see, Lady Jersey introduced the waltz only this spring when she returned from a visit to the Continent—it hadn't previously been danced in England. It shocked the staider elements of our society; they thought that it was scandalous for a young man to put his arm around a young lady in *public*. When the prince regent included the waltz in the program of a ball that he very recently gave, the *Times* commented '. . . this indecent foreign dance . . . is deserving of severe reprobation and we trust it will never again be tolerated in any moral English society.' Of course, I'm sure that your morals are above reproach, Your Highness." Lyndock gazed down at her with a teasing grin. "I can't tell you how relieved I am to know that you're not really Frau Steinach. I *am* a little surprised, I own, to discover that you're actually a princess."

"Only a serene highness," she corrected him automatically.

"Yes, but still, most impressive. Tell me, Durchlaucht, do you always travel under a nom de plume?"

"Not always," she retorted. "Only when it suits me. In general, however, I believe that advertising rank or fortune is foolhardy when one is travelling, especially in Italy, where it is just an invitation to thieves and bandits. May I ask if it is *your* practice to travel under an assumed name, Lord Lyndock? Or do you do so only if you contemplate dalliance with a strange lady and wish to remain anonymous?"

Lyndock hunched his shoulders in a mock gesture of defense. "Touché!" he said good-naturedly. "You're your father's daughter, I see—always carry the attack to the enemy! But seriously, when I last met you, I hadn't yet become accustomed to being called Lord Lyndock. I had never expected to inherit the title. My uncle, the fourth marquis, died of a heart attack shortly after the Battle of Waterloo, only days after his only son was killed in a hunting accident. Until shortly before our dramatic meeting in the Ligurian Alps I was plain Major Stretton."

"In effect, Lord Lyndock, you would like me to believe that your withholding of your real identity was a mere slip of the memory?" Anthea said with a touch of acid.

"Not at all," said Lyndock insouciantly. "You know perfectly well that I had every intention of spending the evening in pleasant —and anonymous—dalliance, as you put it. Until you very properly put me in my place." His expression sobered. "I've been wanting to make amends for my coxcombical behavior that night at the inn. I must have seemed to you like the callowest of Bond Street loungers."

Anthea's voice had an edge to it. "No, indeed, my lord. I simply took into account your belief that I was plain Frau Steinach. Of course, I know that you would never have had the bad *ton* to cast out lures to a serene highness."

For just an instant Lyndock's elegant poise deserted him. "Confound it, I would have apologised to you more gracefully the next morning," he spluttered. "But during the commotion of removing the tree from the road and conferring with the landlord about the shortest route to Novi, you never gave me a moment to talk to you privately. That middle-aged Tartar of yours stuck to you like a burr."

"That was on my orders. Though she scarcely needed any encouragement to do so. Hannah suspected from the first that you—as she would put it—had designs on my virtue."

"Which you defended like the impregnable fortress that I'm sure it is," said Lyndock feelingly.

"Indeed I did, sir. And a novel experience it was, beating off the advances of a gentleman of presumed birth and breeding."

Lyndock bit his lip. "I deserve that. I had no right to assume that you were—were available just because you were travelling alone. Confound it, I do know quality when I see it. But you were so beautiful—so irresistible—and we had just been through a hair-raising experience together. I don't see how you can condemn me so harshly for being carried away by my feelings."

Anthea lifted an eyebrow. "Condemn you, my lord? Not at all. I'll gladly put the incident—and you, too, for that matter—entirely out of my mind. Which brings me to the reason I accepted your invitation to dance this evening. If you haven't already done so, I would appreciate your not speaking about the circumstances of our meeting in Italy. I don't particularly wish to be the object of gossip."

"I haven't mentioned our first meeting to anyone, and I won't," said Lyndock promptly. He looked at her pleadingly. "I can't believe that you're as heartless as you sound. Won't you accept my profound apologies for my behaviour in the Alps? Give me a chance to make amends, to show you how perfect a gentleman I can be?"

"You make a great deal too much of this," said Anthea impatiently. "Oh, very well, your apology is accepted."

"And you'll let us be friends?"

"I said nothing about that."

Lyndock broke into a sudden smile. "You aren't really going to keep me in Coventry, are you?" he said cajolingly. "So lovely a lady with a 'heart as soft, a heart as kind, a heart as sound and free . . .' "

" 'As in the whole world thou canst find That heart I'll give to thee.' " Anthea picked up the quotation without thinking. She broke off in some confusion to find Lyndock's eyes brimming with laughter.

"Confess to it, Your Serene Highness, you couldn't have considered my behaviour so very dreadful, or you'd never have looked up that poem."

It was difficult in the extreme to resist the impudent charm of the man, Anthea thought resignedly. "Your actions were quite reprehensible," she retorted with as much severity as she could muster. "I must be going quite soft in the head to even consider forgiving you."

"It's too late, you've already done it," he retorted. His smile deepened. "Do you know, I was very tempted to go on to Vienna after we parted in the Alps, even though you had refused to tell me your real name. I thought that if I went about Vienna describing a ravishing beauty with coal-black hair and Irish blue eyes—there *is* a spot of Irish in you somewhere, am I not right?—I thought that someone would be sure to identify you to me."

Anthea was unable to suppress a dimple at the corner of her mouth. "Then you would have been clapped into the nearest lunatic asylum, and well you would have deserved it," she said, adding primly, "you know as well as I do, Lord Lyndock, that your ridiculous remarks—indeed, virtually every remark that you have made to me this evening—are most improper."

"But you're not really shocked, are you, Madame von Hellenberg?"

Anthea broke into a chuckle. "Perhaps not. And did you go on to Vienna?"

"No. I thought better of it. After all, your manner when we last met was certainly not very encouraging. If I *had* located you in Vienna, would you have allowed me to call?"

"Certainly not. I never wanted to see you again."

"Just as well, perhaps, that I didn't try my luck. But speaking of my luck, it was certainly with me tonight when I discovered that the very latest, most talked about beauty of the season, an Austrian princess, no less, was actually my lady of the Ligurian Alps. And a cousin of my old acquaintance, Phillip Montville. I must tell you that Montville and I were at Eton together and we have neighbouring estates in Rutland. And so, tell me, are you enjoying your visit to London? Have you visited here previously?"

"I daresay that I must have been here briefly as a very small child, but I have no recollection of it. I'm enjoying it very much. It's very different from Viennese society, but pleasant. My young cousin Fanny is being brought out this season and there is some kind of party or entertainment every evening. I'm becoming quite exhausted! I must say, however"—her eye roamed around the ballroom—"that I haven't yet met either Beau Brummell or Lord Byron."

"The poor Beau." Lyndock shook his head sadly. "After his falling out with the regent a few months ago his debtors caught up with him at last and he was forced to flee across the Channel. I hear that he blames his misfortunes on the loss of a lucky sixpence with a hole in it."

"Come now, my lord, that's doing it rather too brown!"

"That's the Beau for you. He'll never admit that he finally went too far, making jokes at the regent's expense. As for Byron"—Lyndock lowered his voice to a murmur—"this isn't for innocent ears, but the truth is that you won't have the opportunity of seeing him either; he's also had to leave England. Society drew the line against an accusation of incest with his own sister."

Shaking her head chidingly, Anthea said, "I must tell you, sir, that I find your remarks more than a trifle warm."

Lyndock grinned down at her. "Don't try to bamboozle me, Your Serene Highness. I haven't shocked you in the least. You're no inexperienced innocent, no Friday-faced prude. Don't forget, when I first came across you, you were travelling the length of Italy with only a handful of servants to accompany you, and I'll wager that if I hadn't come along to rescue you from those bandits, you would have been perfectly capable of extricating yourself from the situation."

"Odious creature!" said Anthea roundly, but the corners of her mouth were quivering.

As the waltz ended, Lyndock said quickly, "I must see you again soon."

"You're welcome to call on me at my aunt's house in Grosvenor Square. But I'm sure that we'll be meeting each other often in any case. The fact that we both have the entrée at Almack's almost guarantees that we will be guests at the same balls and parties. Do you know, I'm told that Lady Jersey has excluded two-thirds of the peerage from attendance at Almack's!"

"Of course we'll be seeing each other," said Lyndock impatiently. "But I don't wish to meet you in the middle of a mob of people."

Cocking her head at him, Anthea feigned puzzlement. "But, surely, you can't have anything of a really private nature to say to me?"

"I have *many* private things to say to you. Tell me, are you riding in London?"

"I *drive* every afternoon in Hyde Park. One must be seen, you know."

"You aren't riding, then," replied Lyndock, disappointed.

"As a matter of fact, I am," Anthea relented. "My young cousin Julian and I have been rising at a frightful hour to ride in

Hyde Park—there is nobody else around then and I can have a real unladylike gallop.''

"Excellent. What time precisely do you mean by a frightful hour?''

As she walked off the dance floor Anthea felt strangely exhilarated, with a sense of lightness and excitement, of almost walking on air, that she had not experienced in years. When she and Lyndock arrived back at Harriet's side, Fanny was there also, and Lyndock greeted her smilingly. After he had gone, Anthea soon noticed that Fanny, usually so bubbling, so talkative, with a lovely rosy tinge to her skin, now looked pale and was unnaturally quiet. Harriet's maternal eye soon zeroed in on her. "My dear, aren't you feeling well?''

"I have a little headache, Mama. It's nothing.''

"I was afraid of this. You've been racketing about entirely too much, Fanny. I've been telling you that you needed more rest, and now I must insist that you take a nap in the afternoons.''

Fanny made the ritual response. "Oh, Mama, I'm not a baby to need naps.'' But Anthea, as she danced every dance for the rest of the evening, including another vigorous waltz with Lord Lyndock, kept an anxious eye on her young cousin, who actually insisted on sitting out several dances, and concluded that Fanny was either ill or quite worn down from the rigours of her first London season.

Later that evening, back in Grosvenor Square, Anthea was sitting before her dressing table while Hannah brushed her hair, when she heard the sounds of altercation from the room next to hers. It was Fanny's bedchamber, and when the voices grew even louder and more strident, Anthea quickly went into the corridor and knocked at her cousin's door. After a brief pause, Fanny's middle-aged maid opened the door. "Oh, it's you, ma'am,'' she said, her harassed expression somewhat lightening. "I was afeared that it might be Miss Harriet. Do come in. I'm quite at my wits' end to know what to do.''

"What's the problem, Sinton? It *is* Sinton, is it not?''

"Yes, ma'am. Well, you see, Miss Fanny's in such a state—she made me bring down her large portmanteau from the attics, and now she's in there throwing all her belongings into it, every which way—and what it will do to her new sarcenet morning gown and her beautiful ball dress I really don't know. And now she wants me to go to the stables and order the carriage brought around—''

"Merciful heavens," said Anthea in astonishment. "Why does she want the carriage at this time of night?"

"To go home to Rutland, ma'am. I can't rightly make out exactly what she's saying, but she seems very unhappy."

"Don't worry about it, Sinton. You may go now. Just leave Miss Fanny to me."

Anthea entered the bedchamber, where Fanny, her hair disheveled and her face wet with tears, was attempting to stuff a swansdown muff into an already bulging portmanteau. Before Fanny had quite grasped that she was even there, Anthea removed the muff from her cousin's fingers and shut the portmanteau, saying calmly, "Now, my dear, will you tell me what this is all about?"

"Leave me be, Cousin Anthea," cried Fanny, jamming a bonnet over her curls and reaching for a fur-trimmed pelisse. "I'm going home to Ashby House and you can't stop me."

Realising that Fanny was very close to hysteria, Anthea grabbed her by the shoulder with one hand and with the other administered a hard slap to her cheek.

"Oh!" gasped Fanny, her features twisted with surprise; it was probably the first time, Anthea reflected, that anyone had lifted a finger to the Montvilles' pampered oldest daughter. Surprise gave way to a flood of stormy tears, and Anthea put her arms around Fanny, holding her close, making soothing little sounds of comfort, waiting for the tears to subside. When Fanny had wept herself out from sheer exhaustion, Anthea mopped her face, brushed her hair back and settled her against the pillows.

Drawing up a chair, Anthea sat down beside the bed. "I'm sorry that I slapped you, Fanny, but I really felt that I had to do something."

Fanny flushed a bright red. Her eyes were clear now, and she was much calmer. "Oh, Cousin Anthea, I'm so unhappy." Tears welled up into her eyes again.

"I can see that," said Anthea gently. "Would it help, do you think, to tell me about it?"

Biting her lip, Fanny hesitated. Then the words rushed out. "It was seeing Lord Lyndock. I watched him dancing with you, smiling and flirting . . . I could see him starting it all over again, breaking your heart the way he broke mine."

Anthea drew a startled breath. She had gathered, during the brief time that she had known her, that Fanny was a romantic, immersing herself in the Gothic novels of Mrs. Radcliffe and Monk Lewis, dreaming away the hours with a book of Lord Byron's poetry. But the girl's statement about Lord Lyndock seemed wildly melodramatic. "I don't think that I quite understand you, Fanny. Could you explain a little?"

Fanny lowered her eyes. "I—I thought that I was in love with Lord Lyndock." She raised her head, staring defiantly at Anthea. "I *was* in love with him. After he came home to claim his new estates after Waterloo—he lives near us in Rutland, you know—we met at several assemblies in Oakham and at private parties, nothing really formal, of course, because I wasn't out yet, and sometimes we would meet when I went riding around the estate. He was so attentive and charming, he paid me all sorts of compliments, he always asked me to dance with him at least once every evening. And once he said, with that wonderful smile of his, 'You're quite enchanting, little Fanny. I've made up my mind to wait for you until you're all grown up.'"

Anthea, privately reflecting on that beguiling smile of Lyndock's, and thinking also that he should not have paid such decided attentions to so young a girl, playful though those attentions probably were, said placatingly, "Perhaps you read too much into what Lord Lyndock said. It's really too bad, I know, but I do think that he's something of a flirt."

Fanny shook her head emphatically. "No, no, he did mean what he said. Because when we met again, after he returned from his tour of the Continent—after the season had started here in

57

London—he was more attentive to me than ever. For several weeks he singled me out on every occasion; his attentions were so marked that I—I really began to think that he was preparing to offer for me. I know that Phillip thought so, too, because I overheard him talking to Mama about the possibility, and he seemed quite put out about it. I don't think that Phillip cares much for Geoffrey—Lord Lyndock.''

"I see," said Anthea, beginning to feel chilled. "So what happened then?"

Fanny looked desolate. "Nothing happened. Nothing at all. Suddenly he just—he just dropped me and started giving all his attention to Miss Millson. *She* was the great belle of this season until *you* came along, Cousin." Fanny paused, an uncharitable gleam lighting up her eyes. "He merely bowed to Flora Millson tonight at Almack's, however. I expect that he will now concentrate on you, since you've quite put her in the shade."

Utterly taken aback, Anthea considered her reply carefully. Certainly Fanny seemed convinced that what she was saying about Lyndock was true, but she was very young, impressionable and inexperienced; it was likely that she had greatly exaggerated his actions, making far more of his attentions than the situation actually warranted. She said tentatively, "I can't believe that Lord Lyndock would deliberately lead you on to expect an offer. Isn't it at least possible that you misunderstood him? For we've agreed, have we not, that he's a dreadful flirt, quite reprehensible, of course, but—"

"No, no," exclaimed Fanny vehemently. "He's more than just a flirt. He gets great pleasure from breaking hearts. He collects impressionable young females like—like my Uncle Hubert collects butterflies."

"Fanny! You can't realise what you're saying," said Anthea with real horror.

Fanny shook her head unrepentantly. "Yes, I do so realise. You see, I was talking recently with Eliza Vincent—she's become my particular friend during the season—and she told me the truth about Lord Lyndock. For years, it seems, he's had a terrible reputation for fickleness, chasing after the leading beauty of the moment, dropping her as soon as his eye lighted on someone else.''

"Fanny, you must know that you're repeating gossip, mere hearsay," said Anthea with real distaste. "And gossip, I might add, that sounds very unbecoming on the lips of a young girl."

Fanny bridled at Anthea's criticism. "It may be just gossip," she flared, "but everybody in London seems to believe it. I know that you're older than I am, Cousin Anthea, and more—more experienced in the ways of the world, and very beautiful and immensely rich, but you don't know *everything*. Don't say that I didn't warn you about Lord Lyndock when you become his latest victim."

As Fanny was finishing, her voice rose stridently, and Anthea, hoping to avoid another hysterical outburst, deliberately kept her own tone matter-of-fact as she said, "Thank you for telling me this. I'll remember what you said, but I must tell you that I'm in no danger from Lord Lyndock." She smiled brightly at Fanny. "I'm far too downy a bird, as my father used to say, to be taken in by a loose fish of a Guards' officer!" She took Fanny's hands, saying gently, 'I'm sorry that you suffered any pain from knowing Lord Lyndock, Fanny, but I'm sure that it won't be long at all before you find someone more worthy of you."

"You say that so easily, but I know that I'll never love anyone again the way I loved him," said Fanny woefully, tears filling her eyes.

Recognising that only the passage of time would help cure Fanny's lovesickness, Anthea continued to speak with a determined cheerfulness as she tucked the girl under the coverlets, brushed her tangled hair and promised to send in Sinton with some warm milk. "And mind now," she said as she paused in the doorway on her way out, "if you should ever want to talk about this problem again, or any other, please feel free to come to me. Good night, my dear."

Outside the room, she paused in some surprise as she found both Sinton and Phillip Montville standing beside the door.

"Oh, Sinton, please bring Miss Fanny some warm milk. I think that it might help her to sleep."

As Sinton left, Phillip said, "I heard the commotion and came straight to Fanny's room, hoping to reach her before my step-mother was disturbed. Lady Montville is troubled by excruciating headaches and badly needs her rest. When I arrived here, Sinton told me that you were with Fanny."

He paused, obviously waiting for an explanation. Anthea hesitated, unwilling to betray Fanny's confidence even to a compassionate older brother.

"It's Lyndock, isn't it?" Phillip said, his eyes narrowing. "I saw Fanny's face when Lyndock brought you back to your seat after your waltz together. Is my sister very upset?"

It was clear that Phillip had already guessed the reason for Fanny's outburst. Anthea made a sudden decision. "We can't talk here," she said in a low voice. "Fanny might hear us."

"Yes. I suggest that we go down to the morning room." Phillip glanced at her pretty, ruffled silk dressing gown and smiled slightly. "You're somewhat unconventionally dressed for a tête-à-tête, Cousin, but no one will see us. The servants are all in bed."

In the morning room, Phillip said, "I'm going to fetch myself a glass of cognac. Will you join me?" When he returned he handed Anthea her brandy and settled down opposite her, glass in hand. Sipping slowly, he looked at her over the brandy glass, raising his eyebrow. "Well, Cousin Anthea?"

"I'm afraid that Fanny fancies herself head over heels in love with Lord Lyndock. She feels that he definitely encouraged her to think that he was going to offer for her. When she saw him dancing with me tonight she apparently thought that he was now becoming interested in me, and it made her so unhappy that she was packing a bag and threatening to leave London immediately."

A look of outrage settled over Phillip's face, but he did not seem surprised at Anthea's remarks. "I've been worried about the situation since last autumn," he said with a sigh, "when I observed that Lyndock seemed to be paying marked attention to Fanny at our little informal parties in Rutland."

"He seems to be a great flirt, of course. I imagine that it would be very easy to turn the head of an inexperienced young girl."

"It's much more than that," Phillip interrupted. "The man has practically made a career of breaking hearts. It has gotten to the point where every well informed and responsible mother of a young girl about to start her first London season automatically warns her daughter against Lord Lyndock."

"You don't feel that you're exaggerating?" Anthea ventured.

"No, not at all. I really believe that he delights in leading these young women on, making them believe that he is readying a proposal of marriage; then he drops them, leaving them exposed to the most spiteful gossip and innuendo." Phillip brooded for a moment. "I blame myself for much of this. I've known Lyndock for many years—we were at Eton and Cambridge together and we have estates near each other in Rutland—and he's always been selfish and irresponsible, without a serious thought in his head, using that easy charm of his to get whatever he wanted from life. I warned my stepmother about him when he first started throwing out lures to Fanny, and I realize now that I should have been much more emphatic; Lady Montville found it hard to believe that such a charming, friendly young man, practically our next door neighbour, would have designs on her daughter; in fact"—Phillip made a little moué of disgust—"in fact, I believe that my stepmother actually welcomed the thought of a match between Fanny and Lyndock. I hope that Fanny will get over her hurt. I did think for a while that she had ceased to think about Lyndock. She's so pretty, so popular—she seemed to be really enjoying her season."

He looked so despondent that Anthea hastened to reassure him. "Look on the bright side. Fanny has youth and health and energy. She'll probably spring back very quickly from this disappointment. Perhaps she was just overwrought this evening. Aunt Harriet tells me that she thinks that Fanny has been overdoing her activities. And—for what it's worth—I promise to keep an eye on her and to be available if she should want to confide in me again.''

Phillip sat down beside her, taking both her hands in his. ''Now I have even more reason to be glad that you've come to visit us, Cousin Anthea,'' he said gratefully.

There was a decidedly warm light in Phillip's normally cool blue eyes, and the pressure of his hands on hers was anything but cousinly. Withdrawing her hands, Anthea said with a slightly nervous smile, ''You've no need to thank me. I've grown very fond of Fanny. I'm very happy to do anything that I can to help her.''

Later, as she climbed into bed and sank back against her pillows, Anthea found herself enmeshed in conflicting emotions. Had she been too quick to pardon Lyndock for his cavalier treatment of her in the Alps? Had she merely succumbed to the same graceful charm that had always persuaded her to excuse her weakling father's excesses? It was obvious that Lyndock now felt that he had a clear road to a more intimate relationship, a relationship that would be very difficult to maintain in the face of Phillip's intense dislike and poor Fanny's jealousy.

Anthea stirred uneasily in her bed. Tonight in Lyndock's company she had felt vibrantly alive, intensely aware of her own youth and beauty, filled with the heady sensation that a new and breathtaking chapter of her life was opening before her. Was it possible that Phillip, who seemed to have been outshone by Lyndock since boyhood, and Fanny, perhaps dazzled by the attentions of a very personable and much older man, were simply exaggerating the flaws in Lyndock's character? In her own case, wounding though the thought might be, perhaps Lyndock had made a perfectly natural mistake in assuming that Anthea was receptive to a one-night love affair. As he had pointed out, respectable, highborn women customarily travelled with a suitable male escort and a large entourage of servants.

Anthea came to a decision. She did not want to close her heart to these new feelings that Lyndock had awakened in her. But neither was she prepared, on the strength of two brief meetings, to plunge headlong into a love affair with him. She would continue to see him, to enjoy his exhilarating attentions. Then, if he were to become important in her life, it would happen naturally. She would not go out of her way to welcome his advances, but neither would she discourage him.

= 5 =

"WELL, NOW, THIS this is much more the thing," said Julian, drawing a deep breath of the cool morning air as he cantered with Anthea through the gates of Hyde Park. "Why, when one can do this, would anyone want to spend his time at a place like Almack's, I ask you?"

"Some of us would like to have the best of both worlds," retorted Anthea, laughing.

"Hullo—there's Lord Lyndock, by Jove."

As she spotted the tall, rangy figure waiting for them just inside the park, mounted on a magnificent chestnut stallion, Anthea's heart leaped, to her chagrin. She saw that it was going to be difficult to maintain a cool facade in her relationship with him, to have it appear that his company was something that she took very much for granted.

Bringing his mount up beside hers, Lyndock exclaimed gaily, "Your Serene Highness, what an unexpected pleasure. May I join you?"

While Julian was muttering to himself, "Unexpected pleasure, my eye and Betty Martin!" Anthea said demurely, "By all means, Lord Lyndock. The more the merrier."

"May I compliment you on your riding habit?" He appreciatively eyed the Parisian masterpiece that she was wearing, a bright green coat *à la militaire* with a hat in black beaver topped with long green ostrich plumes and black half-boots laced in green.

"What a rider you are!" he exclaimed a few moments later, his eyes kindling in an even more heartfelt compliment after a furious gallop down the length of Rotten Row.

"Yes, indeed, Cousin," chimed in Julian. "You ride better than any female I've ever met!"

"I thank both of you, but if I do ride well, it's no credit to me. John Potter—my father's old groom and now mine—put me on a horse almost before I could walk. Of course, it was a necessity to ride well in the Peninsula. One never knew when the French would chase us out of town!"

Julian turned his attention to Lyndock. "You were at the Battle of Waterloo, were you not, my lord?"

"Yes—along with many thousands of others."

"Is it true that during the great cavalry charge you actually dueled with a French officer so that you could wrest away from him the eagle standard that he was carrying?"

Lyndock opened his eyes wide in a good-natured grin. "Now, wherever did you hear about that?"

"Oh, I've read everything that I could put my hands on about the battle. But I've never actually met anyone who had fought at Waterloo. Is it really true that Lord Uxbridge had the recall sounded, after the initial English cavalry charge had broken d'Erlon's great assault, but that nobody heard the trumpets?"

"Well," said Lyndock, his brown eyes dancing with amusement, "I think that many of us did hear the recall, but we just pretended that we didn't!"

Julian ploughed ahead with his questioning. "I've heard that your regiment, the Blues, wasn't even supposed to take part in the engagement. Your orders were just to cover the retirement of the other regiments." He sighed. "Oh, how I wish I could have been there," he burst out. "For the rest of my life I could say that I fought in the battle that changed the course of history."

Lyndock's sympathetic smile disappeared and he said quietly, "Don't forget, by the time our cavalry reached the French guns, we were reduced to mere remnants of squads and sections. Lord

Wellington lost a quarter of his entire cavalry in that action, over twenty-five hundred of his best troopers. The glory of victory fades just a bit when you see your friends dying beside you and you ride over a field of mangled bodies.''

Julian appeared unconvinced by Lyndock's little lecture. He retreated into his own thoughts, leaving Anthea and Lyndock to talk and flirt amiably. Anthea thought gaily that there was no reason to allow Lyndock to have all the fun; she discovered a new talent within herself, the ability to parry his practiced thrusts with an expertise that brought an appreciative gleam to his eyes and a redoubling of his efforts to ingratiate himself.

"Will you be attending Lady Alliston's rout party this evening?" he asked.

"I'm not sure. Lady Alliston has a very grand house in Portman Square, and apparently she has the entrée everywhere, but I do think that she may be a bit of a parvenu. Do you know, I've heard that she won't invite anybody to her house who doesn't sport a title! So, I've almost decided not to go—unless, that is, I might expect to find some *very* interesting people there." She tossed him a mischievous sideways glance. "*Will* I find some interesting people there, do you think?"

"I can guarantee that there will be at least one person there who is very interested in *you*. As to how interesting he is himself, I'll leave that entirely to you."

"I'll think about it," replied Anthea, laughing.

As they said good-bye to Lyndock at the park gates and started home, Anthea remarked to Julian, "You seemed very interested in Lord Lyndock's military career. Have you ever thought of entering the army yourself?"

Julian's expressive young face darkened. "I've thought of nothing else for years," he said bitterly. "I know, from what my brother Edmund tells me about his experiences in the Seventh Hussars, that I would like it beyond everything. But Phillip will hear nothing of it. He intends me for the Church."

"The Church!"

"There, you find the thought as ridiculous as I do. But Phillip says since I'm not the eldest son, or even the second son, that some provision must be made for my future. My godfather has offered me the living on his estate. It's a fine living with a very good stipend. So I'm to study with my tutor this spring and summer, and then in the autumn I'm to go up to Cambridge to study to be a clergyman."

Anthea listened, appalled. It did not seem to her, from what she had observed of Julian, that the fun-loving boy was a likely candidate for the clergy. But she kept silent. She knew how deep was Phillip's concern for all his brothers and sisters and she did not want to put herself in the position of publicly criticising him. Later that day, however, she sought Phillip out.

"Julian tells me that you wish him to take holy orders," she said tentatively. "Forgive me if I'm being intrusive, but I did just wonder why you feel that he would be a good clergyman."

Phillip smiled. "You're not being intrusive in the least. I'm glad that you take such interest in him. Well, Cousin, it is really very simple. I will undoubtedly marry and have sons to inherit the baronetcy and the family estates, my half-brother Edmund is doing well in the army, and with Julian's godfather willing to provide a living for him, I can only believe that this is the most prudent course to follow."

"But if Julian is not temperamentally suited for the ministry," began Anthea, "if he has no real calling to serve God in this way—"

"Oh, come now, we're not asking him to become an anchorite or a tonsured monk, after all. A career in the Church isn't very much different from any other career. You'll see, Julian's living is located in prime hunt country, and, once he settles in, he'll wonder why he ever made such a fuss about taking orders."

With that, Anthea had to subside, though she still did not agree with Phillip and even felt somewhat shocked at his matter-of-fact attitude toward the ministry.

At breakfast that same morning, Anthea was relieved to find

that Fanny had weathered the emotional storm of the previous night, though she looked a little wan and was far less talkative than usual. Fortunately Harriet never came down for breakfast and so failed to note the signs of strain in her daughter's behaviour.

As the days wore on, Fanny seemed to be making a determined effort to put her failed love affair behind her, and Anthea, admiring the girl's spunky courage, made it a point to spend as much time as possible with her young cousin. The two of them spent many hours turning over the wares at the fashionable shops in Oxford Street; Fanny loved pretty clothes and never tired of visiting the linen drapers, the silk mercers, the milliners and dressmakers in Mayfair. They visited Hatchard's bookshop too, drove in Hyde Park at five every afternoon, of course, and sampled the water ices at Gunther's. It was as she and Fanny sat over white currant ices under the plane trees of Berkeley Square across the road from Gunther's that Anthea received a small shock. She looked up to see the elegant figure of Karl von Westendorf, picking his way between the waiters dashing across the road with laden trays.

"Durchlaucht." He bowed with a smart click of his heels that elicited a muffled laugh from Fanny.

"Karl! You're the very last person in the world that I expected to see," gasped Anthea. "What on earth are you doing here? Oh, Fanny, may I introduce an old friend from Vienna, Graf von Westendorf. Karl, my cousin, Fanny Montville. And do sit down, before you cause one of these poor waiters to drop his tray all over you."

"I've just come from Grosvenor Square, where they told me that you were out. I was planning to return later this afternoon, but now there's no need," said Karl happily. "Imagine my joy when I looked across the street and found you sitting there under the trees."

"Yes, but Karl, what *are* you doing here?"

"Without her most beautiful, her most accomplished, her most interesting hostess, Vienna is a sad bore," replied Karl with a grin, reaching for her hand. "So I did the logical thing: I came here looking for you."

Anthea pulled her hand away. "Really, Karl, you might try for a little more formality in public."

"Why?" asked Karl innocently. "I don't object at all to being known as your very determined suitor." He turned to Fanny, who looked mildly scandalised. "I've been asking Princess von Hellenberg to marry me at least once a week for months. Except, of course, when she's being her very elusive self, jaunting around Italy, visiting her English relatives—"

Anthea threw up her hands. "Fanny, pay no attention to Karl. He has no manners at all."

Though Anthea had periodically to dampen down Karl's irrepressible spirits, she really did not object to his being in London, where, by virtue of his good looks, engaging personality and ancient title, he soon had the entrée to every house of any consequence, and his single-minded pursuit of Anthea occasioned only the lifting of amused eyebrows.

During the next few weeks Anthea often felt that she was living in a sort of dream world, her days filled to the brim with social activities, which, though she occasionally granted their superficiality, she enjoyed immensely. She had never really had a youth; her years of constant worry about her father's mounting problems, the perpetual scrabbling for enough money to pay the bills, her brief marriage during which she catered entirely to her aging husband's whims, even her months of widowhood where she was always conscious of the need to preserve her image as Princess von Hellenberg—all these were behind her now, and for the first time in her life she felt young and free, living in her own country at last, sought after, admired, with no necessity to please anyone but herself.

She went to all the fashionable haunts of society. To Drury Lane, with its old crones in rusty black bonnets and long cloaks, hovering in the foyer behind the fresh young girls they hoped to sell to the highest bidder, where Anthea, in the Montville box, laughed with the rest of London at the off-stage remarks of the famous Mrs. Grundy in *Speed the Plough*. To the Royal Opera House, where music took second place to the dandies and fops, who strolled in the pit during performances, showing off their clothes, rattling their canes, chatting so loudly that the people in the galleries shouted at them to be quiet. And to a Royal Drawing Room, where, though the old, mad king was absent, she met Queen Charlotte and accepted the commiserations of those who regretted that she had just missed—by a matter of weeks—the wedding of the year, that of the regent's daughter, Princess Charlotte, to Leopold of Saxe-Coburg.

Anthea met, too, the famous figures of London society. Lady Holland, the great political hostess of the day. The eccentric and spendthrift Lord Alvanley, who once complained that he had wasted his entire fortune paying tradesmen's bills when he might better have lost it in a gambling hell, and who was the terror of country house parties because he insisted on extinguishing his bedchamber candle by tossing it on the floor and throwing a pillow at it. Lord Petersham, his only interest in life his vast collection of snuffs and exotic teas, who once said solemnly that a delicate Sèvres snuffbox was suitable only for summer wear. Sir Lumley Skeffington, who wrote bad plays, painted his face and used scent. Lord Barrymore, club-footed, dissolute and profane, who was one of the notable whips of the Four-in-Hand Club. Anthea always regretted not having met the celebrated Beau Brummell: She could not approve his single-minded concentration on his own person, but a man who spent five hours each day on his appearance, who once resigned an army commission because his regiment was transferred from London to the provinces, and who, for a considerable time, ruled over London society by the sheer force of self-confident arrogance, must have been fascinating to know.

As evening fell every day during the height of the season, the streets of the West End came to glittering life; there was a great rumble of wheels on cobbled streets as streams of lighted carriages began drawing up before the tall houses, every window ablaze, with powdered and gold-laced footmen lining the steps of the mansions and curious crowds gathering around the marquees, straining for a look at the famous and high-born.

Every evening there were balls, routs, assemblies, masqued balls, musical galas, *fêtes champêtres* in the gardens of Mayfair mansions, often ending in the early hours with a breakfast party in one of the great estates of nearby Surrey. The affairs were often very crowded, with a thousand people invited to a house where only six hundred could be accommodated, and often, too, they provided no entertainment, no cards or music, for the guests. Many a party was simply a showcase for the display of one's clothing or jewels or social standing, but for a long while Anthea failed to see that London society could be every bit as trivial, as artificial, as empty, as that of Vienna. It was only in rare moments of introspection that she forced herself to admit that her sense of perpetual excitement, her feeling of being poised on the brink of some poignantly thrilling experience, were caused by her constant association with Lyndock, who was a fellow guest at virtually every gathering to which she was invited. Often in the small hours of the night, as she lay in bed remembering the details of the evening just past—waltzing in the secure circle of Geoffrey's arm, exchanging a secret grin with him over some incidence of idiocy or social pretension, feeling the slight pressure of his shoulder against hers as they glided along the Thames in a carpeted boat with coloured awnings and fairy lanterns to guide the way as they sipped champagne from Gunther's—Anthea would draw a deep breath and wonder a little uneasily how far and how swiftly the relationship with Lyndock would go.

It was during this period that Anthea met a woman, who, though not as prominent as Lady Holland or Lady Jersey, made far more of an impact on her. At a ball given by the Duchess of Margate, Anthea was accosted by a Lady Fenwick, a very pretty, rather elaborately dressed woman, seeming to be in her late twenties or early thirties. Anthea vaguely recalled having seen her at various social events.

"I think that we should know each other better, Your Highness," Lady Fenwick had gushed. "We have such a great mutual friend—Lord Lyndock," she added in response to Anthea's look of frozen surprise. "Oh, yes, my dear, I've known Geoffrey for donkey's years."

"Indeed. I don't recall that Lord Lyndock ever mentioned your name."

"Oh, that naughty boy," exclaimed Lady Fenwick archly. "Well, all the more reason for us to meet. We have so much to talk about! Won't you come to tea with me one day soon? I'm just around the corner from you in Brook Street."

"I'm afraid that my engagement calendar is full for the next few weeks, Lady Fenwick. And now, won't you excuse me? I see that my aunt is trying to get my attention."

With that, Anthea managed to make her escape. Later that evening, back in Grosvenor Square, Harriet had commented delicately, "I didn't realise that you were acquainted with Sarah Fenwick."

"I'm not—nor do I wish to be," Anthea had replied shortly, a small frown furrowing her forehead. "I think that, in her own vulgar way, she was trying to warn me off Lord Lyndock."

"Oh." Harriet's eyes had widened at Anthea's bluntness. In common with most of London, she had observed Lyndock's increasing attentions to her niece.

"Tell me, Aunt," Anthea had inquired abruptly. "Is Lady Fenwick Lyndock's mistress?"

Harriet had been overcome with confusion. "Oh, my dear, I don't think—I'm not sure that we should be talking about such matters, but—well, yes, they do say that Lord Lyndock once had an affair with Lady Fenwick. Last year, some time, I think it was. I shouldn't—I shouldn't let it concern me at all, if I were you. I can assure you that it doesn't seem to bother the lady's husband!"

Her frown disappearing, Anthea had laughed at her aunt's

anxious expression. "Lord, Aunt, it's nothing to me if Lord Lyndock has a harem!" Inwardly she did not feel quite so insouciant, though she was a woman of the world enough to realise that it would be strange indeed if a man of Lyndock's calibre had not had a number of affairs with married ladies. But the incident had the effect of making her slightly more cautious with Lyndock for the next several days.

Anthea was seeing almost as much of Karl von Westendorf as she was of Lyndock. Because he was a friend of Anthea's, Harriet made sure that Karl was invited to every prominent house in Mayfair, where he amused himself mightily with pretty females and commented on Lyndock's pursuit of Anthea with a good-natured "My dear, I see that it's not enough for you to break every heart in Vienna." He even showed up occasionally for an early morning ride in Hyde Park, complaining bitterly about the barbarity of the hour. With his usual quickness, Lyndock realized that Karl was no real threat to him, remarking to Anthea with a grin, "If this keeps up, I'll have to challenge your Austrian friend to a duel to get him out of the way."

That Anthea was meeting Lyndock virtually every morning in Hyde Park gradually became known to all the Montvilles through a chance remark dropped by Julian. Fanny said nothing, but her wistfully reproachful glance caused Anthea more than a pang of guilt. And though it obviously cost him a great deal of effort, Phillip made it a point to discuss the relationship with her. "It has come to my attention, Cousin, that you are seeing a great deal of Lord Lyndock," he began gravely. "I suppose that one could say that it doesn't concern me, but you are a close relative and a guest in my house, and I would feel very remiss if I did not remind you of the shoddiness of the man's reputation."

Anthea found herself in a dilemma. She was not prepared to admit to anyone her growing feelings for Lyndock. She would have preferred to have her relationship with him regarded as no more than a casual acquaintance, no more important than the many other friendships that she had formed since her arrival in London.

"I really don't think that I see Lord Lyndock more often than other people," she said rather defensively. "If you're referring to our rides in the park—well, that's none of my doing, Cousin. After Lord Lyndock chanced to find out about my early morning rides he simply began appearing at the park each day as Julian and I were starting out. I could hardly forbid him to ride there. It *is* a public place."

"But surely you could have discouraged him from riding with *you*, public place or no."

Phillip's observation was entirely reasonable, Anthea thought. Phillip was almost always most reasonable and logical. She could think of no counter to his remark except an outright fib. "Well, I did hint to Lord Lyndock that I would rather ride alone. But he's not an easy man to discourage. And really, Phillip, I'm sure that you will agree that if I were to make an issue of it, it would give the matter an importance that it doesn't deserve."

His colour rising, Phillip snapped, "I still say the man has unmitigated gall. Leave this to me. I'll give him such a set-down that he'll think twice before inflicting his unwanted presence on you."

"Oh, no, you mustn't do that," exclaimed Anthea, aghast. "It might"—she searched her mind for a convincing argument—"it might cause a great deal of unpleasantness." She ended on a note of pathos. "I don't think I could bear any hint of scandal, Cousin."

Chagrined, Phillip said quickly, "Forgive me, I spoke without thinking. It goes without saying that we cannot allow any kind of embarrassing gossip about you. Perhaps I refined too much on the subject. Lyndock is such a flighty creature, he'll very likely soon drop his pursuit of you and start chasing after some other female."

"Yes, very likely," said Anthea, trying to sound indifferent. If Lyndock were the fickle philanderer that Phillip considered him to be, she thought, it was really not impossible that his roving eye might shortly alight on some other young woman.

Her aunt's complaisant reaction to the news of Anthea's daily rides rather surprised her niece, until Anthea reflected that Harriet had never known the full story of Fanny's infatuation for Lyndock.

"Of course, my dear, Geoffrey Lyndock has always had the reputation for being a very great rake," Harriet had said pensively. "But somehow, you know, I've always had a great fondness for him. There was a time, early in the season, when I actually thought that he might offer for Fanny. But Phillip was so opposed to the very thought of it, and I daresay that Geoffrey *is* too experienced, too worldly, for an innocent like Fanny. But he might be just the match for you, Anthea. I would so much like to see you settled down here in England." She added, "I don't suppose that you've noticed it, but Geoffrey does remind me, just a little, of my brother Jack when he was young, before he married your mother. Their smiles are so alike, their happy outlook on life . . ."

How odd, Anthea thought, that Harriet should see a resemblance between Lyndock and her father. Anthea had seen it too, but of course Lyndock possessed a strength of character lacking in John Blanchard.

Rather to the amazement of her relatives and many of her new acquaintances, Anthea had also become something of a sightseer, an activity that, except for the obligatory annual visit to the Royal Academy to view the latest portraits or perhaps a trip to the British Museum to see the newly arrived Elgin Marbles, was reserved for the children. No great culture hound himself, Julian, however, usually accompanied his cousin on these excursions as a welcome excuse to get away from his studies. At the Tower of London he showed a mild interest in the sword that had decapitated Anne Boleyn, and at the British Museum, though he did not care for either the Elgin Marbles or the famous Rosetta Stone, he was fascinated by a pair of stuffed giraffes.

Unlike Vienna, Anthea discovered, London was not a place of great public buildings. Westminster Abbey itself, with its sooty walls and crumbling monuments, was situated in an area of narrow, grimy streets, and the newly erected Bank of England was perhaps the handsomest building in the city, rather than some royal palace. But she did enjoy seeing the great Thameside docks, built by the East and West India merchants during the recent wars, the Royal Exchange with its great piazza and its bustling traders in their colourful garb of every nation, and the House of Commons, which she was surprised to find was a rather modest-sized chamber, some 90 feet in length, with plain panelling and tiers of green leather benches.

When Lyndock caught up with her and Julian at the House of Commons one day—a frequent happening, since he generally learned of her daily plans during their morning rides—he laughed aloud at her shock as she observed the honourable members' behaviour during the session; some members were lying down on the benches, napping during speeches, others were eating oranges and various other snacks, some—when they particularly disliked a speech—were howling like dogs.

"We English have a much healthier attitude toward politics than, say, the French," he commented airily. "If our members reacted as dramatically as did the delegates to the Estates General at the beginning of the French Revolution, for example, we'd soon have no king and possibly no country. Regard all this schoolboy behaviour as an escape valve."

"I say, Geoffrey," began Julian with a touch of gentle malice —he had now graduated to a comfortable first name relationship with Lyndock—"I simply had no idea that you were so historically minded. Somehow, I always thought that your interests lay elsewhere."

"Yes, indeed," Anthea joined in laughingly, "I had the impression that you spent all your time taking boxing lessons from Gentleman Jackson, or buying prime horseflesh at Tattersall's, or—horror of horrors—gambling away your fortune at White's."

"You wrong me, Your Serene Highness," said Lyndock in mock hurt. "I do other constructive things as well. I must keep up my wardrobe, you know; that involves a rather fatiguing round of visits to Weston to be measured for a new coat, and to Harboro and Acock's for my shirts. And my boots! You'll hardly credit the trouble that I must undergo for the sake of my boots."

"Hoby's, of course," said Julian, eying Lyndock's gleaming Hessians with a touch of envy. "Tell me, is it true that Brummell used champagne in his boot polish?"

"I have no idea. I never asked the Beau. My valet rather fancies his own secret formula for polish. It is true, though, my military-minded young friend, that Hoby once told the Duke of York that if Wellington had patronised any other bootmaker, he could scarcely have won the Battle of Waterloo. But that's enough about my wardrobe," Lyndock added, turning his attention to Anthea. "The last time that I spoke to you, you hadn't made up your mind about attending Countess Lieven's ball tonight."

"I do hope that you haven't let my plans influence your own decision about whether to go."

"I dislike contradicting you, but if you aren't going to be present, I wouldn't set foot in the place," replied Lyndock firmly. "That woman has rather too high an opinion of herself. She admittedly is one of the powers at Almack's, but she also fancies herself the supreme arbiter of society. Do you know that she recently said, 'It is not fashionable where I am not'?"

"Yes, Madame Lieven is rather insufferable," agreed Anthea, "but she does give very interesting parties. I rather think that I will go."

The Russian ambassador and his socially powerful wife lived at Ashburnham House in Dover Street. Moving away from the receiving line that evening after curtseying to the Lievens, Fanny glanced at Anthea's gown and said admiringly, "You look absolutely stunning tonight, Cousin Anthea. All the rest of us will be quite eclipsed."

Anthea placed an affectionate hand on Fanny's arm. "Nonsense, my dear. You'll be the most beautiful girl here tonight." She was thankful that she and Fanny, tacitly agreeing not to bring up Lyndock's name, had returned to their old friendly footing after the slight setback that had occurred when Fanny learned about the daily rides in Hyde Park.

As Anthea entered the ballroom Lyndock came up to her immediately, obviously having lain in wait for her arrival.

"Now, if that isn't complete to a shade," he said, gazing at her gown. Anthea was wearing a white lace robe over a white satin slip, topped by a bodice of rose satin, very tight and high waisted, with tiny puff sleeves and trimmed on the skirt with a drapery of white lace intertwined with pearls and full-blown pink roses. "There's not another woman in the room who could bring off such a costume, but you have an unfailing sense of what suits you. You look absolutely superb."

Anthea was well aware that every eye in the ballroom was on the pair of them. Even though it was not generally known that she and Lyndock rode together every morning, it had become crystal clear to London society that she was the marquis's latest flirt. Contriving to be present at every activity that she attended, he stood up to her at every ball, sat or stood next to her at every available opportunity. But despite the frequency of their meetings, they were never actually alone together, and Lyndock's behaviour and remarks had always been properly discreet. Tonight, however, his voice was deeper, his eyes more ardent, and Anthea felt a shiver of excitement as his arm closed around her for the first waltz. As the music ended, he said suddenly, "Let's go out for a bit of fresh air in the garden. I hear that Countess Lieven has outdone herself there tonight."

Anthea glanced at her program. "Oh, but I have the next quadrille with my cousin Phillip."

"Montville sees you every day. We can't allow him to monopolise your evenings too," said Lyndock callously.

Their progress toward the ballroom door was interrupted when Sarah Fenwick suddenly appeared at Lyndock's elbow. The sight of the woman's malicious smile gave Anthea a jolt, since she had been able to put out of her mind completely her recent unpleasant encounter with the lady.

"Good evening, Your Highness, Lord Lyndock. How pleasant to meet you again, Princess. I've been admiring your gown—Paris,

I suppose? And by the by, my invitation to tea is still very much open! Geoffrey, my dear"—Lady Fenwick placed a possessive hand on Lyndock's arm—"I was going to send a note around to you tomorrow, but now that I have you here—I'm planning a small supper party for next Thursday. Can you come?"

"Why, thank you, Lady Fenwick. May I let you know?"

With an easy smile and a bow to Sarah Fenwick, Lyndock continued on into the garden with Anthea, who had no doubt at all that the woman had engineered the incident to display her close acquaintance with Lyndock and to make Anthea jealous. Lyndock himself did not seem in the least embarrassed, although he said casually, "Do you frequently enjoy Lady Fenwick's hospitality?"

"No, I have yet to accept her invitations," said Anthea composedly. "She seems to wish to be friendly, but I don't think that we would suit."

"You're right. She's the last person in the world that you should befriend," said Lyndock much too quickly, and Anthea smiled to herself in the darkness. Lyndock, for all his sophistication, was rather transparent.

Countess Lieven's garden was a magical sight on this late June evening. The temperature was pleasantly warm and there was a soft breeze intermingling the perfumes from a myriad of flowers; it was one of those rare occasions, in what was beginning to be called the worst summer in memory, when cold and rain had not cast a damper over the festivities. Lamps in jewellike colours swayed from the trees or glowed half-concealed among the flowers. At the back of the gardens hung a great transparent landscape, depicting moonlight shimmering on water, which turned into a real cascade flowing among the scented shrubs and along the mossy paths.

"It's lovely, like a fairy land," said Anthea softly, breathing deeply of the scented air, acutely aware of Lyndock's arm brushing against her bare shoulder.

Lyndock, casting a quick glance around him, drew her into a secluded path at the rear of the garden. "Alone at last," he said lightly, "and safe, for the moment, from your horde of admirers. I wanted an opportunity to invite you to a small party that I plan to give at Vauxhall Gardens next week. I hope you won't mind, I've already spoken to Lady Montville about it, and she was pleased to accept. I can't entertain your family at my house, of course, because I have no hostess, a situation, I'm bound to say, that I hope to rectify very soon!"

Anthea pretended to ignore his last remark. She looked up at him with a pleased smile. "Why, thank you, my lord. I haven't yet visited Vauxhall Gardens. I shall look forward to your party immensely."

Drawing a sudden deep breath, Lyndock grasped her shoulders, saying huskily, "The night intoxicates me—*you* intoxicate me. Anthea, you're the most beautiful, the most desirable, the most tempting woman that I've ever met." He crushed her against him, bruising her lips in a savagely hard kiss, leaving her spent while somewhere deep inside her a great burst of warmth exploded and began to course through her veins. She felt herself drowning in a deep velvet pool of languorous passion, coming to her senses only when Lyndock lifted his mouth at last. Pulling away, she gathered her shawl around her shoulders with fumbling fingers, saying, "I think that we should go back to the ballroom, my lord. I'm sure that you wouldn't want to occasion any gossip about us."

Lyndock sounded slightly dazed. "But Anthea, I thought . . ."

"No, really, we must go back. My aunt will be wondering where I am."

Anthea walked quickly toward the main path of the garden, leaving Lyndock to follow after an uncertain pause. Near the entrance to the ballroom she met Phillip, looking around him with an expression of mingled anger and irritation. "There you are, Cousin Anthea. I couldn't find you when the quadrille started."

"I'm so sorry, Phillip, to have missed our dance. I was feeling just a trifle warm, and Lord Lyndock very kindly offered to take me for a stroll in the gardens."

Phillip looked past her to Lyndock's approaching figure, his mouth hardening. He was obviously exercising great control as he replied, "Forgive me if I sound preachy, but I would be neglecting my duty if I didn't tell you how unwise it is for you to allow Lyndock to inveigle you into a tête-à-tête."

"Thank you for your concern, but truly, we were just catching a breath of cool air."

Phillip continued to look disapproving, but Anthea was glad of his presence as Lyndock came up to them. Until she could sort out her emotions, decide just how deeply she wanted to plunge into a romance with Lyndock, she did not want to be alone with him.

=6=

"Your Serene Highness, will you see Lady Henrietta Orwell?"

Anthea looked up from her book at Hastings, the Montville butler, as he stood in the door of the morning room.

"Lady Henrietta Orwell?" Anthea frowned. "I don't recognise the name. Are you sure that she wants to see me? Perhaps she's a friend of Lady Montville's."

"No, Your Highness. The young lady particularly asked for you." There was a faintly apprehensive cast to Hastings' normally imperturbable face, but before Anthea could question him further a slight figure rushed past him into the room.

"Are you the Princess von Hellenberg?"

"I am," said Anthea. She gazed curiously at the girl standing before her. Lady Henrietta was small and slender, with a tiny heart-shaped face that would have been exceptionally pretty had it not been puffed and blotched from an apparent bout of heavy weeping. Her fine blond hair was carelessly arranged and her fashionable clothes showed signs of having been very hastily pulled on. Her hands were twisting together nervously as she said in a high, wispy voice, "Please, could I talk to you for a few moments, Your Highness?"

"Yes, of course. Please sit down, Lady Henrietta. That will be all, Hastings." Anthea turned back to her guest to find the girl staring at her with an unblinking intensity.

"You look kind," said the girl abruptly. "I can't think that you would deliberately ruin another person's life."

"I certainly hope not," said Anthea uneasily. There was a wild light in Henrietta's eyes, an impression of unbearable tension in her slim figure.

"Then will you give up Lord Lyndock?"

"Give up . . . ? What do you mean?"

"Are you telling me that he's never even mentioned me to you? Oh—oh . . ." Tears gushed from Lady Henrietta's eyes, streaming unwiped down her cheeks as she lifted her hands imploringly to Anthea. "He can't have forgotten me, no matter what Papa and Mama say. Princess, if you'll just give him up, I know that he'll come back to me. Because he loved me once, loved me better than any of the others, I'm sure of it. And I—if I can't have him, then my life isn't worth living."

Her eyes wide with distaste, Anthea rose, saying, "I think you must be . . ." She bit her lip. The girl might not be mad, but she was obviously very close to a mental breakdown. Anthea crossed the room to tug at the bell rope. "Lady Henrietta, did you come in your own carriage? If not, I'll have Hastings put you into a hackney. You should go home and rest."

The girl threw herself to her knees in front of Anthea, clutching at Anthea's hands in a renewed paroxysm of scalding tears. "No, no, I won't go—I can't go—not until you promise to give up Lord Lyndock."

Anthea sighed with relief as the door opened to admit, not Hastings as she had expected, but a tall, middle-aged stranger followed by a concerned-looking Phillip.

"Henrietta, my dear little one." The girl looked up at the stranger's words, then rushed across the room to hurl herself into the man's arms. "Papa, Papa, what shall I do?"

"Hush, my love, let Papa see to everything." The man stroked Henrietta's hair, his soothing, quiet voice belying his drawn, worn face. "Dearest, here's Sir Phillip Montville. You remember him, don't you? You met him several years ago when we visited his Rutland estate. Now, he's going to take you out to the carriage and wait with you until I come out. I won't be long, I promise. Will you do that for me?"

Suddenly Henrietta seemed to collapse. Without speaking,

without glancing at Anthea, she allowed Phillip to take her arm and walked with him, as in a trance, out of the morning room.

Her father said sadly, "Pray allow me to introduce myself, Madame von Hellenberg. I am the Earl of Netherton. I wish that we might have met under happier circumstances. Please accept my apologies. I assure you that my daughter had no wish to offend you, or to harm you in any way."

"I quite understand, Lord Netherton. I could see that Lady Henrietta was very upset."

"In view of the embarrassment that you've been caused, I feel that I owe you an explanation. If I might sit down?"

"Yes, please do. But you certainly need offer me no explanation. Except . . ."

"Yes?"

"Well, I was somewhat puzzled by your daughter's mention of a—a good friend of mine, Lord Lyndock."

"Ah, yes, Lyndock," said Lord Netherton heavily. "If it weren't for his involvement I might have been tempted to ask you just to ignore this incident, without giving you any reason for Henrietta's behaviour. God knows that I have done my best for the better part of a year to keep this miserable affair secret. But since you, too, seem to have been drawn into Lord Lyndock's clutches, I feel it to be my duty to warn you against him."

"I don't understand you, my lord," said Anthea, her back stiffening.

"No, I see that you don't, more's the pity. Well, to put it bluntly, Lord Lyndock is a heartless philanderer who actually seems to enjoy leading young women on and then dropping them. No, hear me out," Netherton added, as Anthea opened her mouth to protest. "My wife and I brought Henrietta to London for her debut at the beginning of last season. She was very happy at first, much sought after, making many friends. Then she met Lord Lyndock. He was Major Stretton then, of course, on duty with the Blues here in London before the start of the Waterloo campaign. We knew that he had the reputation of being a hardened flirt—and he would have been an ineligible suitor in any event, since he was penniless. So, quite frankly, we warned Henrietta off of him when he began to pay her decided attentions. But in no time at all she had formed a deep attachment to him. I grant you that this was unseemly on her part, but we seem to live in different circumstances these days, with young girls of good family 'falling in love' like common servant girls. Perhaps it's the unsettling effect of the recent wars, or more probably the influence of that infernal Lord Byron. . . .

"Well, no matter," Lord Netherton continued with a sigh. "Henrietta fell deeply 'in love' with Lyndock and believed that he reciprocated her feelings. She confided to her mother that she expected Lyndock to offer for her hand at any time. And then, nothing. He dropped her to chase after someone else. Henrietta was crushed. She moped in her bedchamber, refusing to go out or to see her friends. And one day we found her unconscious. She had consumed the contents of a large bottle of laudanum. A doctor saved her life, and we managed to conceal the incident from the public and even from our closest acquaintances. We took Henrietta home to the country, where she has been in seclusion ever since, listless, uninterested in any of her former activities, spending most of her time behind the locked doors of her bedchamber. Late this spring, however, she did seem to be regaining some of her spirits, and we decided that it might hasten her recovery if we brought her up to London to shop, go to the theatre, anything to bring her out of herself. Unfortunately, she soon heard—I don't know who told her—of Lyndock's determined pursuit of the season's latest beauty—yourself, Princess. Her mother found her dissolved in tears over the news. And today her abigail very properly informed me that Henrietta had been talking wildly about you, Your Highness, ordering a carriage to be brought around so that she could visit you and 'have it out with you.' "

Lord Netherton paused, straightening his drooping shoulders. "Would you mind telling me what Henrietta said to you?" he asked after a moment. "If I knew, it might help me to deal with her."

"She asked me—she begged me—to give up Lord Lyndock," replied Anthea shortly.

"I see. And what did you tell her?"

"I told her nothing, my lord. I simply asked her to leave." A touch of belligerence entered Anthea's voice as she said, "I know that you are perfectly sincere in what you've told me, sir, but is it possible that you've misjudged Lord Lyndock? Lady Henrietta —forgive my bluntness—obviously needs medical care. Do you think that it is really fair to brand a man's reputation on the word of a young girl who is—is . . ."

"Henrietta may seem deranged to you now, but I can assure you that she was perfectly sane, perfectly normal before she met Lord Lyndock," Netherton cut in angrily. He rose, reaching for his hat and stick. "Good day to you, Madame von Hellenberg. I apologise again for my daughter's intrusion. And call it interference if you like, but I ask you again to consider carefully whether you should continue your friendship with Geoffrey Lyndock."

Shortly after Lord Netherton had bowed himself out, Phillip entered the morning room. He gazed closely at Anthea, noting the bright spot of colour high on either cheek and her tightly clenched hands. "Lord Netherton asked me to give you a message, Cousin. He says that he forgot to ask you not to speak of his daughter's visit to you."

"Yes, of course. I've no desire to speak of it to *anyone*," said Anthea tightly. She lifted her head. "Not even to you, Phillip."

"I quite understand." Phillip looked grave. "But I should tell you, Anthea, that I overheard Lady Henrietta's use of Lyndock's name as I came into the morning room, and it wasn't hard for me to put two and two together. Last season before the news of the Belgian campaign put everything else out of our minds, there was considerable speculation about the reason for Lady Henrietta's hasty exit from London."

Anthea was rather glad to set out alone, several days later, when an unscheduled dress fitting prevented Fanny from accompanying her on a shopping expedition to Bond Street. Since Lady Henrietta's visit, virtually every waking moment had been filled with engagements, from morning till late at night, and Anthea had had little time to reflect privately on her reaction to the distressing encounter. She could not bring herself to believe that Lyndock had set out callously and deliberately to ensnare Henrietta with no intention of returning the girl's affection. Yet she could not forget Fanny's account of her relations with Lyndock, so unpleasantly similar to Henrietta's experience except for the near-fatal aftermath. Of course, Lyndock was a flirt—perhaps an incorrigible flirt; Anthea had realised this from the first moment that she had been exposed to that confident charm of his. But she had come to believe that his flirtatious ways merely reflected the fact that he had not yet met a woman who could seriously engage his heart.

In Bond Street, Anthea left Hatchard's bookshop well before the 45 minutes that she had allotted to herself on the premises. Somehow, today, she took little of her usual pleasure in browsing through the shelves, even though she had come upon a new book by a favourite author. She paid the clerk for her copy of *Emma* and stepped out of the shop, glancing up the street for her carriage.

"Princess von Hellenberg! How delightful to see you again. I vow, it's been ages since we met."

With an inward sigh of resignation, Anthea turned to greet Lady Fenwick. Though they were often guests at the same functions, Anthea had caught only passing glimpses of Lyndock's former mistress in the past several weeks, and she was more than content to have it so. "Surely it hasn't been very long since we last met," Anthea said now. "Didn't I see you only a few days ago at Lady Sanditon's rout?"

Sarah Fenwick smiled, careful, Anthea noted uncharitably, to keep her head lifted against the tiniest hint of fullness beneath her chin. "Oh, I don't count a dreadful squeeze like Lady Sanditon's rout, Your Highness. What I had in mind was a quieter occasion, an opportunity to have a long, comfortable chat." A sudden thought seemed to strike her. "What about now? Won't you accompany me in my carriage to Madame d'Albret's and help me choose a new gown?"

"Another time, perhaps. I really must be getting back to Grosvenor Square."

"Oh, I think that you can spare the time for just a short talk. You see, I have something very important to tell you. And believe me, with this nasty little rumour making the rounds, you need all the helpful advice that you can get."

Anthea stiffened. Sarah Fenwick's lips were still smiling, but beneath the overly elaborate coiffure and the fashionable bonnet her prominent blue eyes sparkled with malicious amusement.

"Rumour?" said Anthea. "What rumour?"

"My dear, you surely couldn't have expected that your little run-in with the Orwell chit would go unnoticed?"

Anthea felt cold. Despite her own silence and that of Phillip, despite the best efforts of Lord Netherton, Lady Henrietta's sad story was apparently the latest *on-dit*. Perhaps a gossipy servant had leaked the news, or a member of Henrietta's family may have dropped an indiscreet remark. "I don't know what you're talking about," Anthea snapped. "And I don't care for gossip, Lady Fenwick, so I'll bid you good-bye—" She broke off with a gasp of affronted amazement as Sarah Fenwick shot out her hand to grasp Anthea's arm.

"Not so fast, Your Serene Highness. If you don't listen to me you'll be very sorry."

"Are you quite mad? Release me immediately," Anthea muttered angrily as she tried to jerk her arm away, casting a hurried glance around her to see if they were being observed.

Maintaining her grip, Lady Fenwick eyed her coolly. "I don't care a fig if we make a scene. But you do, I fancy. Wouldn't it be wiser to come with me for a short drive while we have that little chat that I mentioned?"

Hesitating for only an instant, Anthea gave in. "Very well. Anything to allow me to see the last of you."

"I thought you might see the light. Jasper"—she raised her

voice to her coachman—"drive a little through the park, please."

"Well, Lady Fenwick?" said Anthea a few moments later, as they drove past the Green Park. "Please get on with what you have to say."

Lady Fenwick laughed a little tingling laugh. "All in good time. First let me tell you how very sorry I was to hear that the Orwell child had created such a scene. My dear, wouldn't you think that her family would have had the good sense to keep her cooped up in the country?"

Anthea stared at her in cold silence.

"Ah, well, I can understand how painful it must be for you to talk of Lyndock's connection with the girl," said Lady Fenwick. "Frankly, it was hearing about the incident that finally prompted me to do what my conscience has been nudging me to do for weeks: to make you acquainted with Lord Lyndock's true nature."

"You need say no more. My aunt, Lady Montville, has already told me about your—your friendship with Lord Lyndock. Which is now past history, I believe."

"Then your belief is wrong. We don't see each other as often as we once did—we both like a little change of scene now and then, you understand. But only a few days ago he sat in my boudoir, sending me into positive gales of laughter with his anecdotes of his latest romantic conquest—you, Your Serene Highness. Oh, yes," she nodded as Anthea looked at her unbelievingly. "Geoffrey has been amusing himself—and me—for years now, by telling me all the details of his romantic flings. Pleasures, I'm sure that you would agree, are more enjoyable if you share them! There was the Russian baroness last year, for instance. Geoffrey avoided being shot by her husband only by diving out her bedchamber window into some rose bushes below. And Lady Jersey—how she would hate people to know that he made an assignation with her at his shooting box and then failed to arrive."

Reaching for the handle of the carriage door Anthea interrupted her. "I've heard quite enough of your spiteful lies. Pray order your coachman to stop the carriage."

"Lies, Madame von Hellenberg?" purred Lady Fenwick. "Was

Geoffrey lying when he told me about rescuing you from those dreadful Italian bandits? Or about your delightfully intimate dinner afterwards in the inn, so romantic that you quite forgot about your miserable surroundings? I understand that you gave each other false names—what a delicious surprise for both of you it must have been when you met this spring in London!"

Later Anthea decided that she must have fallen into a sort of daze from the shock of Sarah Fenwick's revelations. She sat in numbed silence as the older woman rambled on maliciously.

"Poor Geoffrey, he's a little like myself. He does so enjoy the opening stages of a new romance, the thrill of the chase, so to speak. But he gets bored once he's fixed the lady's interest, and then he has to begin all over again with a new object of his affections. And sometimes, you know, even I consider that he goes a bit too far. Your little cousin, Fanny Montville, for instance. Did you know that he promised her that he would wait for her to grow up—and she believed it? I gave him quite a scolding about Fanny, told him that such a peagoose innocent was really not fair game for him. He agreed with me and dropped her, I understand. Now you, my dear, are older than your cousin and certainly not inexperienced. After all, you're a widow. But if rumour is correct and you plan to marry Lord Lyndock, I really think that you should know that he isn't capable of loving anyone for very long. Now that he's come into the title he will want an heir, naturally. And if, along with a breeder for his children, he acquires an enormous fortune, why so much the better! Because everyone knows that his cousin Harry—Lord Vansittart, the previous heir—had very nearly bankrupted the Lyndock estate before the foolish boy mercifully broke his neck in a hunting accident."

Afterwards, Anthea could never quite remember leaving Lady Fenwick's carriage to transfer to her own vehicle for the drive back to Grosvenor Square. Her thoughts were so chaotic, her feelings so lacerated, that she could concentrate only on what the woman had said. With every fibre of her being Anthea wanted to believe that Sarah Fenwick's accusations were the spiteful lies of a jealous woman. But Anthea had told no one about her first meeting with

Lyndock in the Alps. The Fenwick woman could only have learned the details of that meeting from Lyndock himself. And then there was Fenwick's mention of Lyndock's laughing promise to poor little Fanny that he would wait for her to grow up! Anthea's face flamed as the pictures flashed through her mind: Lyndock holding Sarah Fenwick in his arms, sniggering as he told his mistress about his latest romance with the princess from Vienna.

Arriving back at the Montville house, Anthea maintained a frozen composure as she brushed past the butler and climbed the stairs to the haven of her own bedchamber. There she tore off her bonnet and her short Spencer jacket, throwing the garments to the floor, where she stamped on them vigorously with both feet in a fury of self-loathing, and then dissolved into a long bout of angry weeping.

Half an hour later, drained but calm, Anthea wiped her eyes and thought back over her relationship with Lyndock. Even though she had been on guard against him, even though she had promised herself that she would never again fall victim to her selfish father's brand of irresponsible charm, she had somehow fallen in love with Lyndock. She clenched her fists until her nails dug into the palms of her hands, marveling at her own gullibility, her naïve lack of discernment, in not seeing Lyndock for what he really was. He had shown his true colours at their first meeting in the Alps, when he had arrogantly set out to seduce her to while away a few hours of boredom. Why had she allowed her initial correct perception of him to be obscured? Why, on the very night when she and Lyndock had met again in London, had she disregarded the warnings of Phillip and Fanny about his libertine ways? It should have been so obvious to her, after talking to her cousins, that Lyndock was pursuing her because she was the latest beauty to appear on the scene, a prize all the more alluring because she carried a semi-royal title and had inherited a fabulous fortune. Thanks to Sarah Fenwick, as it happened, Anthea now knew that it was the Hellenberg fortune, above all, that had appealed to Lyndock.

Anthea smiled grimly to herself. She ought to be—she was—

very grateful to Sarah Fenwick for opening her eyes to Lyndock. The woman had meant no kindness, of course. She had been motivated by pure malice, by an impulse to watch her victim squirm. Undoubtedly, too, by eliminating a glamourous, wealthy—and above all, much younger—woman from Lyndock's life, she could hope to keep him more securely in her clutches.

Anthea drew a deep breath. The crushing humiliation of learning that Lyndock was nothing but a common fortune hunter had destroyed every shred of affection that she had ever felt for him. She was possessed now with a fierce hate and an iron determination to pay him back in his own coin. She would lead him on, pretend that she was falling in love with him, induce him to propose marriage to her. Then, when he was fully ensnared, she would throw him over.

=7=

THE DATE OF Lyndock's excursion to Vauxhall Gardens arrived, and Anthea grew increasingly nervous as the day wore on. Tonight would mark the first round in her campaign to conquer Lyndock, and she was not entirely sure of her ability to carry out her scheme.

They were a smaller party than originally planned. Lyndock had invited the entire Montville family, but Phillip had declined to go, pleading a prior engagement, which Anthea suspected was merely a plan to visit White's for supper and gambling; he had said nothing overt about Anthea's acceptance of Lyndock's invitation, but it was clear from his distant manner of the past few days that he disapproved. Fanny had declined to attend also, though in her case there was the genuine excuse of a long awaited ball at Devonshire House, one of the great events of the season; but Fanny had given her cousin a long questioning look with a hint of hurt behind the soft gray eyes, and Anthea had had to steel her heart with the thought that soon the girl would have no reason to grieve over Lyndock's fickleness. Harriet, of course, *was* among the guests, together with Julian and Edmund, Harriet's older son, in town briefly on leave from his regiment, and a shy young girl, a Miss Susan Peabody, the late Sir Josiah Montville's godchild, who had been invited along as company for Edmund.

As the Montville party arrived at the Chelsea landing place, Lyndock was waiting to escort them on the boat ride across the Thames to the Vauxhall Gardens across the river. As it happened, he and Anthea had not met since the Countess Lieven's ball several days before. To Anthea, the interval seemed much longer than that. She found it hard to believe that a few days—a few hours, really—had so altered her perception of this man. The flashing smile, the warmly intimate gaze that had so nearly brought her to the point of enthrallment now seemed hollow and hypocritical.

Dusk was falling as they left their boat at the Vauxhall landing. In the gardens, hundreds of multicoloured lanterns illuminated the long tree-lined avenues and the many fountains and cascades. All classes of society could mingle in the pleasure gardens, which had been a favourite haunt of Londoners for many years, though Vauxhall was not perhaps quite as fashionable now as it had been during the later years of the previous century; but the attractions of the great pavillion, which included a ballroom, a concert hall and gaming rooms, and the lure of special events such as masquerade balls, balloon ascents, fireworks displays and concerts by famous opera singers, were sufficient to maintain its popularity.

After a brief stroll among the secluded paths, fragrant with the scent of flowering shrubs, where Miss Peabody was thrown into a fit of nervous giggles at the occasional sight of laughing girls tussling with their swains on the half concealed benches among the trees, and a tour of the pavillion to catch a glimpse of the dancers in the ballroom and to listen to a few strains of the Handel oratorio being played in the concert hall, Lyndock led his guests to a supper box beautifully situated in a leafy bower. With his usual flair, he had ordered a supper that was a near work of art; it included turbot with lobster sauce, a goose pie and the famous Vauxhall powdered beef and custards, with arrak punch and syllabub laced with wine.

"I really don't know when I have enjoyed myself so much, Lord Lyndock," sighed Harriet, as she sipped the last of her punch. "I know that some folk are beginning to say that Vauxhall is vulgar, but I can only think that they must be very difficult to please. What could be better for every member of the family, from the young to the very old, than a place like this?"

"Thank you, Lady Montville. I hope that you will give me the pleasure of inviting you here often in the future." Lyndock turned to Anthea. "There's a rather interesting temple at the end of the Long Walk. Would you care to see it with me?"

"A capital idea," said Julian promptly. "I'll come with you."

With only the briefest of hesitations, Lyndock said warmly, "We would, naturally, be glad of your company, but the fireworks display by Madame Saqui is about to start, and I wonder if you wouldn't prefer to see that."

"Oh, yes, Julian," said Harriet. "I understand that Madame Saqui ascends a rope to the top of a high platform and comes down in a shower of Chinese fire. I feel sure that you and Edmund and Susan would not want to miss it. I declare, I feel quite excited at the prospect myself."

As they strolled away from the rest of the party, Lyndock said with a grin, "What a delightful person, your Aunt Montville. Such tact, such discernment."

"Yes, Aunt Harriet has obviously succumbed to your charms," teased Anthea. "She becomes one of a large company, so I hear."

Lyndock seemed slightly taken back. "Someone has been maligning me," he protested, smiling but with a tinge of underlying concern. "I'm no Casanova at all, not in the same class with somebody like, say, Colonel Dan MacKinnon . . ." He stopped, quirking his eyebrow. "I do beg your pardon, Your Serene Highness. I mustn't relay gossipy tales unsuited for virtuous female ears."

Anthea glanced at him composedly. "You forget that I'm a widow accustomed to a *very* racy Viennese society—or so old Lady Ffolliot intimated the other evening when she was asking me about my life in Vienna."

"Oh, well, in that case: the *on-dit* goes that Colonel Dan, having cast off a certain high-born lady to whom he had been paying court, was asked by this lady to return a lock of her hair that she had given him as a keepsake. Upon which he had his manservant deliver to his ex-love a large packet of assorted locks, ranging in color from black to auburn to purest white, with a note instructing her to pick out her own property."

It was another of those rarities in the miserable summer of 1816, a perfect June evening. Darkness had completely fallen so that the lanterns in the trees glimmered like many-hued stars and the fountains and cascades reflected their light in sparkling jewels of spray. The little temple at the end of the Long Walk, itself festooned with lamps, was surrounded by flowering shrubs, making the air heavy with the rich scent of roses and honeysuckle and peonies. Mounting the shallow steps of the little temple and entering through the pillared archway, Anthea and Lyndock stood looking back at the swaying fairy lanterns in the trees bordering the Long Walk. He stirred, looking down at her, his face reflecting an unwonted uncertainty in the flickering light of the lanterns.

"Anthea, I presume—I hope—that you were only joking when you spoke about women succumbing to my charms. But I'm afraid—" There was an awkward pause. "I've just heard that Lady Henrietta Orwell paid you a very unpleasant visit the other day."

Anthea found herself thoroughly enjoying his obvious discomfiture, but she was careful to sound merely politely concerned as she said, "Oh, dear, I did so hope that her father could whisk Henrietta out of London without creating a scandal. I hadn't meant to tell you, Geoffrey, but it really was the most dreadful thing. Lord Netherton told me that Henrietta had convinced herself that you had treated her badly and actually tried to commit suicide by swallowing laudanum."

"He said that, did he?" Lyndock sounded appalled. "There's some sort of story making the rounds, but I hadn't dreamed . . . Anthea, I swear to you that this is the first I've heard of this suicide attempt. I hope that you don't think that I ever meant any harm to the girl."

Anthea spoke reassuringly. "Of course not. I don't see how anyone could blame you for Lady Henrietta's plight. Her father, I'll admit, does seem very resentful—but there, it's plain that the young woman is unbalanced."

Lyndock breathed a sigh of relief. "I might have known that I could count on your good sense. I *was* a bit worried, I'll confess. Well, I daresay you've heard that I'm something of a Lothario."

"Oh, not that, precisely. An incorrigible flirt, perhaps," Anthea said lightly.

Lyndock grasped her by her shoulders, giving her a little shake. "Be serious. I'm trying to tell you something. I admit that I've —admired—many females, but I want you to know that since I first met you I haven't had a thought for any other woman. Anthea, I adore you. And I know—there is too strong a current flowing between us for me to be wrong—that you feel something for me, too. But, my heart, do you care enough to marry me? Could you possibly leave behind Her Serene Highness the Princess von Hellenberg to become the next Marchioness of Lyndock?"

He put his arms around her, and Anthea's pulse began to race as she felt the tumultuous uneven beat of his heart beneath the fine broadcloth and crisp white linen. She brought her errant impulses under quick control, however, with the steely thought that, during the very time that he had sworn that he was thinking of no one else but her, he was busily breaking Fanny's heart, laying court to the popular Miss Millson—the toast of the current season until Anthea had come along to supplant her—and laughing over his numerous conquests with his mistress, Lady Fenwick. She forced herself to relax, to nestle her head against his chest as she said softly, "You foolish man, I've been angling to become the Marchioness of Lyndock ever since I first met you in the Ligurian Alps, when you were repelling those dreadful bandits."

A tremor ran through Lyndock's body and his lips swept down on hers. After a long moment, Lyndock lifted his head and said, with an attempt at lightness though his voice was still husky with passion, "But you didn't know that I was the Marquis of Lyndock when we first met, my love."

She put up her hands, running her fingers through his crisp chestnut curls. "Well, no, I didn't of course," she admitted, feigning a loving smile. "And to tell the truth, I really didn't want to marry anyone. My marriage to the prince had been such a disaster that I had vowed never to marry again. But then I met you, Geoffrey, and that night in that repulsive little Italian inn I was so tempted to become plain Mrs. Stretton that it took all my willpower to drag myself away from you the next morning."

Lyndock snatched her back again into his arms. "If I had guessed—if I had had the slightest inkling of your feelings, my darling, my dearest love—whole regiments couldn't have dragged you away from me. I would have been like Alexander the Great, or Julius Caesar, or William the Conqueror—"

"Please, Geoffrey," murmured Anthea, smothering a mischievous desire to laugh, "I want a lover, not a general."

=8=

PHILLIP CAST AN affronted eye at the rather charred beefsteak reposing on his breakfast plate. "Do we have a new cook?" he demanded. "Or, indeed, any cook? This meat is quite inedible."

From her place down the table Anthea looked up with a laugh. "We have the very same cook, Cousin," she said merrily, "but she's getting quite flustered about Fanny's ball. The great event is only a few days away, you know. And Cook vows and swears that it will be a miracle, to quote her very words, if she survives the ball without being carted off to Bedlam. So it's really no wonder that she can't concentrate on your beefsteak."

"I find it very difficult to understand why my house should be torn completely apart merely to prepare for one evening's entertainment," complained Phillip. "There's virtually no corner to which I can retreat. Why, even my own library—"

"I'm so sorry, Cousin," said Anthea contritely. "I didn't know that you were in the library yesterday when I came in to estimate how many card tables we might set up in there."

"Oh, well, I suppose that there's no help for it," said Phillip, rising from the table. "I do hope, my dear Fanny," he said to his sister, "that after all this commotion the event will live up to your expectations. Julian, I rather fancy that a house on the eve of a party is no place for gentlemen. Do you care to accompany me this morning to Angelo's to cup a wafer or two?"

His thin young face flushed with pleasure, Julian rose with alacrity. Anthea suspected that he would have gladly partnered his elder brother even to such a dull event as a showing at the Royal

Academy to escape from the grind of his studies for a few hours.

Fanny's ball would be the last important event of the season. Two days later the great houses of the West End would be shuttered and empty as their inhabitants scattered to spend the summer on their country estates.

Phillip had been exaggerating only slightly when he complained about the inconveniences spawned by the preparations for the ball. There had been a frenzy of concentrated activity for some days now, as the entire house had been cleaned and polished to the last square inch, with special emphasis on the ballroom, where the fire lustres had been taken down for a painstaking cleaning and the floor had been waxed to a diamond brightness. Harriet, whose enthusiasm often outran her strength, had been warmly grateful to Anthea, who volunteered to take over much of the work involved in hiring an orchestra, arranging for extra servants, ordering the gala ices and confections from Gunther's and champagne from Berry Brothers in St. James Street, and accompanying Fanny for special fittings on her ball gown.

"I wonder if we will have enough champagne after all," fretted Harriet later that morning as she sat with Anthea in the morning room going over the checklist for the ball. "It would be such a catastrophe to run out of champagne, especially now"—her face brightened—"that Fanny's ball really seems to be shaping up as one of *the* events of the season."

"Yes, I do think that it will be a great success," agreed Anthea. "We've received hardly any regrets."

"Well, I fancy that we would have had virtually a total acceptance in any event," said Harriet complacently. "The Montvilles are not nobodies, after all. But with everyone expecting also to hear such important news . . ." She paused, looking at Anthea hopefully.

Keeping her eyes cast down on the list in front of her, Anthea waited deliberately for some moments before lifting her head to say with an absentminded frown, "I'm sorry, Aunt. What were you saying?"

Harriet sighed, tacitly admitting her defeat in her latest attempt to discover Anthea's marital intentions. Growing stronger by the day, rumours had been flooding London for almost a week now to the effect that Anthea's betrothal to Lyndock was imminent and would probably be announced at Fanny's ball. With a deliberate slip of the tongue Anthea herself had started the ball rolling in a conversation with old Lady Allenby, Mayfair's most tireless prattle-box. Thereafter Anthea proceeded laughingly to deny the rumour, with just a hint of dainty embarrassment, every time the subject was broached to her, which only served to fan the flames of speculation even higher. Necessarily, since she could never pin Anthea down, Harriet also had to deny the rumour to all her numerous acquaintances, and the effort was rapidly bringing her to a fever pitch of frustration.

Fanny, too, had heard the rumour. She brought it up that afternoon, as Anthea watched her trying on the ball gown that had just been delivered from Madame Ebert's chic establishment in Bond Street. Her eyes just a trifle blurry, Fanny managed a determined smile as she said, "Please let me wish you and Lord Lyndock very happy, Cousin Anthea. He must truly love you very much, since you've been able to pin him down to a proposal—" She gasped, flushing a deep red. "Oh—I'm so sorry. What a vulgar thing to say. What I meant was . . ."

Feeling once again like a very monster of deception, Anthea said reassuringly, "My dear, you couldn't be vulgar if you tried. But whatever made you think that Lyndock had offered for me?"

"Why, everyone talks of it. Your betrothal, in fact, is the only subject that people *are* talking about."

"Oh, dear, whatever will the gossips think to say next?" Anthea exclaimed angrily. "It's simply the outside of enough, that one cannot say a civil word to a gentleman without being accused of being in his pocket. No, Fanny, Lord Lyndock and I are not planning marriage. We're simply friends."

Thus having muddied the waters with Fanny, and having done the same thing earlier in the day with Harriet, Anthea next sought out Phillip in the library on his return to Grosvenor Square in the afternoon.

"Phillip, I do hope that you won't disapprove too much, but I think that I should tell you that I have just accepted Geoffrey Lyndock's proposal of marriage, and I would like you to announce our betrothal at Fanny's ball."

Recoiling a step, as though Anthea had launched a physical blow at him, Phillip struggled for a moment to recover his customary poise. At length he said, "I can't say that I am happy to hear your news. In fact, I can't bring myself to believe that you're actually contemplating such a step, that you're disregarding everything that I have told you about the man's vicious reputation. In my opinion, Lyndock's character hasn't changed; if he's dropped his philandering ways to offer marriage to you, Anthea, it's only because, having come into a title, he must now think of having an heir. That being the case, what better candidate for the position of Marchioness of Lyndock could there be than yourself: a reigning beauty with a great social position and an even greater fortune?"

Anthea thought grimly that Phillip, with his usual incisive common sense, had pegged Lyndock's motives precisely. But, pretending to be both hurt and angry, she said to Phillip, "I think that you're being most unjust, Cousin, and very unflattering to me personally. Whatever Lord Lyndock's faults may have been in the past, is it impossible for you to believe that he's fallen in love with me? And may I remind you that you haven't the slightest right to dictate what my behaviour should be?"

"You're quite right. Please accept my apologies. I will, of course, do as you ask," replied Phillip stiffly.

Impulsively, Anthea went up to him, taking his hand. "No, let me apologise. I didn't mean to speak so sharply to you. Please, Phillip, try to be happy for me."

He turned away from her. "Yes, I'll try," he said in strangled tones. "But it won't be easy."

Anthea eyed him remorsefully, aware that his feelings for her went much deeper than she had imagined. But she said merely,

"Thank you, Phillip, I knew that I could count on you. Oh, and could I ask one more thing? Please don't mention my betrothal to anyone until you actually announce it at Fanny's ball. I so much dislike being the subject of gossipy speculation."

On the evening of Fanny's ball, as they stood with Phillip and Julian in the receiving line, the women of the family presented a handsome appearance: Fanny ethereal in white net over satin with a rouleau of white satin intertwined with seed pearls on the skirt; Harriet in her favourite shade of mauve and a turban topped with formidable plumes; and Anthea in a striking gown of poppy-coloured India muslin trimmed with double bands of gold lace on the skirt.

Anthea began to tense as she observed Lyndock coming slowly up the steps. He spoke nothing but commonplace as he paused in front of her, but flashed her a smile of incandescent brilliance and gave her hand a quick, secret little squeeze. She returned his smile, blocking from her mind the climax that she had planned for the evening, and proceeded with a feverish excitement to enjoy the ball, rather as though she were on reprieve from her own execution.

Karl von Westendorf, performing expertly opposite her in the first quadrille, murmured, "Everyone seems to be expecting an interesting announcement this evening, chérie. I do hope that they are all wrong."

"You should never listen to gossip, Karl."

"But why not? It's one of the great pleasures of life. But seriously, my dear Anthea, if you really do intend to announce your betrothal this evening, I must tell you that my life will be blighted. I will have lost the only woman that I ever really loved."

"Nonsense. You've been cutting a swath through female hearts ever since you arrived in London. I know of at least one heiress and two near-heiresses who would be only too happy to become Gräfin von Westerdorf."

"I do try to keep up my spirits, *bien entendu*," grinned Karl. "But, my sweet, I'm not just sad because of my own broken hopes. It's you, Anthea—I can't bear to think of you spending the rest of your life in a dull place like this. Marry me and let me take you back to Vienna where you belong.''

Anthea was still smiling at Karl's amiable persiflage when Lyndock claimed her for the first waltz. "I can't wait to send that Austrian fop packing,'' he teased, as he held her more closely than the patronesses at Almack's would have countenanced. "I can't wait for the moment when I can have you all to myself and not let a single admirer get near to you. Tonight, for example, if only you hadn't insisted on keeping our betrothal a secret until Montville's surprise announcement, I would have refused to allow you to dance with anyone but me.''

Recoiling inwardly as she glimpsed, despite his smiling manner, the naked longing in Lyndock's eyes, Anthea tried hard to sound carefree and flirtatious as she chided, "I warn you, my lord, that I won't have a jealous husband.''

"Have no fear. After we've been married for—oh, say, five years—I'll allow you to stand up to a partner in the country dance, and I may even permit another man to take you into dinner.'' His smile faded as he added, "I hope that you're not having any difficulties with your cousin Phillip. He caused considerable talk last night at White's when he gave me the direct cut. He'd been drinking—he wasn't actually foxed, just a trifle above par—and I think that I covered up pretty well when I told the bystanders that we'd had an argument about a horse. You didn't tell me, by the way, that Montville had joined the ranks of your suitors. He's such a cold fish, I hadn't noticed it myself. . . . But I don't know what else except jealousy could have caused him to act like that.''

Anthea fought back a sharp spurt of anger and said carelessly, "Of course Phillip isn't one of my suitors. He's simply not overly fond of acquiring you as a cousin-in-law. You're not a prime favourite of his, you know.''

As the orchestra struck up for the last dance before the supper interval, Phillip walked up to the leader, asking him in a low voice to stop playing. A little ripple of rising excitement ran through the crowd of guests as they stopped in their places on the ballroom floor. All through the evening Anthea had been conscious of curious side glances, of murmured conversations that broke off as she approached. Now, as she stood beside Lyndock near the orchestra, she was the object of every unabashed stare in the room.

Phillip, somewhat pale but quite calm, lifted his hand to quell the buzz of speculative voices. "Ladies and gentlemen, I have something to tell you—" He interrupted himself in surprise as Anthea darted up to him, drawing him aside to whisper urgently, "I've changed my mind. Don't announce my betrothal."

"I don't understand," Phillip stammered. "What—couldn't you have told me this a little earlier?"

"Yes—no—it doesn't matter," hissed Anthea. "Just don't make the announcement."

"But what will I say?" murmured Phillip, looking strangely indecisive.

"You'll think of something," gritted Anthea under her breath. "Go to it, Phillip." She moved away from him as Phillip, drawing a deep breath, went back to stand in front of the orchestra. Clearing his throat in obvious embarrassment, he stood silent for several dragging moments. At length he said lamely, "Ah—please excuse me for keeping you waiting. As I was saying, I have something to tell you. I would like to thank you, first of all, for coming here to make my sister's coming out ball such an enjoyable occasion. And my cousin, the Princess von Hellenberg, has asked me also to extend to you her gratitude for the warm welcome you have given to her on this, her first visit in many years to the land of her birth."

A wave of sound erupted through the ballroom, compounded of various elements of shock, spiteful amusement and incomprehension. Anthea stood by herself, her face a frozen mask, wondering why, instead of a sense of triumph, she felt only a grinding emptiness. Belatedly the orchestra leader lifted his baton, and as the strains of a waltz drifted over the floor, Lyndock came up to her. She could see signs of unwonted strain around his eyes, but his lips wore their usual buoyant smile as he said, "This waltz is ours, I believe, Your Highness." The smile remained on his face as they danced away; to the casual observer he would have appeared to be his usual self. But his voice was savage as he murmured, "You did tell me that you had asked your cousin to announce our betrothal tonight, did you not? I can't believe that I misunderstood you, because at least half of the people here this evening have intimated to me that they, too, expected an announcement. May I ask what made you change your mind?"

Anthea looked straight into his eyes, saying coldly, "I didn't change my mind. I never intended to allow Phillip to announce our betrothal."

His grasp around her waist tightened convulsively. "You mean that you deliberately planned this mean little exhibition? You accepted my proposal of marriage, allowed half of London to anticipate our betrothal, without ever planning to go through with it? Why, Anthea? Why would you do such a cruel thing?"

Anthea's throat felt constricted and momentarily she could think of nothing to say. She berated herself for not having prepared an answer for this inevitable confrontation. But deep down, in her inmost being, she had not been prepared to admit to Lyndock her knowledge that he had discussed with Sarah Fenwick the details of his relationship with her. To admit this knowledge would be to admit the depth of the wound to her pride. No, she wanted Lyndock to believe that her feelings had never been seriously engaged. Her voice was composed, even flippant, as she replied, "I wanted to give you just a dose of your own medicine, my lord. Perhaps now you can appreciate the feelings of all those women that you've discarded during your career as a Don Juan."

For a moment Lyndock could only stare at her, stupefied. Then, his lips tightening, he snapped, "I think that you'd better explain yourself. Am I to understand that you've set about to reform—and yes, punish—what you consider to be my reprehensible conduct toward the female sex?"

The acid ridicule in Lyndock's voice stiffened Anthea's resolve. "Yes, I meant to do exactly that. You've become a heartless philanderer with a string of broken hearts trailing behind you, and I thought that someone should bring you to your senses. I won't dwell on your treatment of my young cousin, Fanny; she's very inexperienced, very impressionable, but I have hopes that she will recover with only a few scars to show for her encounter with you. But Lady Henrietta Orwell is another matter entirely; she tried to kill herself last year when you dropped her, and I don't suppose that she will ever really be herself again. I don't know, naturally, how many other young girls you may have driven to near suicide, but it is certainly a fact that every wise and responsible mother in London society has warned her daughter off of you. I only wish that my Aunt Harriet had had the wisdom to do it in Fanny's case; then her first season might have been the unmitigated joy that it ought to have been, instead of the dreary little tragedy that it almost became."

Lyndock's face had now gone completely blank. He spoke carefully, as if holding an incredibly tight rein on himself. "I understand you, I believe, Princess von Hellenberg. I'm to be punished for my crimes against lovesick young females, and you've appointed yourself the chosen instrument of that revenge. Allow me to thank you for all the trouble that you've taken. It must have required great sacrifice on your part to overcome your distaste of me personally to associate with me. And let me thank you also for your considerate staging of your scheme this evening; you might as easily have allowed Montville to make the announcement of our betrothal and then denied it to my face. Why didn't you do it that way, incidentally? My public humiliation would have been such an apt climax to your campaign."

"Such behaviour would have been seen as a trifle lacking in finesse, not to say good taste," replied Anthea bitingly. "And then, too, if I had cried off in public it would have been very bad for my reputation. I have no desire to be known as a common jilt."

"Ah, of course. Your Serene Highness is the epitome of good taste. Perish the thought that you should ever be branded a jilt," said Lyndock brutally. "Well, now, my dear, our waltz is ending, and since I believe that we've said to each other all that there is to say, I'll bid you good night—or, better yet, good-bye. For your peace of mind I can promise you that you need not fear any future intimacy with me."

Lyndock took Anthea to her seat, bowed and walked off to spend the rest of the evening dancing with the prettiest girls in the room without, apparently, a care in the world. Pulling herself together, Anthea, too, assumed a merry smile and an air of unclouded enjoyment as she blandly ignored a battery of inquisitive glances.

Karl was the only guest who dared to put a direct question to her. During the next waltz he said softly, "Changed your mind at the last minute, eh? Playing it rather fine, weren't you?" Then, as he observed her expression change ever so subtly, his eye grew keener and he added quickly, "It was deliberate, wasn't it? You led Lyndock on and then you pulled the rug from under him. Why, Anthea? The man obviously adores you, he's got an old title and a vast fortune, from what I hear, and I thought that you had a case on him, too. Matter of fact, I'd given up all hope for myself."

Anthea felt her brittle composure cracking along the edges. "Please don't, Karl. I don't want to speak of it."

"Oh, very well." Karl shrugged. "It's your own affair, after all. But let me tell you this, my dear Anthea: You may have done yourself a vast disservice tonight. If you won't take me—and I'm still convinced that I'm the only man for you, if I could only make you realize it—then you'd better have Lyndock. Because I can already see Phillip Montville waiting in the wings for you, and I *know* that he's not the man you want for a husband."

=9=

REINING IN AFTER a long, satisfying gallop, Anthea paused on a low hill, breathing in with sheer delight the fragrant early August air, mercifully freed from the oppressive humidity that had marked so much of the summer. Her eyes roamed with pleasure over the lovely rolling Rutland terrain: broad, intensely green fields sloping down to narrow, winding, willow-fringed streams, quiet roads edged with flourishing hedgerows of ash and flowering hawthorn, and, off in the distance to the south, the luminous line of a range of higher hills. She lifted her head to savour the warmth of the sun on her face, remarking to her groom, "How wonderful to see the sun out at last, Matt. I was beginning to think that it would never shine again for the rest of the summer."

The groom, Matt Corby, a raw-boned young man in his early twenties, returned her smile rather diffidently. Anthea's long-time groom, John Potter, who had served her father in that capacity during John Blanchard's army career, had, shortly after their arrival in Rutland, taken a toss from his horse and had broken his leg, much to his discomfiture, for he firmly believed that his adored mistress could not manage without him. His assistant Josef, homesick and unhappy at the prospect of a pro-tracted stay in a country where he spoke not a word of the lan-guage, had already been sent back to Anthea's Burgenland estate. And so, during John Potter's convalescence, Matt Corby, a groom in Phillip's stables, had been selected to accompany Anthea on her daily rides. She had taken a great liking to Corby, especially after she discovered that he had seen Peninsular service, returning to his home in Rutland after being mustered out at the close of the Napoleonic Wars. It had been necessary for Anthea to make a continuing effort to put the young ex-trooper at ease: He was shy and inarticulate, and obviously found it hard to adjust to her rather informal friendliness, which came so naturally to her after her wandering army years but which was rare in the caste-bound local county society.

"Yes, indeed, ma'am," said Corby in the slow, flat Midlands drawl that Anthea had initially found so hard to understand. "It's a marvelous pretty day. Happen we'll have some real summer now, after such a bad start—in the spring we had snow here that killed off many a lamb, and July was so rainy that the crops aroundabouts are pretty fair ruined. Whatever happens now's bound to be an improvement in the weather. Couldn't get much worse."

"No, I fancy not," sighed Anthea, recalling the torrential July rains and hailstorms and the perpetual dank fog and mist that had enveloped the countryside. "Were your family's crops destroyed, too?"

"No, ma'am. My father don't have any land."

"But I thought—I've been told that all the villagers in England cultivate strips of land outside their villages. Do you have a different system here?"

"No, ma'am. Some of the villagers do own or rent plots of land. But my father, he just rents our cottage. He's allowed to cut fuel in the woodland, and he could pasture a cow, if he had one, on the common, but he's always earned his living by hiring out as a field labourer."

"Oh. That sounds like a hard life."

"Yes, ma'am."

It was clear that Matt felt uncomfortable discussing his family with a member of the gentry, so to change the subject, Anthea said, "Do let's go on a little farther today. I hate to waste even a part of this lovely day by spending it indoors."

On the whole, Anthea decided as she rode on, it had been a good idea to come here to the Montvilles' Rutland estate to spend the summer, though she had been hesitant at first to accept Harriet's invitation. Karl von Westendorf's remarks to her at Fanny's ball had reinforced her own impression that Phillip was beginning to care for her very deeply. She was still very unsure of her own feelings and had wondered if a long stay at the Montville country estate might signal to Phillip that she was encouraging his suit. She was quite certain that a gossipy London society already had her betrothed to her cousin! But, aside from her concern about Phillip's romantic state of mind, she had found that being in the midst of a large and lively family, pursuing a variety of country activities, had helped her to put out of her thoughts the discomfort of her severed relationship with Geoffrey Lyndock. In unguarded moments she would recall the searing flame of his embrace, or she would look up instinctively to share with him a smile over some passing instance of the ridiculous, but in the main her feelings of bleak regret were for the loss of what had originally seemed to her a nearly perfect mingling of physical passion with strong mutual tastes and a lively sense of the absurd.

Rather surprisingly, having anticipated a distinct social lull after the London season, when invitations had left hardly a minute of her days unaccounted for, Anthea discovered that there was more than enough to keep her busy in the quiet confines of Rutland. Her army years had precluded the acquiring of the accomplishments usual to girls of her class—fine embroidery work, painting on fans, shellwork and lacework, collecting and arranging mineral specimens, playing the pianoforte, or gardening—nor was she given, as most English girls seemed to be, to long walks in the countryside. But she rode every day, usually in Matt Corby's company, and her scholarly governess had instilled in her a love of reading that she was well able to satisfy in the vast collection of the Montville library. There was also a very full, if somewhat informal, country social life. There were morning calls to be paid and received, small dances for six to eight couples, card parties for whist, quadrille, picquet and loo, and casual outings for the young people of the vicinity to visit the local sights: the famous Bede House in Liddington, Belvoir Castle near Grantham, the great Normal Banqueting Hall of Oakham Castle, its walls curiously hung with a vast display of horseshoes of all sizes.

During her stay in the country, however, it had been impossible to avoid seeing Lyndock occasionally. His estate, Stretton Priory, its great stretches of parkland a fitting setting for the immense Palladian mansion built in the last century on the foundations of an earlier monastic establishment, was situated only a few miles from the Montville estate; this proximity had contributed to her reluctance to accept her aunt's invitation. But to date all her meetings with Lyndock had been without incident. Anthea was certain, from the curious glances that she had intercepted and the whispered speculations cut off when she entered a room, that there must be some gossip about her friendship with Lyndock. But he himself never added any fuel to the gossip. When they were in the same company he always made it a point to greet Anthea with casual politeness; at least once during an evening he would ask her to dance, but always as a partner in the fast and lively country dance, never for a waltz. Since the night of Fanny's ball they had not exchanged more than a few impersonal words. Anthea suspected that he was carefully cultivating the impression that they had been only friendly acquaintances, in order to forestall any suspicion that he had been jilted, an occurrence, Anthea thought scornfully, that would be galling indeed to such an accomplished Lothario. Meanwhile, as was his normal mode of behavior, he was cheerfully charming every pretty girl in sight. Watching Lyndock at his most flirtatious, Anthea would grimly congratulate herself on having unmasked him before it was too late to turn back.

Returning from her ride, Anthea passed through the centre of the quaintly pretty little village of Upton, situated in the rolling hills above the River Gwash, with a sweeping view of the fertile level fields of the Vale of Catmose. The village comprised a cluster of thatched cottages constructed of ironstone, the local dark brown limestone, surrounded by neatly tended fenced gardens abloom with flowers. Matt Corby had previously pointed out to her the little cottage occupied by his twice-widowed father and a swarm of younger half-brothers and sisters, and now, as they passed by the cottage, one of Matt's sisters, a thin, shabbily dressed little girl, came out to the gate to wave at them. With a muttered excuse, Matt slipped off his horse to go to his sister with something clumsily wrapped in a bit of old sacking.

As she watched them together, Anthea remembered that Matt had mentioned his father's frequent recent bouts of illness, and she wondered suddenly how the elder Corby, if he were not able to work and neither owned nor rented any land, could support his numerous children. Could it be that Matt was reduced to bringing food to his family from Ashby House, the Montville home? She recalled now that this was not the first time she had seen Matt slip a packet to his sister. She resolved to find out, without actually asking Matt himself, if the Corbys were in want.

The gates of Ashby House—so called from the family that had long lived there before the sale of the property to Sir Josiah Montville—opened, as did so many of the great Tudor manor houses, directly on to the village street. As the house came into view at the end of the long drive, Anthea was conscious of a familiar feeling of delight at the gracious beauty of the building, a massive, many-gabled "black and white" mansion of plaster and framework built around a system of four large courtyards. She had been surprised, early in her stay here, to hear Harriet speak deprecatingly of the house; apparently her husband, with her full agreement, had initially wanted to tear it down and build anew when he first bought the property. This was a fate, Anthea later learned from Phillip, that had happened to many an Elizabethan manor house; they were considered too old-fashioned, in these modern times, for the gentry.

Phillip, however, aware that there was a reawakening interest in these Tudor houses, had persuaded his father to refurbish Ashby House instead, for which Anthea was very glad. It would have been criminal, she thought, to destroy the great beams and black oak carvings, the long gallery hung with swords and armour, the grand staircase with heraldic beasts perched on the newel posts, the remaining pieces of elaborately carved, large-scale Elizabethan furniture. Anthea had been especially charmed by the bed in her chamber: a monumental bed, over 12 feet square, surmounted by a panelled wooden canopy.

As Anthea entered her bedchamber she was greeted by Hannah Simms's familiar scolding tones. "I thought that something must have happened to you, Miss Anthea. You'll be very late for breakfast."

"It's such a glorious day outside that I just hated to come in," Anthea sighed as she sat down before her dressing table.

"There, now, you've been galloping again," grumbled Hannah. "Your hair is all snarls. How often must I remind you that you're not a harum-scarum girl anymore, with nothing better to do than to ride all over the Portuguese countryside?"

"Hannah, dear, I don't think that you'll ever admit that I've grown up," laughed Anthea, as Hannah helped her into a morning gown of yellow jaconet muslin with yellow slippers to match. "I'm not a green girl any longer, you know. I *have* cut my eyeteeth." She patted Hannah's hand affectionately as the elderly abigail draped a light shawl over her shoulders.

In the corridor outside her bedchamber she encountered Julian, just emerging from his own room. She had seen comparatively little of the youngster since her arrival at Ashby House. Sometimes he would join her on her early morning rides, but, despite the boy's passionate love for fishing and other outdoor activities, he was very little in evidence during the daytime. Here in the country it was possible for Phillip to keep a much closer eye on his brother's doings than he could in London, and poor reports from the boy's tutor on Julian's progress during the family's stay in town during the season had prompted Phillip to enforce a much more stringent schedule in the classroom.

This morning as Anthea looked keenly at Julian she found the boy distressingly changed. There were signs of strain about his mouth and the happy-go-lucky sparkle was missing from his eyes. She tried for a cheerful tone as she said, "Good morning, Julian. How are the studies going?"

"Pretty well, I guess, Cousin Anthea," he replied listlessly.

"I've missed your company on my morning rides. Today I had a glorious gallop on that long, low incline south of the village. Wouldn't you like to come out with me tomorrow if the weather holds?"

"I thank you, but I really can't spare the time. I have two hundred lines of Virgil to translate by Wednesday."

"I'd offer to help, but all that I can remember from my Latin is 'amo, amas, amat,' " Anthea smiled. She added gently, "Julian, dear, I hate to see you like this, so sad and miserable. Can't you try to look a little more on the cheerful side of things?"

Briefly the expression of subdued resignation faded from Julian's face as he flared despairingly, "It's all so useless. I'm not a scholar, and no amount of study will ever make me one. And I'd be an absolute disaster as a clergyman. The only thing that I want to do—the only thing that I would be any good at—is to join the cavalry."

Anthea gazed at him with silent sympathy. After a moment she asked, "Are you sure that Phillip really understands how deeply you feel about all this? Perhaps if you went to him for a frank talk—"

"It wouldn't do the least bit of good," retorted Julian scornfully. "Phillip doesn't care how anyone feels. All that he's interested in is making sure that you do exactly what he says is right for you."

"Oh, I think that you must be wrong. I've never found Phillip to be uncaring, or domineering."

"Well, of course you haven't. For one thing, Phillip has no right to tell you what to do, has he? He's not even related to you by blood. And he's much too anxious to turn you up sweet to risk offending you by telling you how to conduct yourself."

Feeling embarrassed, Anthea refrained from replying, unwilling both to condone any criticism of Phillip or to take notice of Julian's comment on his brother's feeling for her. She placed her hand on Julian's arm, saying, "Do let's go down to breakfast. I'm simply famished."

She was sitting in the morning room after breakfast, looking over the latest edition of the *Morning Post* to arrive at Ashby House, when Harriet, who never came down for the morning meal, trailed in. "Ah, there you are, my dear. You look so fresh and charming this morning, but I daresay that you've already been out for your usual long ride before breakfast," she said to Anthea with a fond smile. "I sometimes wonder where all your boundless energy comes from. I do hope that you will at least take a short nap this afternoon before going with us to the assembly at Oakham."

"Dear Aunt, I don't need naps. Hannah tells me reproachfully that I didn't like to take naps even when I was an infant." At the back of her mind Anthea wondered if she should say a word to Harriet about Julian's profound unhappiness, but decided against it. Much better not to distress her aunt since, she conceded ruefully, it was Phillip who always made the final decisions in the family.

"My dear, I've been wanting to tell you how much we've all enjoyed having you with us this summer," said Harriet. "In fact, I've begun to hope that your stay here will be permanent, that you'll eventually take my place as the next Lady Montville—" She clapped her hand over her mouth. "Oh dear, oh dear, Phillip will be so angry with me if he ever finds out that I said that."

Andrea replied quickly, "I'm flattered, Aunt, that you would like to have me as a member of the family. But I've no thought of marriage, at least for the present. Once seems quite enough! I suspect that Phillip hasn't thought of marriage, either. At least I've seen no sign of it."

"Oh, but *I* have," said Harriet promptly. "It's clear to any eye that he's head over heels in love with you!" Once more she clapped her hand over her mouth, peering at Anthea with dismayed eyes. "My wretched tongue, sometimes I'd like to cut it off!"

"Let's just pretend that you never said it," said Anthea hastily. "What are you planning to wear to the Assembly tonight?"

After a delightful quarter hour spent in discussing wardrobes, present and future, with the easily distractible Harriet, Anthea wandered into the library for a quiet read, as was her usual morning custom, but after only a few minutes she became restless. Her book tucked under her arm, she wandered outside to one of the several walled gardens on the property; this one, Phillip had told her, had been restored to look as it did during the reign of Queen Elizabeth. Here, only recently, the gardeners had uncovered an almost perfectly preserved bit of tesselated pavement, proving, Phillip had said triumphantly, that there had been a Roman villa on the site of Ashby House in the first century.

As she neared the entrance to the garden Anthea could hear the sound of muted shrieks and excited laughter. Stepping through the gate she saw Fanny in the act of chasing energetically after Rob Sinclair, a young officer in her brother Edmund's regiment who had been invited to spend his leave at Ashby House. Catching sight of Anthea, Fanny came up to her cousin. "I'm so glad that you've come, Cousin Anthea. Perhaps you can make Ensign Sinclair give me back my property." At Anthea's inquiring look, Fanny added, dimpling, "He's snipped off a lock of my hair, you see, and he refuses to give it back. I'm sure I don't know what he could possibly want with such a useless thing, but there it is."

It was clear to Anthea, however, taking in Fanny's demurely coquettish smile and the ardent gaze of the darkly handsome Ensign Sinclair, that her young cousin knew perfectly well why Rob Sinclair wanted the lock of her hair.

"Do guess what, Cousin," said Fanny. "Rob is going to give me a lesson in driving his phaeton today. Won't that be a lark? It's a high-perch phaeton, you know, so dashing. Perhaps I could even drive it in Hyde Park one day."

"*Not* in Hyde Park," came Phillip's amused tones from behind them. "Driving a carriage is quite all right here in the country, Fanny, but it's not at all what I would care to see my sister do in London. Mind, now, Ensign Sinclair, that you don't allow Fanny to go too fast. Those grays of yours, I've observed, are sweet goers, but they may be just a little too strong for a lady."

"Oh, I assure you, sir, that I will take the greatest care of Miss Montville," said Rob Sinclair earnestly.

As she watched Fanny go off with the young officer, Anthea observed to Phillip, "Is a match being made there, do you think?" She refrained from mentioning to Phillip the incident of the purloined curl, feeling that his conservative soul would not approve of such frivolous behaviour. She was also vaguely annoyed with herself for being embarrassed at being alone with him as she recalled Harriet's remarks to her earlier in the morning. Phillip was normally so quiet and reserved that it was never easy to discern any particular emotion in him. But for some time now, she admitted to herself, there had been a warmth in his eyes and in his voice when he spoke to her that she had never observed in him when he conversed with anyone else.

"A match between Fanny and young Sinclair?" Phillip nodded. "I shouldn't be at all surprised. Nor would I be averse to it, truth to tell. The boy comes from an excellent family. And even though he's not Lord Billington's heir, I understand that he will inherit a substantial fortune from a bachelor uncle on his mother's side of the family. Actually, it would be a very good thing for Fanny, in view of the—ah—unfortunate situation of last spring," he added delicately, not mentioning Lyndock's name, though it was undoubtedly much in both his and Anthea's thoughts. For that matter, he had not once brought up the subject of Anthea's never announced betrothal to Lyndock since the night of Fanny's ball, an oddly curious omission for which Anthea had nevertheless been most grateful.

"Yes, I believe that it would be a very good match," agreed Anthea rather absently. She was happy, of course, that Fanny seemed to be recovering from the unhappiness that she had suffered at Lyndock's careless hands, but she had to force herself to dismiss as unworthy the fledgling suspicion that the girl's emotions were much shallower than she had previously supposed, or else that Fanny's feelings had never been seriously engaged.

"You're looking forward, I trust, to the dance at Oakham tonight," said Phillip after a moment. "I know, of course, that it won't be anything out of the ordinary, especially to someone like you, Cousin. I imagine that you must miss, at least occasionally, your glamourous life in Vienna."

"No, not at all. I won't deny that my life in Vienna was exciting and interesting, but at bottom, you know, I was always a foreigner there."

Phillip's face lit up with one of his rare smiles. "Well, here you're certainly not a foreigner. You're as much at home in the midst of your family as Fanny, or Julian. I'm sure that my step-mother thinks of you almost as another daughter."

On the spur of the moment, taking advantage of Phillip's genial frame of mind, Anthea asked impulsively, "Could we talk a little about Julian? He's so unhappy, Phillip, and I'm sure that if you just realised—"

"Has that brother of mine been complaining to you?" demanded Phillip with a look of extreme displeasure. "Really, I can't understand the boy. You'd think that I was putting him to the martyr's screws by requiring him to study for a few hours every day in order to prepare himself for a distinguished—and yes, well-paying—position."

"Yes, but Phillip, he doesn't believe that this position, as you put it, is the least bit suitable for him. He doesn't think that he's cut out to be a clergyman. All he wants to do, with every fibre of his being, is to join a mounted regiment. And I'm bound to say, from my brief acquaintance with him, that I agree that he doesn't have the makings of a priest." Anthea paused, her heart sinking as she observed Phillip's expression grow ever more obdurate.

"My apologies, Cousin, but I believe that I am a far better judge of my brother's capabilities than you could be."

Anthea bit her lip. "You're quite right. I shouldn't have inter-fered." She turned away, about to leave the garden, when Phillip caught her hand. "This time I really mean my apology," he said remorsefully. "I should have never spoken to you so sharply. I know that you only have Julian's interests at heart." He looked down at her, smiling with some trepidation. "Can we be friends again?"

Anthea returned his smile. "Yes, of course. We were never *not* friends."

That evening as she entered the Assembly Rooms in Oakham, the county seat, with the adult members of the Montville family, Anthea was, as usual, the target of every female eye in another of her Paris dresses. Also as usual, she was besieged by all the local swains, each of them eager to be able to report that he had danced with the dazzling visiting Viennese princess—so much so that Phillip complained smilingly during their waltz that he felt quite deprived because she had saved only one dance for him.

Anthea had caught sight of Lyndock several times during the evening as he paid his effortless court to the prettiest and most charming girls in the room. After Phillip had left her at her seat to fetch her a glass of ratafia, Lyndock came up to her with a bow. "May I sit here, Your Serene Highness?"

"I can't prevent you," she replied coldly, "but I would much prefer that you do not."

"Anthea, can't we call a truce?" he said quietly. "There must be a little friendliness left between us, even if you persist in thinking of me as a heartless flirt."

"I have no desire to be friendly with you, my lord," said Anthea, thinking that it must be very seldom that Lyndock's over-tures had ever been rebuffed, and happily aware that the ardent gaze of his dark eyes no longer had the power to move her.

"So be it, then," Lyndock shrugged. Gazing across the room at Fanny, seated in absorbed conversation with Rob Sinclair, he remarked casually, "Miss Fanny seems to be in very good spirits tonight. "The *on-dit* about the county is that a marriage is about to be announced."

"Ensign Sinclair seems very attentive, certainly," agreed Anthea levelly. "It would be a very happy development for the Montvilles, in view of the unfortunate circumstances . . ." She broke off, reddening.

"In view of the emotional havoc that I am presumed to have caused," Lyndock said with a wry smile. His brown eyes, usually snapping with wickedly amused glints, narrowed into cold slits. "I wish that I could convince you and your cousin Phillip that my Casanova-like reputation is vastly overrated. In the case of Lady Henrietta Orwell, for example—you may believe me as you choose—I would much dislike having to believe that I had driven a young lady to attempt suicide. So I've been looking into the situation—oh, never fear, very discreetly—and the general impression seems to be that Lady Henrietta has always been considered rather unstable."

"Oh, you're in prime twig, my lord," exclaimed Anthea angrily. "I'm sure that if you put your mind to it you can ferret out any amount of gossip to justify your behaviour, but you needn't think that you're bamming me. Lady Henrietta's father assured me that she was a perfectly normal, happy girl before she fell into your hands."

"And Lady Henrietta's father is, of course, an unprejudiced witness," retorted Lyndock with a touch of acid. "Tell me, speaking of gossip, is there any truth to the newest rumour that you are about to become Lady Montville?"

"That, Lord Lyndock, is nothing to you."

"Oh, admittedly! But for the sake of our old—shall we say friendship?—allow me to give you a little warning: you won't enjoy being Lady Montville. Life with the worthy Phillip would be predictable, correct, praiseworthy—and deadly dull. Actually, with all my faults, you would have done far better to marry me, my dear Anthea."

"You seems to have forgotten that I once had the opportunity to marry you and declined the honour," Anthea snapped.

Lyndock's face turned to stone. "I've been meaning to tell you, Your Highness, that I think that your decision will be much more tragic for you than for me. At the very least, if you married me, your primary function would not be to breed a new generation of little Montvilles who just might make the world forget that their grandfather was a semi-literate farmer from Lancashire.''

Gasping at the snobbery, the sheer vulgarity of Lyndock's remark, Anthea completely overlooked the possibility that he might simply be striking back at her in retaliation for her own wounding words. She stared at him in blind fury, unable to think of a sufficiently scathing reply. Her eyes smarting with angry tears, she jumped up from her chair and walked away from him, narrowly avoiding bumping into Phillip, who was returning with her ratafia.

''Cousin—what on earth—are you ill?'' Phillip exclaimed, handing the glasses that he was carrying to a passing servant.

''No—no, not at all. I'm—I'm just a trifle warm. It's very close in here.''

''Let me take you outside. You'll feel much more the thing.'' Taking her arm and drawing her toward the door, Phillip explained to a solicitous acquaintance that Madame von Hellenberg was feeling faint from the stuffiness of the overheated room. Once outside the doors of the Assembly Rooms he took her by the shoulder, saying, ''Out with it, Anthea. What's wrong? I saw you talking to Lyndock. Did he say something to disturb you?''

Anthea hesitated for a moment. Then she burst out, ''Lord Lyndock's been horribly, deliberately rude to me. I suppose it shouldn't surprise me, knowing what he's like, but it's upset me. Let me stay out here for a little while to calm myself. There's no need for you to stay, Phillip.''

Curbing a sudden, impulsive move to dash back into the ballroom, Phillip exclaimed in frustrated anger, ''I'd call him out in a shot but that would only cause disagreeable attention to be directed to you, Cousin. Cousin!'' he repeated heavily. ''Actually, I don't have the right to do anything in your behalf. I'm not really related to you in any way. Anthea, my dearest Anthea, won't you give me that right? Please say that you'll marry me. I was going to wait a little longer to ask you, to give you the opportunity to know me—all of us—better, but I can't hold back my feelings any longer."

Looking up into his loving, troubled face, Anthea thought back to Lyndock's crude remark about Phillip's humble ancestry. She felt another surge of anger and said, despite a warning inner voice urging caution, "Yes, Phillip, I will marry you."

=10=

ANTHEA TRAILED LISTLESSLY into the stable yard the following morning, feeling little enthusiasm for her usual early ride and half inclined to turn around and return to her bedchamber. A dull headache pressed against the back of her eyes, the result of a sleepless night spent agonising over the wisdom of accepting Phillip's proposal of marriage. She had tossed and turned, had risen from her bed to sit at the window and stare out at the moonlight-silvered park, had paced the floor until her legs ached, and she was no more resolved after all this expenditure of energy than she had been the night before.

She knew that she did not care for Phillip in the accepted romantic sense; her heart did not lilt at his touch, she did not yearn for his presence during every brief absence. But she was very fond of him and of his entire family, she had great respect for his sturdy strength of character, she admired his feeling of responsibility for his stepmother and his younger brothers and sisters. And she was well aware, of course, that in their position in life it was considered rather vulgar to base a marriage on mere feelings of romantic love. Certainly on the surface her marriage to Phillip would be an excellent match; her fortune united to his would enable them to live in almost princely comfort, and she knew that Phillip's rocklike dependability would never fail her in any crisis. And yet . . . Periodically during the night, despite her desperate efforts to beat back her errant thoughts, she had found herself remembering the hard clasp of Lyndock's arms, the pressure of his lips on hers. Was it fair to marry Phillip if she did not feel for him the overwhelming passion that she had once shared with Lyndock?

As she spotted Matt Corby across the stable yard, Anthea straightened her shoulders resolutely. If she went back to her bedchamber she would only keep mulling over the problem of her betrothal to Phillip. It was better to keep to her usual routine and hope that a fast ride in the bracing morning air would clear her mind and enable her to see the situation from a fresh slant.

Matt Corby was standing in absorbed conversation with a young man whom Anthea had never seen before. She had to call to Matt to make known her presence, and when he turned to her he seemed flustered. The strange young man, glancing nervously in her direction, quickly left the stable yard.

During the course of their ride Corby was much preoccupied, totally lacking in his usually rather shy friendliness. After he had failed for the second time to respond to one of her remarks, Anthea tapped him lightly on the shoulder with her riding crop. As he turned his startled face toward her, she said, "Something is troubling you, Matt. Do you care to talk about it? Perhaps I could help in some way."

The groom averted his eyes. "No, I thank you, ma'am. If there's summat amiss, there's naught you could do about it."

"Well, but you can't be sure of that. If there's something wrong in your family, for instance . . .Who was the young man in the stable yard? It seemed to upset you to talk with him."

"Oh—that was my brother Aaron."

"Really? I don't believe that I've seen him before."

"No, ma'am. He's been working up Nottingham way. Just came back here a few days ago."

Anthea eyed the young groom with exasperated concern. She had no right at all to pry apart his stubborn reserve, but she had become fond of the boy and it was obvious that he had serious problems. "You know, it sometimes helps to talk about one's difficulties," she persisted.

"Yes, ma'am. But the master wouldn't like my coming to you with my concerns. And really, Miss—Your Highness—it's all settled, no'un can change it."

"Change what, for heaven's sake? What's settled?"

"Why, the razing of the village," came Matt's answer in a rush of words as he became resigned to the fact that Anthea would interrogate him until he revealed what was troubling him. "Aaron just came to tell me this morning that Mr. Howard—Sir Phillip's steward—notified my father and the other villagers late yesterday that their cottages were to be vacated in two weeks time."

"The villagers are being vacated from their cottages? The village itself is going to be razed? How can that be?"

"It's an enclosed village, ma'am," said Corby patiently. "Most of the land hereabouts is enclosed. All those hedgerows that you're always admiring—they weren't here twenty years ago before the land was enclosed. Sir Phillip owns the whole village of Upton, the land and everything on it. And he wants to raze it and turn it into grazing pastures for his cattle. The notice was put up on the church door a month ago, but my father has been hoping that the master might change his mind. I knew that Sir Phillip wasn't about to do that, but Father and the other villagers, they was so used to old Mr. Hampton, do you see—they couldn't rightly believe that they would ever be thrown out of their cottages. Squire Hampton's family had owned the village and the land around for hunerds of years, so I've heard, and the squire, he was a right softhearted man. He didn't like the idea of enclosing the village and turning all the folk out of their homes. But he died some months back and his heirs, they sold the whole property to Sir Phillip."

"But Matt, didn't you tell me that your father's family has occupied their cottage for several generations back? What about their rights of tenancy?"

"Oh, my father is only a tenant at will. The lease could be terminated at any time Sir Phillip wanted."

"I see." Anthea hesitated, not wanting to pursue the subject of enclosures, lest she inadvertently criticise Phillip to one of his servants. "What will your family do now, Matt?"

The groom's shoulders slumped. "Dunno, ma'am. When I was growing up we weren't too bad off. My father worked as a labourer for the farmers roundabout, and he kept a pig and some chickens and grew vegetables in the garden behind the cottage, and my stepmother, before she died, made articles out of straw that she was able to sell. But she's been dead a while now, and my father has been sick more often than not lately, so him and the little 'uns have been depending mostly on poor relief, which I'm bound to say wouldn't be near enough to live on without a roof over their heads. Nine shillings a week won't stretch far these days."

"Nine shillings a week?" exclaimed Anthea, horrified. "For a grown man and four young children?"

"Yes, ma'am. A' course, out of that Father paid three guineas a year rent on the cottage, too. I've tried to help out as best I could, though just starting out, like, since I come back from the army, I don't get paid very much. But even a bit of extra bread helps, I reckon."

"I'm sure that it does," said Anthea compassionately, remembering the times that Matt had stopped off at his father's cottage with an awkwardly-wrapped parcel. "How about your brother—Aaron, is that his name? Can't he help too?"

"Not very likely. Aaron—he was a stockinger up near Nottingham—he's been thrown out of work, that's why he come home. Times are terrible bad for finding work, now that the war's over. I counted myself very lucky to be taken on in Sir Phillip's stables after I was mustered out. Lots of Peninsular veterans—" Corby eyed Anthea challengingly as he said, "Your father now, he'd be very grieved to see the numbers of mustered out soldiers and sailors who are begging for a scrap of food on the highways of this country. We're of no use to anybody, do you see, now that Boney's beaten and sent off to that island in the Atlantic Ocean."

Surprised at the unexpected bitterness in the groom's voice and anxious to prevent his saying anything further that he might regret later, Anthea said hastily, "Do you know, Matt, I cannot believe that you and your father have understood the situation completely. Sir Phillip, I'm sure, would never turn a whole village of people out on the roads. I'll speak to him this evening after dinner and see if I can't clear up this misunderstanding."

"Yes, ma'am. Thank you, ma'am." But Matt did not look her straight in the eye, and his voice was politely skeptical.

Presented now with a fresh source of worry—distress over the villagers' predicament—to add to her gnawing doubts about the wisdom of her betrothal to Phillip, Anthea went to her bedchamber after her ride in a very subdued frame of mind. She had to make a distinct effort to appear cheerful when Harriet, up unusually early, knocked at her door.

"My dearest Anthea, I can't begin to tell you how happy I am this morning!" exclaimed Harriet, wiping tears of joy from her eyes. "Phillip has just told me the wonderful news. I vow, my heart is pounding so hard, I'll have palpitations. To think of marrying off two of my children virtually at the same time. It's really enough to make one's senses swim!"

"Two of your children, Aunt?"

"Why, yes. Phillip tells me that Ensign Sinclair asked him for Fanny's hand last night at the Assembly ball. Of course, we can't actually announce it yet. Mr. Sinclair must write to his own parents first. But there is no doubt at all that the connection with the Montville family will be more than welcome, you know."

"Yes, I'm sure that the Sinclairs will be very happy to have Fanny as a daughter-in-law," said Anthea politely, feeling a real regret that she could not summon more enthusiasm at the news of Fanny's betrothal.

"Phillip didn't say when you were to be married," said Harriet, "but I presume some time this autumn. For a wedding of this size we really should begin to plan almost immediately, my dear, especially allowing for the fact that so many of your invitations must go all the way to Vienna."

Suddenly Anthea felt as if her limbs were being immobilised by an invisible but inexorably strong set of silken bonds. "I hadn't even though about the wedding, Aunt," she said lamely. "But now that you mention it, I'm inclined to favour a date in the spring."

"In the spring! But that's very nearly a whole year from now."

"Yes, in the spring," repeated Anthea firmly, feeling a surge of relief. "Consider, Aunt, that Phillip and I have known each other for only a few months. It really wouldn't be seemly to rush into marriage, don't you agree?"

It was clear that Harriet was far from agreeing, but she was too well bred to press her opinions on her niece. She lingered for only a short while longer, discussing Fanny's engagement, and Anthea was rather glad to see her go.

Later that day, feeling tired and stale from several more hours of soul searching about her acceptance of Phillip's offer, Anthea determined to drive into Oakham to shop for some ribbon with which to trim the chemises that Hannah was stitching for her. She spent a happy half hour turning over the merchandise at the silk mercer's shop. As she was leaving with her purchases, she spotted Julian some distance away, carrying a heavy portmanteau and standing with a group of people who were waiting to board the stagecoach that had just come into sight at the end of the street. She had last seen him at breakfast, when he had stated his intention to spend the entire day on his Virgil. Before she could recover from her surprise and speak to him, Lyndock appeared as if from nowhere, grasped Julian's arm and whisked him through the door of a nearby tavern.

"Well!" murmured Anthea to herself. "I wonder what all that is about?" She walked up and down the street for some time, pretending to examine an occasional shop window while keeping half an eye on the door of the tavern, but she did not see either Julian or Lyndock come out. Finally she tired of her wait and returned to her carriage for the drive back to Ashby House. A mile or so out of Oakham she heard the sound of a vehicle behind her and turned her head just as Lyndock's curricle, his magnificent matched bays going at a smart pace, was passing her carriage. She met Julian's startled eyes as he sat beside Lyndock in the curricle, and nodded stiffly to Lyndock when he touched his hat to her as he went by.

A little later, approaching the first cottages in the village of Upton, her coachman stopped the carriage as he spotted Julian, waiting by the roadside with his arm raised.

"I'll just ride with you to the house," said the boy with a

sideways glance at Anthea as he climbed into the carriage and settled himself beside her. "Didn't think that it was a good idea to have Lord Lyndock drive me all the way home, don't you know. Phillip—or somebody—might ask questions. Actually, Cousin Anthea, I'd appreciate it no end if you didn't mention that you saw me driving out of Oakham today."

"Yes, Oakham did seem rather an odd place to study one's Virgil," replied Anthea drily. "Where is your portmanteau?"

"I hid it in the bushes—oh," he broke off, looking hopelessly confused. "I didn't realise—that is to say—I daresay that you saw me waiting for the stagecoach."

"I did."

"Well, you see, I thought that I might just take a short trip to—to . . ." Julian reddened as he met Anthea's politely expectant gaze. "Oh, hang it all, Cousin, if you must know, I was on my way to join up with the First Dragoon Guards as a common trooper," he burst out. "I did what you suggested and spoke to Phillip about how much I hated the thought of becoming a clergyman, but I knew how it would be, he simply refused to budge an inch. So I decided to take matters into my own hands. It's my life, after all, the only one that I'll ever have, and I won't spend it marrying and burying people or preaching boring sermons!"

Anthea sighed. "But you changed your mind, obviously," she said after a pause. "Did—did Lord Lyndock have anything to do with that?"

"Well, yes, he did. Your word of honour that you won't say a word to anyone about this, but Lord Lyndock promised to buy me a pair of colours on my birthday next month if I would just go home today, settle down to my lessons for the rest of the summer and really do some hard thinking about my situation. Lord Lyndock said that I should consider all the pros and cons; he pointed out, for example, that if I took orders and accepted the living that my godfather has offered to me, I would enjoy a handsome income, far larger, he said, than I have any right to expect as a second son. And then, since the living is in the hunt country, I could live more or less like any country squire, hunting, shooting, all of that. He also suggested that I should think about the possible consequences of refusing to go into the Church; Phillip might be so angry that he would cut me off, forbid me the house, and that would break Mama's heart, because, you know, fond as she is of me and indeed of all her children, I don't think that she could bring herself to go against Phillip's wishes.''

Anthea agreed silently. In any contest between Harriet and her stepson, there was no question of who the victor would be. Anthea knit her brow, wondering why Lyndock had exerted himself to foil Julian's rash scheme of running away to enlist as a common trooper. It was true that Lyndock had seemed to become casually fond of the boy as a result of their many meetings during the London season. And indeed, his arguments in favor of Julian's accepting his godfather's gift of the living were practically identical to those that Phillip himself had used. It was ironic that Julian had apparently listened thoughtfully to Lyndock's comments when those same words coming from his brother had occasioned only a mulish resentment. But was Lyndock's only reason for so drastic an intervention in Julian's life a mere fondness for the boy? For drastic was really the only word that one could use to describe Lyndock's offer to buy Julian a commission against the opposition of his brother. Could it be that Lyndock was simply responding to a malicious urge to retaliate against Anthea for throwing him over by causing a serious rift in the Montville family? She sighed again, voicing her misgivings.

"Julian, you know that I sympathise with your unwillingness to enter the Church. But do you really think that you should allow yourself to accept such a great favour from Lord Lyndock? He's not much more than a friendly acquaintance, and I know that most people would condemn what they would perceive as meddling in another family's affairs.''

Squaring his shoulders, Julian said grimly, "Cousin Anthea, I would accept help from the devil himself if it would rescue me from taking holy orders!''

Realising the futility of trying to change Julian's mind, Anthea lapsed into silence, but she was still deeply troubled as she dressed for dinner, her concern for Julian overshadowing her own personal problems for the moment. In the drawing room before dinner, however, she relegated her worries to the back of her mind as she gave her good wishes to Fanny and Rob Sinclair, who entered the room together so self-consciously that it required no mental exertion at all to guess that only moments before they had been holding hands.

"My dear Fanny, allow me to wish you happy," Anthea smiled, kissing her young cousin lightly on the cheek. Extending her hand to Rob Sinclair, she said, "No need to wish *you* happy, I'll warrant. Having Fanny for your wife guarantees your future happiness."

"Oh, thank you, Cousin Anthea. I don't think that we've quite taken it all in yet," beamed Fanny. "But what makes this day even more wonderful is the news that we're to be sisters. Mama just told me that you and Phillip are to be married too." She caught sight of Phillip coming into the drawing room and danced over to him, giving him a quick hug as she said excitedly, "We've just heard, Phillip—and we're so happy for you. You couldn't have chosen anyone to be your wife who would have pleased us more. Mama says that the announcement of your betrothal will be the greatest news of the year."

"A little more dignity would be in order, my dear sister," said Phillip composedly as he unclasped Fanny's arms from around his neck. "You sound more like a gushing schoolgirl than a young woman about to be married." A slight smile softened his words. "But then, I suppose that your excitement is understandable. It *is* a very happy day." His smile deepened as he turned to Anthea. "Good evening, my love. Have you had a good day?"

To those who did not know him well, Anthea reflected, Phillip might seem to be his usual reserved, intensely serious self, but there were little signs that revealed to the practiced observer that he was a supremely happy man—the kindling of his eye when he looked at Anthea, a slight lilt to his gravely measured voice, a softened expression on his face in moments of repose. And Julian escaped lightly this evening from what normally would have been a blast of displeasure when Phillip discovered from the tutor that the boy had disappeared from the classroom for most of the day. Phillip merely informed Julian not to let it happen again, and the young boy turned briefly to Anthea with a smile of guilty relief.

At dinner there was no great talk of weddings, though Harriet tried her best to steer the conversation to ordering champagne from Gunther's and the wisdom of an early reservation at St. Margaret's, Westminster. Phillip, once he had gotten over the initial pleasure of seeing Anthea at his table as his acknowledged fiancée, was preoccupied with a more mundane subject. "I've just returned from Lord Treanor's," he remarked heavily. "He wanted to talk with me about some disturbing news that he's just received from Northamptonshire. Gangs of poachers have been moving into the county in what seems to be an organised movement to supply the London markets with game. Ruffians are despatched into areas where there are well-stocked game preserves with the understanding that all poached game will be taken off their hands, no questions asked."

"Are these gangs operating only in Northamptonshire?" asked Julian.

"Unfortunately, no. Lord Treanor's informant suspects that the poachers are encroaching on all the hunting country northeast and northwest of London. It's only a matter of time, I fear, before we're faced with the problem here in Rutland. I've arranged to go into Oakham early tomorrow morning to meet with the magistrates to discuss what measures we might take to discourage these criminals from operating here."

"But Phillip, at least some of the proprietors of the London hotels and restaurants who buy this game must suspect that their supplies come from illegal sources," said Anthea, knitting her brow.

"That goes without saying, my dear. Simple greed causes them to shut their eyes to their suspicions."

"Well, I hope that you can come up with something, Phillip," grumbled Julian. "An autumn and winter without shooting just don't bear thinking about."

After dinner, recalling her promise to Matt Corby to discuss the threatened destruction of the village, Anthea sought out Phillip in the drawing room where tea was being served, but soon realised that a family gathering was no place to tackle him on such a subject. Instead, she said with an inviting smile, "Can I persuade you to join me on my ride tomorrow?"

"I'd like nothing better, though I must say that your chosen hour for riding has often seemed to me to be positively barbaric! But I do have a meeting tomorrow morning with the magistrates in Oakham, as I mentioned at dinner."

"Oh, come now, Phillip. You'll return from our ride in ample time to go to Oakham. I—I have something rather important to discuss with you." Anthea flashed a frankly seductive glance at Phillip, who, with only a scant few seconds' pause, smiled back at her, saying indulgently, "You know that I can't refuse you anything, my love, even if it means losing part of a good night's sleep!"

=11=

A LIGHT RAIN was falling as Phillip and Anthea cantered out of the stable yard the following morning.

"It looks like the last of our fine weather," commented Phillip regretfully, gazing up into the gray skies. "I had hoped for a few more days of sun, to salvage a little more of the harvest."

"Perhaps it will clear later," said Anthea hopefully. "There, I do believe that the rain is stopping already."

They were rounding a bend of the lane, and Phillip, casting a quick glance around him, reached over for Anthea's bridle and reined in both their horses. He leaned over, placing his arm over her shoulder as he sought her lips in a long, clinging kiss. "I've been longing to do that," he said huskily, leaning back in his saddle, reaching out for her hand. "Sometimes, when I'm talking to you, I find myself watching your mouth, not paying any attention to what you are saying, just imagining how soft and warm your lips would feel under mine."

Anthea's hand moved a little uneasily in his. The emotion in his voice, the fire in his kiss, unaccountably surprised and unsettled her. He had, of course, kissed her at the time that she had accepted his proposal of marriage, and he had placed a chaste kiss on her brow when they met at breakfast and when they parted at night. But she had grown so used to Phillip's reserved demeanour that she had—foolishly, she now told herself—failed to consider what emotional depths might lie below that controlled exterior. And she wondered uncomfortably if the time would ever come when she would feel the same response to Phillip's caresses that even the slightest touch from Lyndock had always been able to evoke in her.

"You're so beautiful, my dearest Anthea. I always feel like an emperor—or at least a premier duke of the realm!—when I stand beside you in public as your escort. Even if . . ." Some of the warmth faded from Phillip's eyes as he paused, looking faintly embarrassed.

"Even if?"

"Well, it's just—I've been meaning to say a word to you about this." Phillip paused again to look closely at Anthea's riding habit, a close-fitting confection in bright blue, liberally frogged along the sleeves and high standing collar in a darker shade of blue, and worn with a dashing hat resembling a Hussar's headgear and topped with great nodding plumes dyed the brilliant blue of the habit. "It's your wardrobe, Anthea. I've been told that your clothes are all the crack, but I sometimes find them just a trifle—the tiniest bit extreme in cut and colour. Extreme, that is, for the sort of life that you will be leading as Lady Montville," he hastened to add, as he noticed the beginnings of a frown on Anthea's brow. "For Paris, or Vienna, I have no doubt, your wardrobe would be quite perfect."

"I'll bear your opinion in mind," promised Anthea as soon as she recovered her voice. She was seething inwardly at this unexpected criticism coming from a man who had never before seemed anything but totally admiring, but she wanted to collect her thoughts before she allowed the issue to become an open quarrel. And it was perfectly possible, she thought, trying for fairness, that an overly colourful, overly fashionable ex-princess might indeed be out of place in this placid Rutland countryside.

"I was persuaded that you would see my point," said Phillip approvingly. "As I was saying to my stepmother just the other day, it's quite understandable, considering your early life—no mother to care for you, trailing about Europe from one barracks town to another, the necessity of coping with the excesses of a dissolute father—it's quite understandable that your manners and

136

taste and mode of dressing should be a little—shall we say unconventional?"

Scarcely believing what she was hearing—that Phillip had actually discussed her character with Harriet—Anthea had to clench her hands together very tightly over her reins to prevent herself from screeching at Phillip like a fishwife. He was looking at her with an expression of deepest affection, and it was apparent that he had no idea that he was sounding both smug and condescending. Anthea wondered if he had fallen in love with her despite, rather than because, of the sprightliness of her personality. Now that he had official standing in her life as her fiancé he was evidently preparing to mould her into his image of what a dignified county matron should be. Her back stiffened. Was this really the kind of future life she wanted: ordered, uneventful, guided by Phillip's undoubtedly sensible standards? She knew that his managerial streak was an essential part of his character, although based on a genuinely kindly desire to give happiness to those he loved. And she *had* tired of the artificialities of her Austrian life and knew that she needed a strong anchor against the insecurities that continued to haunt her from her rootless childhood years. But one thing she was sure of: She was not going to give up her independence at the price of surrendering her own freedom of mind completely.

She managed a smile and a hint of playful teasing as she said, "Phillip, my dear, I think that we must have an understanding. Peacock I may be—rather an admired peacock, if I may say so!—but I could never turn myself into a house wren even if I wanted to. And I don't."

"Oh." There was a startled silence. Anthea had a fleeting impulse to laugh. Seldom in his solemn, masterful life had Phillip ever been rebuked. He eyed her with a new, more respectful interest. "Well, of course, I really don't know anything about ladies' fashions. . . ."

"That's right, Phillip. You don't."

"Oh." Another startled pause, and then Phillip said with a

rueful twinkle in his eyes, "Piqued, repiqued, slammed and capotted! It's your game, my love. Your wardrobe is and will always be your own affair. And very lovely you always look, too. Am I forgiven for my tactlessness?"

"Yes, certainly." This time Anthea's smile was unforced. She found herself liking Phillip the better for his generous apology, which could not have come easily from a man unaccustomed to finding himself in the wrong.

"And now," said Phillip, looking very willing to change the subject, "what was it that you wanted to talk to me about? Something of great moment, I trust, to warrant forcing me out of bed so early this morning." His smile took the sting out of his words, but Anthea was very serious as she replied, "Why, yes, I think that it is of great moment. At least it seems so to your groom, Matt Corby. He tells me that the entire village of Upton is to be razed."

Phillip looked displeased. "So Corby's been talking to you about that, has he? Really, you know, it's the outside of enough, a servant badgering one of my guests about his personal concerns."

"No, no, Matt didn't complain to me. I simply dragged the information out of him after I observed how distressed he seemed as he was talking to his brother Aaron in the stable yard before our ride yesterday morning."

"Aaron Corby's back in the area? I'm sorry to hear that. The boy's a ne'er-do-well."

"Well, that's as may be," said Anthea impatiently, "but I told Matt that I would talk to you about the village. I'm sure that he misunderstands your intentions. Surely you can't mean to turn all those people out of their homes? Matt said something to me about enclosures, whatever that means."

Sighing, Phillip shook his head. "It's you who doesn't understand, Anthea. Let me just give you a simple explanation of enclosure, which just means putting up a barrier—fences, hedges, even ditches—around land that was formerly held in common. Enclosure has been in progress for centuries in England, coming to this part of the country, however, mostly during the present reign. Old Squire Hampton, who owned the village of Upton and the surrounding land—which I bought recently from his heirs—was the last owner of any consequence in the neighbourhood to resist enclosure.''

Anthea looked perplexed. ''I understand what enclosure *is*, I think, but what does it have to do with razing the village?''

''So that I can use the land on which it sits, together with the rest of Squire Hampton's acreage, fence it in, and unite it to my own holdings.

''You see, Anthea,'' Phillip continued, ''the Hampton estate was farmed under the old, inefficient three-field system, in which each villager or tenant farmed scattered strips of land in each of three fields, plus owning shares in the use of the common pasture and woodlands. But it was impossible under this system to farm scientifically or to breed livestock scientifically; one could not introduce new crops or new strains of seeds without obtaining the consent and cooperation of all these marginal farmers, and I'm sure you can imagine the difficulties of selective breeding of livestock when all your animals must graze on the same pastures with your neighbour's inferior scrubby stock. So enclosure simply makes for more efficient and productive farming, and a good thing it is that so much of the country *was* enclosed by the time of the recent war, when the Continental blockade prevented most foodstuffs from entering our ports. England would have starved without the food grown on her enclosed estates. And of course we go about the process with the greatest regard for legality. I had to get the government's permission to enclose. I sent a petition to Parliament, a Bill of Enclosure was read twice in the Commons, and the petition was turned over to a committee, which, after ascertaining that at least three-quarters of the concerned landowners concurred, reported favourably on my bill.''

''I'm sure that your actions have been entirely legal, but I keep thinking about the plight of the villagers. Some of them, like the Corby family, have lived here for generations.''

''But most of them are simply squatters,'' said Phillip impatiently. ''Corby's father, for example, never had any land in the open fields. Only ancient custom gave him and the other villagers the right to put up a cottage on common land or to graze their pigs and cows on the wasteland. The old squire resisted enclosure mostly because he had a sentimental attachment to these people in the village, but he's dead now and I intend at long last to make the best use of the land.''

''Well, Phillip, scientific farming is all very well, but the lives of these people in the village are important too. Matt Corby's father, for example, is old and ill and has a handful of young children to feed. Surely you don't really intend to turn him and his family out on the roads to starve? The land that the village occupies doesn't amount to a vast acreage, I'm sure. Why can't you just allow these people to occupy their cottages and tend their little garden plots? Would it put you out of pocket all that much?''

Phillip, who had been calmly reasonable during the course of the conversation, reacted to Anthea's accusing tone with an angry flush.

''My dear girl, you're talking utter nonsense. You haven't lived in England since you were a child, and you know nothing at all about economic conditions here. I must tell you that times have been very bad here since the end of the war, especially in agriculture. Foreign wheat has flooded the country and agricultural prices have plummeted. In fact, Anthea, we may be very close to revolution. Even before the end of the war, workers were agitating for higher wages, smashing machines and burning factories to make their point. Entire districts have been convulsed by strikes, and a year ago March, after the passage of the Corn Law Bill, there was actually rioting all over England, and in London a mob marched on Parliament and then broke into the home of the lord chancellor. In my opinion, the very sanctity of private property is at stake. And here you are asking me to—quite literally—*give* away a large plot of land!''

Anthea sighed. ''Very well, Phillip, I do understand now that a larger question of finance is involved here. But please, couldn't you make an exception for the Corby family? Perhaps find a cottage elsewhere on the estate for them?''

Shaking his head, Phillip said regretfully, ''I know that your soft heart prompts this request, but I can't grant it. It simply wouldn't be morally right. Malthus—I'm sure that you haven't read Malthus, but I consider him a genius—Malthus says that populations automatically outrun their food supply, so that nature ruthlessly eliminates extra mouths by starvation. He says, 'We are bound in justice and honour formally to disclaim the *right* of the poor to support.' So if there is no call for his labour, you see, a man has no claim to food or shelter.''

"But Matt's father *can't* work," exclaimed Anthea indignantly. "You know that he's been ill. And even supposing he was able to work, what if there were no jobs? Matt tells me that his brother Aaron has come back to Upton because he was thrown out of work up in Nottingham."

Phillip threw up his hands. "My dear Anthea, I fear that it's useless to attempt to explain economic theory to a female, but let me try once more: If Matt Corby's father can't work, and his brother Aaron can't find work, it's all the same according to Malthus. Neither of them can be expected to be supported by society."

For one of the very few times in her life, Anthea flew into a blinding rage. "Then I say that Malthus is inhuman, *you're* inhuman! If enclosure means denying little children food to put in their mouths or a place to lay their heads, I hope that these rioters and strikers who've been causing all the commotion around the country tear down every fence and hedge and return England to those dreadful medieval times when folk were not allowed to starve on the roads."

Putting her mount to a gallop, Anthea thundered away from Phillip, plunging into a narrow lane edged thickly with a luxuriant growth of hawthorn. As she pulled away from him, Anthea could hear Phillip crying, "Anthea, please wait," but she put her spurs to her horse in an even wilder ride, streaking so swiftly between the thickly massed hawthorn that the lane before her came to resemble a deeply green tunnel. When, a few moments later, the lane debouched into a roadway, Anthea pounded into the intersection without reining in, or glancing about her to see if the way was clear, and missed charging into another rider by scant inches. Instinctively she sawed on her reins, pulling her horse back so deeply on his haunches that she lost her balance on the sidesaddle and fell heavily to the ground. She felt a sudden sharp pain in her head and then oblivion.

"Anthea—can you hear me? Good God, there's blood on your temple, you must have struck your head on a rock. Anthea, please answer me, let me know that you aren't badly hurt. . . ."

Anthea blinked several times to clear her eyes, then focused on Lyndock's face, his brown eyes almost black with anxiety as he knelt beside her, cradling her in his arms on the soft grass of the verge.

"Why don't you look where you're going?" demanded Anthea crossly. "I haven't taken a tumble like that since I first learned to ride."

Lyndock erupted into a whoop of laughter. "So it was all my fault! Now I know that you must be all right—your female illogic is still intact! My dear girl, I was quietly cantering along the road, communing with nature, when you barreled into me as if you were leading the last charge of the Imperial Guard at Waterloo. Seriously, though, your head is bleeding slightly. Let me sponge it with my handkerchief—it just looks like a scratch, really, it isn't bleeding any more. Do you have a headache? Feel dizzy? Do you know where you are, what you were doing just before you fell?"

Anthea struggled away from his supporting arm to a sitting position. "No, I don't feel dizzy and I know exactly where I am. I realise that you're just questioning me to see if my mind is clear, but I don't think that I have a serious head injury. Actually, I think that my shoulder took the brunt of my fall. It's going to be very sore shortly. But my head—such as it is, female and illogical —seems quite all right." She accented the words "female" and "illogical," and Lyndock eyed her quizzically for a moment before saying, "Famous! Let's get you on your feet, then."

He put his hands under her arms, helping her up. For a second or two, still feeling shaky, Anthea was glad to be enfolded in the sheltering strength of his embrace. Then, as his arms began to tighten around her, she pulled away from him. "Where's my horse? Oh, there you are, Busaco. Poor old fellow, you must have thought that you were back in the Peninsula, being chased by French dragoons."

Lyndock sauntered up to her as she stood beside Busaco, crooning into the horse's ear and gently stroking his head.

"What did set you off, Anthea? You're far too good a rider to charge broadside into another horseman. Did something make you angry? Yes, I see that it did," he grinned as Anthea glared at him. "Did you know that you look magnificent when you're angry? Your eyes erupt with violet sparks and that porcelain skin of yours has a warm glow like a sculpture from a master craftsman coming to life."

Turning away from him, Anthea reached for her bridle, saying shortly, "My state of mind, my lord, is nothing to you. Nor do I care in the slightest what effect my appearance, angry or otherwise, has on you. Will you help me to mount, please?"

Laying his hand on her arm, Lyndock said, "In a moment. First, let me offer my felicitations on the occasion of your betrothal to Phillip Montville."

"How did you hear about that?" Anthea blurted. "It's not been announced publicly."

"Good God, don't you realise that her Serene Highness the Princess von Hellenberg is the object of more curiosity in these parts than the honeymoon activities of Princess Charlotte and Prince Leopold? I don't know how the rumour started—perhaps Lady Montville dropped a hint to one of her cronies, or perhaps the county just naturally expected the event to happen as a result of your long stay at Ashby House—but yesterday afternoon at tea at Lady Symington's the only topic of conversation was the date of your wedding and how much your fortune would add to the Montville coffers. So, now that I know that the rumour is, indeed, true, I'd like to wish you happy." He paused, lifting his eyebrow. "You *are* happy? You're looking forward to a life of wedded bliss as Lady Montville?"

Involuntarily biting her lip, Anthea turned her head away from him. Lyndock shot out a long arm to grasp her chin between his slim, strong fingers, forcing her to look at him. "The mystery of your newly atrocious horsemanship is solved," he said with a sudden grin of enlightenment. "You've had a lover's quarrel with the estimable Phillip."

"You have so little sense of propriety, Lord Lyndock," flared Anthea, "that I daresay it's useless for me to tell you that you're being uncommonly rude. Again I must ask you to help me mount. I have better things to do with my time than to listen to any more of your rudeness."

Still retaining his firm grip on her arm, Lyndock raised his eyes to a point above her head, saying thoughtfully, "Now, what could that paragon Phillip Montville have done to enrage you to the point where you would endanger the life of Busaco—because that magnificent horse of yours has to mean more to you than your betrothed. . . ." He renewed his grip, smiling still more broadly as Anthea, in a fury over his reference to Phillip, vainly tried to pull free. He continued placidly. "Could it possibly be that Phillip is neglecting you? Is he spending so much time conscientiously attending to his estate and county duties that he has no time left to be with his future bride?" He paused, as if struck by an illuminating thought. "Have you, so briefly into your betrothal, discovered how dull a husband poor Phillip will be?"

Angry though she was, Anthea was aware in one corner of her mind that Lyndock was deliberately baiting her, and the reference to Phillip's estate duties reminded her suddenly of the reason for her quarrel with him. She ceased struggling against Lyndock's hold and said, with a calmness that evidently surprised him, "I wonder if you would give me your opinion about a certain matter, my lord: Have you heard about the plan to raze the village of Upton?"

His smile fading, his attention sharpening, Lyndock replied, "Yes, I'm aware of it. Notice of enclosure was posted on the village church some time ago." His eyes widened. "Is *that* the cause of your quarrel with Phillip? Because I can tell—don't bother to deny it—that you've just come away from a flaming row with him.''

Anthea fell into a confused silence. She did not want to appear critical of Phillip, especially to Lyndock. Picking her words carefully, she said, "I *have* been talking about the village with Phillip, yes. He tried to explain to me the enclosure system, and I can see that it would make for more efficient farming. He also quoted the theories of somebody called Malthus, which I perhaps don't understand properly. But it does seem very hard on the villagers.''

"It is hard," snapped Lyndock, all traces of amusement gone from his expression. "And I fancy that you've understood Malthus perfectly. It's not just the villagers, you know. There are five or six small freeholders on the former Hampton estate who have been forced to sell out to Phillip; they didn't have the capital to pay their share of the enclosure fees or the cost of fencing in the land.''

"But if that's so, why did they join Phillip in petitioning for enclosure? He tells me that at least three-quarters of the landowners had to agree on enclosure before the Parliamentary committee would report favourably on the petition.''

"The owners of three-quarters of the *acreage* must agree on enclosure," Lyndock corrected her. "And since Phillip now owns more than three-quarters of the Hampton property. . . ." He shrugged. "But you'll never win an argument with your betrothed on the subject of enclosures, my dear girl. He's perfectly within his rights, you know.''

"But if you agree that Phillip is right in his plans for the village, why do I sense this great disapproval of what he's doing?''

"I didn't say that he was right. I said that he was *within* his rights. Your future husband is a man of perfect justice and very little charity.''

Stiffening, Anthea snapped, "I'll ask you to explain that, my lord.''

"With pleasure. I agree in principle that enclosure makes for better agriculture. During the war years Napoleon might have starved England into submission with his blockade without our increased food production from enclosure. My own uncle enclosed his property over forty years ago—that's the estate that I just inherited—but there was one big difference between his procedure and Phillip's: my uncle made sure that all the dispossessed cottagers and small freeholders were not turned out without some sort of provision made for their futures. Phillip not only is not making any such provisions, he believes that it would actually be immoral—there's Malthus speaking—to do so. Come now, isn't that approximately what he told you, and isn't that why you became so angry with him?''

"Well, yes, but you must remember that the Montville family haven't been landowners for generations like your people, the Strettons, and I think it very possible that Phillip hasn't really thought through the effects that his actions will have. I've asked him to consider finding another cottage for the Corbys—Matt Corby is a groom on the estate who's been riding with me every day, and his father is old and ill with a large family of small children.''

Lyndock smiled derisively. "And of course Phillip promptly granted your request? Wondered, in fact, why it hadn't occurred to him earlier?''

"No—no, he didn't. But then, the idea was so new to him—I'll speak to him about it again, naturally.''

His sinewy fingers biting into her shoulders, Lyndock brought her face close to his. "Anthea, think very hard about this betrothal of yours. You're far too much a creature of fire and feeling to give the rest of your life into the keeping of a man who's all head and no heart.'' His dark eyes bored down into hers. With a little groan, he crushed her against him, claiming her mouth in a long, bruising kiss that, for a fleeting instant, erased all sensation, all thought, except the immediacy of his hard body against hers. It was only when he lifted his head momentarily, to murmur in a voice drowned with passion, "Anthea, you've never felt anything like this with Montville, I'm sure,'' that she was able to wrench herself away from him.

She drew a deep breath, saying coldly, "My lord, despite your great experience in matters of the heart, you can have no conception of what I feel for Phillip. I assure you that I love and respect him and have every intention of marrying him. And I must remind you that no real gentleman would try to undermine another man to his betrothed."

He stepped back with a rueful smile. "Well, I can't deny that, can I? I apologise." He eyed her quizzically. "Do you know, I think that you have a gift for bringing out the worst in me." He cocked his head, as if expecting another angry outburst from her, but, snatching up Busaco's reins, she turned her back on him and stalked off down the lane away from him, half expecting him to follow her. But she heard no sound behind her, and, when she ventured a side glance, she saw that he remained standing motionless beside his horse, watching her progress down the lane.

She had made her way almost back to the point where she had originally left Phillip when she saw him trotting toward her. "Anthea," he exclaimed anxiously as he dismounted, "have you had a fall? I didn't want to follow you, not immediately—well, you were so very angry, you know, there was no point in trying to talk to you then—but when you didn't come back—"

"I did fall, Phillip. It was entirely my own fault, not Busaco's. But I'm not hurt, and if you'll just help me up into the saddle I'll be quite all right."

As they rode off together in the direction of Ashby House, Anthea thought of Lyndock's assertion that Phillip had no heart. Certainly his face had expressed panic at the possibility that she might have injured herself in a fall from her horse, and his countenance now was aglow with affection as he said earnestly, "I can't bear the thought that we've quarreled, my love. Are you still angry with me?"

"No, not angry, Phillip. And I'm sorry that I screamed at you. But I'm still very concerned about the village. Is there really no way that you could enclose your new property and still spare the homes of the people of Upton?"

Leaning from his saddle, Phillip placed his hand on hers.

"There is almost nothing that you could ask of me that I would not willingly give you, but this—this is a moral question. If you understood it better—but there, who could expect you to know anything about economic philosophy? I do care very much about your tender feelings, however, so I promise you that I will try to find some way to assist Matt Corby's family. Perhaps I might increase Matt's wages—we would have to make sure that the other servants didn't find out, of course; it *is* unfair to them—so that he could give his father money to supplement what he's getting on the rates, at least until the younger children are a bit older and able to go to work themselves." He paused, looking at her expectantly.

"That would be helpful, certainly, but wouldn't it be better if you could find them a cottage on the estate?"

Phillip's lips clamped shut. After a moment he said, obviously trying to curb his irritability, "No, I could not. You haven't been listening to me, Anthea. Matt's father can't work, he's nonproductive. I can't in conscience give him a cottage that ought to go to a labourer who *is* productive."

Anthea sighed. Phillip was so strongly convinced that he was in the right. Even his tentative offer to increase Matt's wages represented a considerable concession on his part. She could attempt to change his mind—in fact, she had every intention of trying to do so—but she had a hollow feeling that it would be quite useless. For the moment, however, she said quietly, "Well, I'm sure that the Corbys will be grateful for any help that you can give them, Phillip. Thank you."

═12═

"I DECLARE, MY love, you and Fanny are quite the most beautiful females here, as I knew you would be," murmured Harriet complacently as she stood with Anthea on the threshold of the drawing room at Hinton Court, the estate of their neighbour, Lord Ord.

Anthea thanked her aunt absently—she was wearing yet another of her Paris creations—as she gazed at Fanny, who had entered the room just ahead of them with Rob Sinclair. These days only the dullest of observers could fail to note the glow of happiness in the faces of that pair, even though their betrothal had not been formally announced. And judging by the knowing smiles, the frankly curious stares of her fellow guests, her own engagement to Phillip seemed already a matter of public knowledge. This commonly held expectation that she would marry Phillip, Anthea thought suddenly, would make her position extremely awkward if, as she had seriously been contemplating during this past week, she were to break off her engagement to Phillip because of his decision to raze the village of Upton. Their disagreement on this subject represented such widely different concepts of human values that she was beginning to doubt her ability to live peaceably with him while he persisted in such a plan. But until yesterday, Anthea had had hopes of avoiding so radical a course. After much thought, she had hit upon the brilliant notion of solving the problem by buying the property herself under an assumed name. This, she had congratulated herself, would not only save the homes and liveli-

149

hood of the villagers, but would also prevent any friction from arising between herself and Phillip.

Acting immediately upon her inspiration, Anthea had, a week before, made a long drive into the hills to the town of Uppingham to consult a lawyer. She had decided against seeking legal advice in Oakham, though it was so much closer to Ashby House, because the Montville family had so many connections to the town. Mr. Steele, the Uppingham lawyer, had been both flustered and delighted to serve so highly placed and wealthy a client. If, he said, Her Serene Highness were prepared to make a handsome offer considerably above the price that Sir Phillip had just paid for the property, he had no doubt, considering the depressed state of the farm economy, that Sir Phillip would consent to sell. "Just be sure that the offer is high enough," Anthea had urged, explaining that Phillip, with his industrial background, would certainly not be averse to turning a tidy profit, but that he had originally bought the Hampton estate primarily to enlarge his estate to a size more in keeping with his rising social position.

Yesterday Anthea had paid another visit to Mr. Steele, who informed her regretfully that Phillip had refused even to discuss the possibility of selling. So that had been the end of Anthea's single-handed effort to save the village of Upton. She had no idea what her next move should be, except to redouble her efforts to change Phillip's mind.

She collected her wandering thoughts as she heard Harriet asking somewhat insistently, "Don't you think that it would be a good idea, my dear?"

"I'm sorry, Aunt, I'm afraid I wasn't attending. What would be a good idea?"

"Why, now that the Sinclairs have written to give their consent to Rob's marriage—I did tell you, did I not, that Mr. Sinclair will be visiting Ashby House very soon to discuss the settlements? —perhaps we might announce your and Fanny's betrothals at the same time, say early next month. We could have a small ball, would that suit you? Or . . ." She broke off without noticing Anthea's rather feeble enthusiasm as she spotted a crony on the other side of the room. "We can talk later, my love. I simply must ask Lady Ingleside about her tour of the Continent."

Anthea then fell into the clutches of her hostess, who was propelling her over to join a group seated nearby, when they were intercepted by Lyndock, who, it had not escaped Anthea's attention, had just been deep in conversation with a ravishing redhead.

"Lady Ord, may I monopolise Her Serene Highness for just a moment? I'm planning a visit to Vienna, and I simply must have her invaluable advice."

"La, my lord, don't tell us that you're planning yet another foreign tour," teased Lady Ord. "Didn't you just return from Italy last spring?"

"Oh, but I always come back. After a little while I feel the need to see my good friends in Rutland," Lyndock smiled, and it was clear to Anthea that the elderly Lady Ord had fallen as easily a victim to Lyndock's charm as any of his younger conquests.

"Even if your intention to visit Vienna is genuine," Anthea gritted in a low voice, "I prefer not to speak to you on that or any other subject."

"Oh, come now," he said with a wide smile for the benefit of any eavesdroppers as he steered her to a pair of chairs in the corner of the room, "you're being much too uncivil."

"You know that I can't rush away from you without causing comment," said Anthea coldly. "What did you want to say to me? And please make it brief."

"I've been thinking about your disagreement with Montville about the village of Upton," he said quietly. "I can't wave a magic wand to make the problem disappear, of course, but I have some news for you that I hope will make you feel more cheerful about it."

"I can't imagine how you could influence the situation in any way, Lord Lyndock," said Anthea.

"There you are, Lyndock. I was hoping that you would be here."

Lyndock looked up in some surprise to find Phillip standing

over him. Phillip had not come to Hinton Court with the rest of his party, having been detained at the last moment by a request for an interview by his steward, and evidently had just arrived.

Rising, Lyndock bowed. "Pleasure to see you, Montville."

"I don't know that you'll think it such a pleasure when I finish talking to you. My steward has just been telling me that you've offered Joe Corby a cottage on your estate."

An involuntary smile of pleasure wreathed Anthea's face as Lyndock nodded and said, "That's true enough."

"My steward also tells me that you've offered Joe Corby's son Matt a position in your stables."

"True also. Young Corby won't come to me, of course, until his term of employment with you ends at Michaelmas Fair."

"May I ask," jerked out Phillip, "why you've seen fit to interfere with my labourers and tenants?"

His smile fading, Lyndock snapped impatiently, "Don't pitch that gammon to me, Montville. You don't care a fig what happens to Joe Corby. And since you're about to throw him off your estate, it can mean nothing to you if I offer him a roof over his head. And as for young Matt—he'll find it far easier to help his family if he's working near them. You'll have no difficulty replacing him as groom. In these depressed times you'll have a hundred candidates for the position."

"That doesn't signify. You've no right to intervene in my affairs. Especially since—" here Phillip glanced at Anthea—"especially since I suspect that you're trying to exploit any differences of opinion that may exist between me and my betrothed."

"Phillip!" Anthea exclaimed in outrage, looking quickly around her to see if the altercation between the two men had been noticed.

"Don't talk fustian, Montville," said Lyndock. "I'm going to overlook what you've just said, and so, I trust, will Her Serene Highness." Turning to Anthea he said, "I know how concerned you are about the Corbys. If you should think of anything else that might be done to help them, please don't hesitate to call on me."

Bowing to Anthea, nodding to Phillip, he walked away, leaving Phillip nearly inarticulate with rage.

"I'm very sorry that you accused Lord Lyndock of helping the Corbys only out of malice, Phillip," said Anthea in distress. "You must see that such a remark reflects on me, too."

"Please forgive me. I had no intention of insulting you. But Lyndock—I cannot and will not put up with such effrontery." He took a step away from her, and Anthea, alarmed, put a restraining hand on his arm. "Phillip! You can't make a scene here. And I must tell you, I'm glad that Lord Lyndock gave a cottage to the Corbys. I'll sleep easier at night knowing that."

"But you must see that he's only doing it to make me look greedy and uncaring in your eyes," expostulated Phillip. "You've known Lyndock for some time now. When has he ever displayed such loving sympathy for the poor and downtrodden?"

Anthea silently acknowledged Phillip's shot. In a fit of mischief, Lyndock *was* perfectly capable of a dramatic act of altruism aimed at placing Phillip in an unfavourable light. "I don't care what his reasons are," she said at last. "I'm still happy that Matt Corby's family will have a home."

"But I thought that we'd gone into all that," protested Phillip. "I thought that you had seen my point—" But just then dinner was announced and he was forced to compose himself.

Lord and Lady Ord prided themselves on their lavish table, and it was apparent that tonight they had outdone themselves. From her place of honour to Lord Ord's right as the highest ranking guest, Anthea surveyed a dinner that, as she truthfully assured her host, was the equal of anything she had been served on the Continent. There was turbot with lobster sauce, boiled fowls, a turtle, ham and ducks with green peas, a large cod, soup, chicken pies and assorted puddings. And this was only the first course; the second course, Lord Ord informed her, would include pigeons with asparagus, a filet of veal with mushrooms, an apricot tart and a pyramid of syllabubs and jellies. "For I like a good dinner," he told her, "and so, I am sure, do my guests."

Trying to hide a smile, Anthea demurely agreed, but she also thought to herself, as she gazed around the table, that she was beginning to feel comfortable in this county society, provincial though it might seem at times in contrast to her way of life in Vienna.

"Well, now, Your Serene Highness," said Lord Ord genially, glancing down at Fanny, who was chatting animatedly with Rob Sinclair, the pair oblivious to everyone around them, "are we to expect an interesting announcement soon?"

"I couldn't say, sir. You must ask my aunt. But they do make a very attractive couple, do they not?"

"Indeed they do. But what is more important—" he lowered his voice—"I understand that young Sinclair will inherit a tidy little fortune from an uncle, or some such. Add that to Miss Montville's very handsome portion and they can't go wrong, eh?"

Why bother with an official announcement, thought Anthea mirthfully. The entire county already knew all about Fanny's wedding plans and could probably list every item in the marriage contract before it was even drawn up.

Farther down the table, Lord Ingleside, rather deaf and inclined to speak loudly, was saying to Lyndock, "There was a deal of excitement at Stretton Priory the other night, I believe."

"I fancy you might call it that. My gamekeepers intercepted a gang of poachers about to make off with half a cartload of hares, pheasants, partridges—all meant for the London market, I have no doubt." Lyndock began to laugh. "Have you ever thought that, many a time when you've dined at a hotel or a private home in London, you were very probably eating game that came from your own or your neighbours' estates?"

"I wonder that you can laugh about it," said Lord Ingleside austerely. "The way that the game laws are being flouted these days is a scandal. We had a meeting just the other day at Oakham —evidently you weren't able to attend, Lyndock—chaired by Lord Treanor, in which we discussed reports of just such organized gangs operating in nearby areas. But yours seems to be the first estate in the immediate vicinity to be attacked by these criminals.''

"Well, it was very unfortunate, Lyndock, and I'm glad that your preserves weren't plundered," observed Lord Ord. "But I do think that you might do a little more to protect yourself. I understand that you don't use spring guns, or man traps, against these poachers. A mistake, that." He hesitated. "Perhaps I shouldn't say this, but there's a rumour roundabout that you actually caught one of the poachers the other night and let him go scot-free.''

Lyndock looked up, his face serious for once. "The rumour happens to be true," he said levelly. "The poacher was thirteen years old and he was carrying a gun. If I had had him up before the magistrates it would have meant, at the very least, fourteen years' transportation.''

"You caught a poacher and let him go?" Phillip spoke up incredulously. "How could you be so criminally irresponsible? When the word gets out that there is no regard for law and order at Stretton Priory, the whole county, not just your estate, will be swarming with poaching gangs.''

There was an aghast murmur at the vehemence of Phillip's remarks, but his fellow guests remained silent, their eyes fixed on Lyndock. He showed no resentment as he replied to Phillip in quiet, reasonable tones, "I trust that you exaggerate, Montville. I certainly don't intend to turn over my preserves to the poachers, now or in the future. But in the case of this one lad—thirteen years old, as I mentioned—a shot was fired during the melee with my keepers. Nobody was injured, but, as you know perhaps better than I do, since you've been on the magistrates' bench for some years now, any violence committed during the course of one of these crimes automatically increases the penalty to death by hanging. Now, surely, you wouldn't expect me to expose a child to that risk, even though he didn't actually fire the gun?''

"If the boy shared in the crime of poaching with violence, he certainly should have been hanged," Phillip burst out.

Lyndock raised an eyebrow. "You can't mean that. This thirteen-year-old told me that he had turned to poaching because his family was on Poor Relief and was half starving. I don't care to have my game poached any more than the next man, but these are very difficult times economically and I'm prepared to be a little more lenient." He glanced around the table with his engaging smile. "Come, now, Sir Phillip, this is a social occasion—and a very festive one." He raised his glass to his host. "Seldom, Lord Ord, have I eaten a dinner to rival this one. Montville, let's make a little pact not to talk shop when we could be enjoying the company of all these beautiful ladies."

Phillip's lips tightened, but, to Anthea's relief, he turned his head to speak to the lady next to him. Anthea engaged Lord Ord's attention with a question about the fall hunting season, and soon the entire company had seemingly been distracted from the near quarrel. Later, however, when the ladies had retired to the drawing room, leaving the gentlemen to their port, it was clear that the incident had only been covered up, not dismissed. Anthea was very conscious of the curious looks directed at her and Harriet and Fanny, and more than once among the low-voiced conversations around her she caught Lyndock's name coupled with Phillip's.

Harriet's face was clouded as she drew Anthea apart, saying, "My dear, how mortifying. I can't imagine what came over Phillip. For, try as I might to be fair, I can't but think that he was very rude to Lord Lyndock. Although, I must say, Geoffrey does seem to have some very peculiar ideas."

Anthea attempted to soothe her. "Yes, it was very embarrassing, Aunt, but it's all over now. Please try not to let yourself get too upset about it." Inwardly, however, she was far from being as calm as she sounded. She, like her aunt, had been sent into a state of mild shock by Lyndock's unexpectedly liberal remarks about poaching, which seemed so out of character with all that she had ever observed of his flighty and hedonistic way of life. Anthea knit her brows. Was it simply a coincidence that Lyndock was appearing as the champion of the downtrodden so soon after he had learned of her concern for the fate of the villagers? Could it be that he hoped to become reconciled with her by pretending to share her sympathies, by generously arranging a new home for the Corby family while at the same time driving a deeper wedge between her and her fiancé—as Phillip had angrily suggested—by making Phillip's behaviour seem uncaring?

A bright colour darkened Anthea's cheeks. Her suspicions of Lyndock might be unfair—it was at least possible, she supposed, that his feelings for Matt Corby and the child poacher were genuine—but so long as such thoughts were thronging her brain she did not want to be left alone in his company.

"Now, what on earth is Phillip doing here?" her aunt remarked in some surprise, and Anthea looked up to see Phillip entering the drawing room, much earlier than he might have been expected to leave his fellow port drinkers. His face black as a thundercloud, he stalked over to his stepmother. "Pray make your excuses to Lady Ord, ma'am," he said to Harriet. "I wish to leave immediately."

"But Phillip, whatever for?" began Harriet. "Lady Ord will think it so odd if we leave before the gentlemen join us, and I'm sure that she has an evening of cards and games prepared for us."

Observing the grim lines around Phillip's mouth, Anthea intervened, saying, "I think, Aunt, that we should do as Phillip asks."

"But . . ."

"Doubtless Phillip will tell us all about it later," Anthea advised Harriet gently. "Would you like me to speak to Lady Ord for you?"

"Oh, yes, please do, Anthea. I really wouldn't know what to say to Lady Ord," replied Harriet fretfully. "I mean, it's all so very strange. What will she think of us?"

"Thank you for handling my stepmother so adroitly," Phillip murmured to Anthea later as the Montville party waited in the foyer for their carriage to appear. "Sometimes she can be difficult. Ah—what did you say to Lady Ord?"

"Oh—I told her that my aunt was suffering the onset of one of her prostrating headaches and I thought that we ought to get her home as quickly as possible. Phillip, why *did* you ask us to leave so abruptly?"

"I don't wish to speak of it, Anthea."

"But you must have had a serious reason to leave the dinner party so abruptly, Phillip, and I do think that I have the right to know what it is."

But Phillip merely shook his head and clamped his lips together tightly as, the carriage having been announced, he moved to take his stepmother's arm and help her down the steps and into the carriage. Since he and Julian and Rob Sinclair were riding their own mounts, the journey back to Ashby House was a frustrating one for Harriet and Fanny and Anthea, isolated in the carriage, without access to any information that might explain their premature exit from Lady Ord's party.

"Really, you know, I have never seen Phillip act so strangely," Harriet fretted. "Whatever do you suppose Lady Ord is thinking of us? I imagine that Phillip had some more words with Lord Lyndock after the ladies left the table, and then felt just too embarrassed to spend the rest of the evening making small talk and pretending that it never happened. I do hope that it's no more than that, because, Anthea, Phillip is *very* even tempered as a rule, and I cannot believe that his disagreement with Lord Lyndock could have come to an open quarrel."

"No, no, surely not," said Anthea. "Both Phillip and Lord Lyndock are far too well bred to quarrel while they are guests at someone's dinner table." But privately she was not at all sure, and her forebodings increased when she glanced at Fanny, who had been unusually quiet during the drive, and observed how tense and worried the girl appeared.

On their arrival at Ashby House, Harriet rapidly developed the beginnings of a real headache when Phillip, with thoroughly uncustomary rudeness, disappeared into the library after flatly refusing to speak to his stepmother. Anthea and Fanny accompanied Harriet to her bedchamber and after a considerable effort were able to calm her down and to leave her to the ministrations of her devoted abigail.

"Now, then, Fanny," Anthea confronted her young cousin when the two had retired into the corridor. "You know what's behind all this, don't you?"

"I'm afraid that I do. Rob managed to say a few words to me before we got into the carriage. He says that Phillip and Lord Lyndock had a dreadful quarrel after the ladies left the table. He and Julian actually had to hurl themselves on Phillip to prevent him from striking Lord Lyndock."

"I was afraid of that. Oh, well, they will just have to apologise to each other, and before long doubtless it will all blow over."

"I don't think so," said Fanny, her eyes wide. "Rob says that Phillip insulted Lord Lyndock in order to force him into a duel."

Anthea gasped. "Phillip must be out of his mind!" she said roundly. "I'll go speak to him immediately. Somebody will have to bring him to his senses."

As she came down the staircase to the hallway on the ground floor, she observed Julian and Rob Sinclair talking to each other in subdued tones. "Just the people I want to see," she said, and almost laughed in spite of her worry to see the guilty expressions on their faces when they turned to her.

"Your Serene Highness," began Rob, "Julian's been raking me over the coals, and rightly so. I made a huge gaffe when I told Fanny about—Well, I expect that you know what I told Fanny about."

"I certainly do. Do you really mean to tell me that Phillip and Lord Lyndock might fight a duel with each other?"

"Oh, it's true enough, Cousin Anthea," said Julian, his boyish face grave. "But you see, Rob had absolutely no right to tell Fanny about it. Or any female, for that matter."

"Why not, pray?"

"Because it's an affair of honour, dash it, and not fit for the sensibilities of females."

"What flummery!" retorted Anthea. "At least as regards this female, Julian, you needn't fear for my sensibilities. I've seen many a wounded man, and dead bodies, too, when I lived in Portugal."

"I don't doubt that at all, Your Highness," said Rob Sinclair, looking harassed. "But this puts me in a very embarrassing situation. One doesn't speak about a friend's challenge to anyone, let alone the man's female relatives. You would much oblige me if you would say nothing at all about this to Sir Phillip."

"Well, I've no desire to embarrass you, Mr. Sinclair, but I can't promise you not to say anything about this silly duel to Phillip. In fact, I'm going to talk to him about it this instant before this foolishness goes any further. Is Phillip still in the library, Julian?"

"Yes, but—Cousin Anthea!" Julian's voice rose to a wail. "You can't do this, it's just not the thing at all. . . ."

Ignoring her cousin, Anthea walked down the hallway to the library door, knocked perfunctorily and pushed it open. Phillip was standing beside the fireplace, his arm resting on the mantelpiece, his head cast down. "May I speak to you for a moment, Phillip?"

Barely glancing in her direction, Phillip said somberly, "I'm not really fit to speak to at the moment, Anthea. Couldn't it wait until tomorrow?"

"No. We must discuss this ridiculous idea of yours to fight a duel with Lord Lyndock before anything actually happens, like Lord Lyndock's second arriving to present his choice of weapons or whatever stupid routine is customary for duels."

Wheeling on her, Phillip exclaimed angrily, "Well, if that isn't the outside of enough, my own brother blabbing about my affairs to my betrothed."

"It wasn't Julian who told me about the duel. If you must know, it was Rob Sinclair. He was evidently so upset about it that he let it slip to Fanny just before we entered the carriage at Hinton Court."

"Young Sinclair!" exploded Phillip. "Worse and worse. Bad

enough, I suppose, for you to know, but to upset a young girl like Fanny! I thought that he was a man of breeding."

"He *is* a man of breeding, and right now he's out in the hallway stewing about breaking this peculiar code of honour that you men are so fond of talking about. In any case, Phillip, you can't attempt to provoke a man to a duel in front of a whole roomful of people and expect it to remain a secret. This quarrel will be the only topic of conversation tomorrow all over the county."

"That's as may be, but it's not going to be a topic of conversation with you or anybody else in this house."

"You *must* talk about it, Phillip. I may be practically a stranger to England, but I do know that dueling is now against the law. If you fight Lord Lyndock, even if neither of you is badly hurt—for I suppose that both of you would fire into the air, or at the very least aim for a shoulder or an arm—you could both be forced to flee the country."

Phillip kept his mouth mulishly closed, and Anthea, gazing at him in exasperation, burst out, "Very well, then. I'll go to see Lord Lyndock. Perhaps I can make him see reason. And if not—if all else fails—why, I'll be forced to lay an information to the magistrates."

Reacting instantly, Phillip exclaimed, "I utterly forbid you to go see Lyndock. And as for magistrates—Anthea, your father would turn over in his grave if you did anything so demeaning, so outside the . . ." He paused, as if unable to find words for his horror.

"So outside the code of honour?" suggested Anthea. "Well, I happen to think that a human life is more important than any code of honour. If you don't want me to discuss this duel with anyone else, Phillip, you'd better sit down and talk it over with me."

Phillip glared at her indecisively for a moment, finally throwing up his hands in resignation. "If you insist, I'll talk *about* it—but you won't talk me *out* of it." He paused as Anthea looked at him in uncompromising silence before continuing reluctantly. "After the ladies left the table tonight, the question of poaching came up again, with Lyndock continuing his unconscionable defense of these criminals, and I—I simply lost my temper. I told him that irresponsible landowners like him were inciting to revolution. To which Lyndock had the gall to say that perhaps revolution might seem the only recourse to people like the family of the woman who, during a recent food riot, pounced on a cart of butter, sold off the contents, and was hanged for the crime. At that I couldn't restrain myself. I threw a glass of wine in his face and informed him that I would wait on his seconds to call on me.''

"They hanged a woman for stealing butter?" exclaimed Anthea incredulously.

"Stealing butter is theft, and theft is a capital offense," said Phillip impatiently. "It's nothing to do with the matter at hand, anyway. I only told you about the incident to illustrate how monstrous Lyndock's ideas are. It's time—more than time—that somebody brought the man up short.''

Anthea stared at him, shaking her head. It was useless, she saw, to discuss with him the case of the woman who was hanged for stealing butter. Phillip simply had a blind spot—perhaps most Englishmen did, she thought suddenly—when it came to the sacredness of private property. "Well, it's a tempest in a teapot," she said after a moment. "It was childish of you to throw wine in Lord Lyndock's face, Phillip, and I trust that after he's had an opportunity to reflect upon it for a few hours he will just ignore your provocation.''

During their short acquaintance Anthea had never seen Phillip become so angry. His face turned a bright red and his eyes threw out sparks as he spluttered, "No gentleman can ignore such an insult. If Lyndock refuses to meet me, he won't be welcome in any house in the county. He'll be a social leper. And let me tell you, Anthea, the last thing that I need in my life is an interfering female!''

Realising that Phillip was so beside himself with rage that he was not really conscious of what he was saying, Anthea drew a hard breath and walked out of the library. She shook her head silently at Julian and Rob Sinclair, waiting anxiously in the foyer, and started up the staircase. She knew that part of Phillip's anger —perhaps the greater part of it—had been aroused, not merely by Lyndock's unorthodox social and economic ideas, but by sheer primitive jealousy. She could only hope that a night's sleep would restore both men to a measure of sanity.

=13=

"I DECLARE, I don't know why you insist on going out riding this morning," grumbled Hannah, as she handed Anthea her riding crop.

"I go out every morning, silly woman."

"Of course you do, but judging by those dark circles under your eyes, what you need right now is rest, not exercise."

Hannah was quite right, thought Anthea as she went down the stairs. She had come by those dark circles honestly, tossing and squirming wakefully for most of the night, attempting to formulate some plan to prevent Phillip from dueling with Lyndock. Toward morning, she had decided that her only option was to go to Lyndock, strenuously though Phillip would oppose the meeting, and difficult as it would be for her to request the favour —and ask him to let the matter lapse. As the offended party— and she assumed that having a glass of wine thrown in his face made Lyndock the offended party—the challenge to fight was up to him, and if he chose to ignore Phillip's behaviour there was little her cousin could do about it.

Her mind was so busily engaged, casting about for the most persuasive phrases to use in her forthcoming conversation with Lyndock, that it was some time into the ride before she initiated her usual friendly chat with Matt Corby. "I was so happy to hear last evening from Lord Lyndock that your family is to have a cottage at Stretton Priory."

"Oh, that—yes, ma'am. My father is very happy about it," replied Matt with a wan smile, but his manner was so obviously worried and preoccupied that Anthea said, probing, "You're not anticipating any problem with Sir Phillip, are you? About your term of service with him, I mean."

"No, not at all. Lord Lyndock said that he would fix everything. He's a proper gentleman, he is. I asked him—puzzled like, you know—why he was taking all this trouble for us, and he said, 'Why, Matt, we troopers have to stick together.' He knew that I'd served in the Peninsula, do you see."

His reminiscence about Lyndock's kindness seemed to perk up Matt's spirits, but only momentarily, and Anthea, her curiosity aroused, was about to question him further when, as they were passing through an isolated stretch of woodland, Matt pulled up suddenly, spotting sitting beside the road a small dog, which was whining and wagging its tail furiously. "Bowser, old fellow, is Aaron with you?" The little dog ran off a short way, pausing to look back at Matt, intensifying his whining, clearly indicating that he wanted the young groom to follow him. With an apprehensive glance at Anthea, Matt muttered an excuse and strode after the animal. Perplexed, Anthea watched them both disappear among the trees. The moments dragged by, and Anthea, becoming impatient, dismounted in her turn, catching her reins on a convenient branch, and plunged into the woodland. At first she was disoriented, searching for a path in the thick underbrush, disengaging the skirts of her habit from the nettles that caught at the fabric, peering vainly around her for some sign of Corby. "Matt? Matt, where are you?" she called finally, continuing her floundering progress into the woods. "Matt, please answer me," she called again, stopping short as she came upon Corby, kneeling with the little dog beside a prostrate figure lying beneath a great tree.

"Good God, Matt, who—what's happened?" she exclaimed, throwing herself down beside him. She looked aghast at the ominously pale face of Matt's brother Aaron, whose leg was clumsily swathed in what she took to be the boy's own homespun shirt, its gray colour now entirely obscured by blood.

His eyes blank from shock, Matt looked up to mumble, "I was afraid of this. My sister Rose came over this morning to tell me that

Aaron hadn't been home all night, and that my father was very worried because he'd heard talk that there was a pitched battle last evening between Lord Ingleside's keepers and a band of poachers. And when I saw Aaron's dog Bowser . . .''

"Well, don't just stay there doing nothing, man," said Anthea impatiently. "Can't you see that Aaron's in shock from all that loss of blood? Put your coat around him to give him a little warmth. And help me get this shirt off his leg so that we can have a look at it." Removing the shirt and cautiously tearing away the charred fabric of Aaron's breeches from the ugly wound that gaped on his outer leg just above the knee, Anthea breathed a sigh of relief. "I think that it's stopped bleeding for the moment," she said, as Aaron opened his eyes with a groan, struggling to sit up. She pressed his shoulders back against the ground. "Don't try to move, Aaron, we're going to get help for you." Aaron stared at her wildly, redoubling his efforts to move, until he caught sight of Matt. Then, apparently realising that he was safe, he gave a gasp and lapsed again into unconsciousness.

Anthea turned her head to look at Matt. "We must get Aaron to a doctor immediately. He's lost far too much blood already, and if he should start bleeding again—"

"No. No doctor, ma'am," interrupted Matt frantically. "Don't you see, the doctor would inform the magistrates, and then it would be all up with Aaron. It's a hanging offense, poaching with violence. We heard that one of Lord Ingleside's keepers is near death, and they—Lord Ingleside's men—seem to suspect that at least one of the poachers was wounded too."

"Jack—don't leave me, Jack," moaned Aaron, beginning to move restlessly. Anthea pressed her hand soothingly to his forehead as Matt murmured, "Jack must be one of the lads in the gang. Some of them must have carried Aaron this far, and then I expect that they became affrighted, maybe thought that the dogs were on their tracks."

"We're wasting time," said Anthea, standing up and brushing the crushed leaves from the skirt of her habit. "You must go for the doctor, Matt. I'll stay with Aaron until you get back."

"No." Matt faced her defiantly. "Doctor Cardwell would go straight to Lord Ingleside. My sisters and I will take care of Aaron ourselves. There's an old forester's hut near here on the other side of the wood. It's partly roofless, but 'twould do as a shelter until Aaron's leg is better."

"But that's madness. If the wound should start bleeding again, or if it should turn to gangrene . . . And besides, if the authorities are looking for a wounded poacher they'll ransack every abandoned building in the area." As Matt stood looking at her in wordless indecision, Anthea said suddenly, "I know—I'll go to Lord Lyndock. I'm sure that he wouldn't allow Aaron to be hanged for poaching."

"He's gentry, ma'am. In the end he'll stand with his own kind. And besides, if he should find out that—" Matt looked away in some confusion.

Puzzled, Anthea stared at him for a moment. Than, as comprehension dawned, she said, "Matt! Was Aaron involved with that other poaching attempt on Lord Lyndock's property?" Shaking her head at Matt's guilt-ridden face, she asked curiously, "How in God's name did your brother come to be a member of this gang? Surely he must have known how serious the consequences could be."

"He knew, right enough," replied Matt grimly. "But then, he'd lost his employment as a stockinger up in Nottingham. He was already suspected of frame smashing, and of course the authorities knew that he had taken part in the Bread or Blood marches earlier on—so he decided to come home. But here he was bringing in no income at all, he was just one more mouth for my father to feed, so when he was approached by this London gang, why I suppose he thought that it wasn't much worse than bagging an occasional hare. He'd always done that—well, we all have—just to put a little meat on the table."

As Aaron uttered another restless groan, Anthea cut Matt off. "I'm going to Lord Lyndock. No arguing, Matt. Either I call on his lordship for help, or I notify Doctor Cardwell. I'll return as fast as I possibly can."

Holding her mount to a steady trot, Anthea covered the three miles to Stretton Priory feeling considerably less than self-confident about her errand. Even if Lyndock's apparent sympathy for displaced cottagers and poor agricultural laborers was real, not just assumed in a move to get back into her good graces, he might very well draw the line at helping Aaron escape the penalty for wounding Lord Ingleside's keeper.

As she passed by the gatekeeper's house just inside the magnificent gilded gates at the entrance to the estate, Anthea found her attention briefly distracted from Aaron's plight by the beauty and sheer size of the parkland. Majestic oaks lined the long winding driveway, while deer grazed on the smooth turf shaded by many varieties of trees and exotic shrubs, and here and there throughout the grounds she could see a gazebo or a graceful—and no doubt completely artificial—ruin. Owing to the circumstances of her turbulent relationship with Lyndock, she had never before visited his home, and she was quite unprepared for the grandiose pile that greeted her eyes as she emerged from the driveway and entered the courtyard: Stretton Priory was an enormous Palladian building, which, with its huge pillared Corinthian portico, its massive pediment, like that of a Roman temple, its long round-headed Venetian windows set with relieving arches, resembled nothing so much as a Renaissance palace swollen to unwieldy size and looking completely out of place away from the serene classical landscape of Italy.

As she dismounted and looped her reins around a large marble urn adorning the sweeping staircase at the front entrance of the house, Anthea's thoughts returned to the purpose of her visit, and her nervousness was growing by the second as she waited for what seemed an interminable length of time—it was, after all, many hours before the customary hour of morning calls—before an impassive-faced butler answered her ring. "Is Lord Lyndock at home?" she asked, with as much nonchalance as she could summon, considering that an unattended young female did not usually call on a bachelor peer in the very early hours of the morning.

"His lordship is, I believe, still asleep, Madam. Ah—who may I say is calling?"

"I am the Princess von Hellenberg," replied Anthea haughtily. "And I should very much appreciate not being obliged to stand here on the doorstep while you decide whether I am to have the honour of being admitted to the house."

Without the slightest change of expression—or, indeed, without even an instant of further deliberation—the butler bowed respectfully, standing aside to allow Anthea to enter the foyer. "If you will come into the morning room, Your Highness, I will inform his lordship that you are here."

Trying to quell her growing qualms about the wisdom of going to Lyndock, Anthea gazed around the charming morning room, hung in pale gold damask with a delicately moulded ceiling and graceful furniture in gilt or marquetry on satinwood. She was reflecting that the room, which contained none of the classical Egyptian or Roman motifs so much in current fashion, probably represented the tastes of its late owner, Lyndock's uncle, when, rather sooner than she might have expected, the door opened and the current master of Stretton Priory entered the room.

Lyndock was fully dressed in one of his superlatively-cut coats, leather breeches and Hessians, though Anthea noted that the hastiness of his toilet was perhaps betrayed by his cravat, which was far less artfully arranged than usual. His face was politely blank, though there was a lurking glint of laughter at the back of his eyes as he bowed, saying, "Your Serene Highness. To what do I owe the honour of this—ah—early call? Not that I would not be delighted to see you at any time, naturally, but . . ."

Anthea eyed him with active dislike. As surely as if he had spoken, she knew that he was expecting her to intervene in his threatened duel with Phillip, and that he was thoroughly enjoying the situation. She said abruptly, "Lord Lyndock, is it really true that a young man—a boy, really—could be hanged for taking part in poaching with violence?"

His eyes narrowed. "It is."

"Even if a keeper who was injured during the incident didn't die?"

"Even if none of the keepers received so much as a scratch, even if the poachers didn't fire a shot. Come, Anthea, you didn't come here at this hour in the morning to discuss a fictional case. What's happened?"

"It's Matt Corby's brother, Aaron. A gang of poachers was intercepted last night on Lord Ingleside's estate and a keeper was wounded—how badly I don't know—and Aaron was shot too. Matt and I found him this morning. I—I don't like his looks, he's lost a great deal of blood. But Matt won't hear of taking him to Doctor Cardwell. He says that the doctor would turn Aaron over to the magistrates. He wants to take care of Aaron himself until he's well enough to leave the area."

"Young fool, Aaron," said Lyndock shortly. "He might have known that Ingleside and the other landowners hereabouts would have been on guard against poaching gangs so soon after the attempted raid on my estate."

"But surely Matt is wrong. You can't tell me that the magistrates would condemn Aaron to be hanged."

"They would, and with the greatest of pleasure," said Lyndock grimly. "Matt's perfectly right about that, and about Doctor Cardwell cooperating with the magistrates, too." He paused, knitting his eyebrows together. After several moments' thought, he pulled the bell cord. When the butler appeared, Lyndock said, "Have my town chariot brought around immediately, Simpson."

"Yes, my lord. Might I ask when you expect to return?"

"I'm escorting Her Serene Highness to Oakham. I'll be back this evening."

As the door closed behind the butler, Lyndock replied to Anthea's questioning glance, "We'll need a closed carriage, though I'll warrant that Simpson is cudgeling his brains mightily, wondering why I'm not driving you to Oakham in my curricle. Or why you would want to go there at this hour, for that matter. Well, let him wonder. Incidentally, Simpson will never say a word about your visit here, nor will any of his minions. Discretion is one quality that I demand in my servants.''

Anthea coloured, convinced that Lyndock could often read her thoughts. ''Why *are* we going to Oakham?''

''Why, to get young Aaron to a doctor,'' replied Lyndock in some surprise. ''There's a retired regimental surgeon—a Doctor Matson—living in Oakham. Met him in Belgium, when he was taking care of a friend of mine from the Inniskillings, after Waterloo. I just learned recently that Matson has retired here. Been meaning to have a glass of wine with him and refight the Belgian campaign.''

Anthea felt a sense of relief, but her sense of fair play impelled her to say, ''You could be in very serious trouble with the law if your part in helping Aaron becomes known, and you've no obligation to him at all. I suggest that you pretend that I never came here this morning. Matt Corby and I can take Aaron to see Doctor Matson.''

''Don't talk fustian, Anthea. And what obligation do you have, pray, to Aaron?''

''Why—he's Matt's brother. And I just couldn't let him be hauled away to the gallows for shooting a hare, or a partridge, or even a deer!''

''Exactly. So what are we waiting for? Let's be off on our errand of mercy.''

In the town chariot a short while later, her horse, Busaco, on a leading rein behind the carriage, Anthea settled back briefly with the comfortable feeling that most of her burden had been removed from her shoulders. Soon, however, she stirred, saying hesitantly, ''I imagine that you'll think it none of my affair, and I *know* that Phillip will think so—well, of course, that's an understatement, he'll be positively *livid*—''

Lyndock chuckled. His dark eyes were gleaming with laughter as he said, ''Montville's in prime twig, is he? Waiting for me to call him out? Well, my dear Anthea, you may tell your cousin that I have no intention of fighting a duel with him. I have my reputation to consider, after all. Why, what would the *ton* think of me if I engaged in such an unequal match? For I'm obliged to tell you that Montville is the most miserable of shots."

Anthea looked at him uneasily. "Phillip says that you'll be ostracised by the whole county if you don't fight him."

The smile lingered on Lyndock's lips but there was also an edge to his voice as he said, "Allow me to think better of my neighbours' opinion of me than that, Anthea. The Strettons, as perhaps you may know, have been living in this place since the Conquest."

The carriage made several false stops as Anthea had difficulty remembering the exact place where she and Matt had left the road, but at length, leaving the chariot at a spot that looked vaguely familiar to her and floundering through the undergrowth, she and Lyndock located Aaron. Matt was crouched over his brother, oblivious to the noise made by the pair as they crashed through the brush; he looked up, terrified, as Lyndock knelt down beside him. "Aaron's bleeding again," Matt gasped. "He started thrashing about, afraid, I reckon, that the keepers were after him, and the blood fair started to gush out. I've been keeping my fingers pressed tight just above the wound, but—"

"Steady on," said Lyndock calmly, reaching into the pocket of his coat. "I thought that this might happen." He quickly whipped a stout leather cord above the bullet hole in Aaron's leg, keeping it tied tightly for a few moments. "There. I think the bleeding's stopped for the time being. But we've got to get your brother to a doctor right away, Matt. No, there's nothing to worry about," he added, forestalling Matt's protest. "I know a doctor in Oakham who won't whisper a word to the magistrates. He's a good one, too, used to be a surgeon with the Inniskillings. Can't get better than that, now, can you? He saved the life of a good friend of mine at Waterloo. But I'll need you with me in the carriage. If Aaron should start struggling again in his delirium and his wound should reopen, I don't think that I could manage the tourniquet."

"Oh, I don't think that's a good idea," intervened Anthea. "Matt will certainly be missed at the stables. If there's the slightest suspicion that Aaron's mixed up in this poaching affair, they'll come around to question Matt. And if both he and Aaron are nowhere about . . . For all that we know, they'll be calling in the Bow Street Runners.''

Lyndock frowned thoughtfully. "Oh, I don't think so. It would take several days for them to get involved in it, at any rate. But the militia will almost certainly be out. Still, there's nothing for it. I can't manage alone.'' ·

"Then let me go."

Both men stared at her in almost comic disapproval. "Out of the question," snapped Lyndock. "I've just told you, the militia will probably be out, and that means that we could be intercepted at any moment. I can't let you expose yourself to such danger." And Matt stammered, "His lordship is right, ma'am. It's not fitting for a female."

"Men!" exclaimed Anthea. "How can you be so caper-witted? I collect that you think I might swoon dead away at the danger, or the blood, or some such foolishness. Well, let me assure you, I've seen more wounded men—and more enemy soldiers, too—in the Peninsula than either of you, I'll warrant. No, it's settled. I'll go with Lord Lyndock, Matt. Try to get Busaco back to the stables without anyone's noticing that I didn't come back with him. And slip a word to my maid, Hannah, that she's to pretend that I've returned from my ride and am taking a nap."

Lyndock stared at her with knitted brows. Finally he grinned, slapping Matt on the shoulder. "The princess has spoken, lad, and we'll just have to obey her royal commands. Come, let's get Aaron out to the carriage. Gently, now. Anthea, will you keep at Aaron's side, ready to tighten the tourniquet if necessary—that's it." Slowly, guided·by Lyndock's calm, low-voiced orders, the little procession moved out to the road, where Lyndock's coachman was waiting to help them settle Aaron into the chariot.

Anthea kept an anxious watch on Aaron as the coachman closed the carriage door and flicked the horses to a fast trot. The boy was now in a deep coma, his head rolling flaccidly against the back of the seat until Anthea slipped her arm around his shoulders and cradled his head against her. "He looks dreadful," she whispered. "He's white as a ghost and he's breathing so heavily. Geoffrey"—it was a measure of her distress that she did not even notice that she was using Lyndock's Christian name for the first time in many weeks—"Geoffrey, you don't think that he'll . . . ?"

"Will he die?" was Lyndock's cool response. "I don't know. It will be touch and go, I imagine. Pray that the wound doesn't reopen." Then, with no change in his expression, he said, "I expect that the young idiot took part in the raid on my coverts, too, eh?" He laughed as Anthea's eyes dropped guiltily. "There, my girl, you're fairly warned: You'll always catch cold if you try to gammon me."

"But—how did you know that Aaron had been poaching your coverts too?"

Lyndock flashed her his familiar quick grin. "I'd like you to think that I had the sixth sense, but it's really very simple. There can't be more than one large poaching gang operating in the area, or they'd be running into each other in the woods."

Involuntarily Anthea found herself smiling back at him. For a single, tremulous, fleeting moment it was as if all the past weeks of rancour and deep hurt were wiped out and they were back to their old lightly passionate, wittily flirtatious footing.

"Anthea," breathed Lyndock, stretching out his hand to clasp hers. Then he stiffened, craning his neck to peer out of the window as the carriage began slowing. "Trouble," he murmured. "Bad trouble, by the looks of it."

The door of the chariot was wrenched open and an officer in the red and white plumed shako and blue coat of the Dragoons peered in.

Lyndock leaned forward, glancing behind the officer to the file of troopers drawn up behind him. "Yes, Captain? What seems to be the difficulty?"

The officer raised his finger to his hat. "Sorry to trouble you, sir. Doubtless you haven't heard. There was a gun battle very early this morning between Lord Ingleside's keepers and that poaching gang from London that's infiltrated the area. We're patrolling the roads to see if we can't catch some of them. At least one of the gang was wounded, to judge by the keepers' accounts, and it's thought that their henchmen may try to bring him out by road. How far have you come this morning, sir? Have you spotted anything out of the way, anything that might make you suspicious?"

"I'm just coming from my estate, Stretton Priory—a mile or two down the road—and I haven't noticed anything out of the ordinary, Captain."

"Stretton Priory? Why, you must be—it's Major Stretton, isn't it? Lord Lyndock, I mean?"

Lyndock beamed. "I thought that there was something familiar about you. Give me a moment, now. . . ."

The officer smiled. "You'll never recognise me, my lord. My face was streaming blood from a sabre cut over my eyes, half blinding me. If you hadn't grabbed my reins there on the ridge, with Boney's cuirassiers countercharging to recover their guns, I'd likely have been just another corpse with a French lance in my chest. They told me afterwards who it was who had guided me back to our lines. I'd like to take the opportunity now to thank you for saving my life, my lord."

"Nonsense. Your horse would probably have brought you back with no help from me. But I'm very glad indeed to see you safe and sound, Captain. Those were the days, eh? Doubtless we'll all be dining out on the strength of the Waterloo campaign for the rest of our lives."

"Peacetime life can indeed seem a little drab at times," agreed the officer with a smile. "Well, I won't keep you, my lord. A pleasant journey to you." He again saluted Lyndock and bowed politely to Anthea and was about to close the door of the carriage when Aaron groaned loudly and lurched forward, away from Anthea's restraining grasp.

"What's the matter with that man?" asked the officer sharply, thrusting his head into the carriage to see more clearly. "Here, let me have a look at him."

To the petrified Anthea, the Dragoon officer loomed like an Avenging Angel. She was utterly unprepared for Lyndock's reaction: he raised a hand theatrically to his brow, turning to her to say ruefully, "It seems that we're for it, my love. Unless—" He turned back to the officer with an embarrassed cough. "Could I have a private word with you, Captain? I'll just step outside the carriage with you."

The moments dragged by unbearably—mercifully, Aaron lapsed back into unconsciousness—and Anthea, her nerves at the breaking point, was just about to clamber out on the roadway when Lyndock returned. "Thank you, Captain, most considerate of you," he called out as he climbed back into the chariot and closed the door.

Waiting until the last of the troop of Dragoons had trotted past them in the opposite direction, Anthea leaned toward Lyndock to demand, "What in heaven's name did you say to the captain? I can't believe that he's the type of man who could be bribed. Or did he let us off because he owed you a favour for saving his life?"

"My dear Anthea, Captain Anson is a man of irreproachable morals," replied Lyndock calmly. "If he had known that our Aaron was the poacher that he was looking for, no amount of gratitude to me would have prevented him from hauling us all off to the nearest magistrate. No, I simply appealed to his honour as a gentleman." He paused, favouring Anthea with a bland smile, as if his comments were self-explanatory.

She glared at him. "Well?" she said in exasperation. "Just what was this point of honour that you appealed to?"

"Oh, I told the captain that Aaron was your young brother, who, discovering that you and I were about to elope, attempted to interfere with our plans at gunpoint and was wounded when I wrested the weapon away from him. Naturally, we don't wish the affair to become common gossip, so we're conveying your brother to a physician friend in Oakham, where his wound can be treated confidentially."

"Oh!" gasped Anthea. "I never heard such falderal. Captain Anson must be a near idiot to believe such nonsense. Why, pray, would Aaron object to his sister's marriage to one of the most eligible peers in England?"

Lyndock gave her a steady glance, his dark eyes cool and unsmiling. "You and Phillip Montville seem to have serious objections to me."

Anthea looked away from him, unable to think of anything to say in reply.

"Anthea! Tighten the tourniquet!" She turned back to Aaron, finding him struggling against Lyndock's firm grasp while an ominous red stream poured from his reopened wound. For the remainder of the journey to Oakham she continued to alternately tighten and relax the leather cord above the bullet hole, while Lyndock, after leaning out the window to urge his driver to a full gallop, managed to hold Aaron's threshing limbs immobile. The carriage ground to a halt in the stable yard of a modest house on the outskirts of town and the driver leaped from his seat to dash up the rear steps of the house and pound furiously on the door. An elderly maidservant appeared and the driver ran back to assist Lyndock in removing Aaron from the carriage, with Anthea stumbling along beside them, keeping her grasp on the tourniquet. They were met at the door by a grizzled, sinewy-figured man in early middle age, who peered at them with narrowed eyes. "Well, now, what have we got here?" he barked.

"Dr. Matson, I'm sorry to meet you again under such circumstances, but my young friend here has met with an unfortunate accident. I hope that you'll do as well by him as if he were one of your own Inniskillings."

Grunting, the doctor waved them past him into his surgery at the end of the hall. To Anthea, when Aaron had been deposited on the examining table, the doctor said, "We won't need you any more, ma'am. My housekeeper will take care of you, if you'll just follow her into the parlour. You two"—motioning to Lyndock and the driver—"see if you can make yourself useful to me." He squinted sourly at Lyndock. "Now that I see you more closely, you do have a familiar look about you. The Blues, wasn't it? I had hoped that I wouldn't have anything more to do with you Hyde Park soldiers, once I retired.''

After the excitement and the worry of the past few hours, Anthea collapsed, half dazed, into a chair in Dr. Matson's little parlour. She sat, sipping a cup of strong tea, while the doctor's elderly housekeeper pressed some cakes on her and clucked concernedly about her torn and bloodstained riding habit. "If you was to take it off I could sponge it off a bit, take a stitch or two, but I really don't know if you'll be wanting to wear it again, Miss.''

Braced by the restorative effects of the tea, Anthea roused herself to say, ''Please don't worry about my habit. I fear that it's beyond repair.'' She sat up straight, keeping her eyes fixed on the door of the parlour, expecting at any moment to hear that Aaron had died on the table; the boy's frenzied threshing in the chaise had been succeeded by a frightening limpness and a corpselike pallour that made Anthea fear for the worst. But within the half hour Lyndock entered the parlour, pulling down and fastening the torn and stained sleeves of his fine white cambric shirt. She rose, looking at him in silent anxiety.

''No, he's not dead, Anthea. Doctor Matson thinks he has a chance. Even a fairly good chance. He'll keep the boy under close watch until—well, let's hope until he's out of danger.''

''Thank God,'' said Anthea fervently. She took an impulsive step toward the doctor, who came into the room a few moments later. "I can't thank you enough for helping my brother,'' she began, pausing as she observed the sudden look of disapproval on the doctor's craggy features.

''It won't wash, Anthea,'' said Lyndock with a wry grin. ''Doctor Matson knows that Aaron isn't your brother.''

''But I thought that you were going to tell him the same story,'' Anthea blurted.

''Well, now, ma'am, you must give me credit for using the few brains that the good Lord gave me,'' said the doctor frostily. ''No duelling pistol made that wound in young Aaron's thigh. It was a musket ball, and you're surely not going to tell me that a Pink of the *ton* would take a musket to his sister's lover! And then, too, the boy recovered consciousness briefly on the table, and I'm bound to say that I never heard a rustic accent like his in any drawing room in which *I* was a guest. If he's your brother, ma'am, you must surely have been reared in vastly different circumstances."

"Oh," said Anthea in acute embarrassment.

"I had to tell Doctor Matson the whole story," said Lyndock. "But don't worry," he added hastily as she glanced at him in alarm. "He's not going to turn Aaron over to the authorities. He'll keep the lad here until—or if—he's recovered. And then I think that it might be as well if Aaron were to leave the area very quietly. I'll try to find him something to do in London."

"Where I trust he will forget that he ever set foot in my surgery," said Dr. Matson shortly. "I came to Oakham for a quiet retirement, not to run the risk of winding up on the gallows as an accessory to a felony."

Later, driving out of Oakham after a quick change of teams at a posting inn in the center of town, Anthea found herself experiencing a feeling of anticlimax. "I keep thinking about what the doctor said about the gallows," she shivered. "If I had stopped to think of how dangerous it might be to help Aaron, I'm not sure that I would have done it. And I certainly had no right to involve you."

"Think nothing of it, Your Highness. I was getting quite bored with my existence as a country gentleman. There's nothing like a spot of danger to add a little spice to one's life. Unless it's a beautiful woman," he added, with a glance so intimately caressing that it might as well have been an actual touch.

Anthea stiffened, all her original suspicions of Lyndock's motives reviving. Did he really think that he could wipe the slate clean between them by this one daring act of altruism? Had he risked his neck and his reputation simply to put the Hellenberg fortune once more within his grasp? She said coolly, "I think that it would be best if you left me off at the gates of Ashby House. So that Phillip wouldn't see me with you, you know. He'll be so upset if he knows that I've intervened to stop you fighting the duel."

Lyndock's body did not move, and he hesitated only a fraction of a second before replying, but when he did speak it seemed to Anthea that a physical gulf had opened between them. All trace of warmth had left his voice as he said, "I quite understand that you would not wish to upset Montville."

"No, indeed. I must tell you that Phillip feels this rather irrational jealousy toward you, based, I presume, on the fact that you and I were once—were once closer than we are now."

"Yes, I *was* aware of that. By all means, let us make sure that Montville has no future cause for vexation on that score."

There was no further conversation between them on the remainder of the drive to Ashby House, with Lyndock retiring behind the blank wall of his own thoughts and Anthea huddling into her corner of the carriage. As they passed through the village of Upton and neared the gates of Ashby House, Anthea stirred, saying, "I really meant what I said, Lord Lyndock. I should much prefer to be left off here at the gates."

"As you wish." Lyndock lifted his stick to knock at the roof panel. As the driver opened the door and helped her to the ground, Anthea turned back to Lyndock. "Please believe that I appreciate immensely what you've done today. I don't—I really don't know whom else I could have called upon."

"Not at all, Your Serene Highness. Delighted to have been of service."

Trudging along the winding driveway leading to Ashby House, Anthea was reviewing with a considerable sense of disbelief the events of the morning when she stumbled over a pebble, and, her eye falling on her torn and bedraggled riding habit, she realized with a shock that she could not possibly enter the front door of the mansion in such a condition. Cautiously she skirted the curving sweep of the drive as it circled the front of the house and made her way to the stable area, glancing around and behind her at nearly every step to make sure that she was not being observed from one of the windows. She entered the gate of the stable yard, intending to make use of the secluded side door that led by a narrow back staircase to her corridor. To her dismay, she was confronted by Phillip, about to mount his horse for his customary daily ride about the estate.

"Anthea! Good God, what's happened to you?" he exclaimed, gazing in horror at her torn habit, bedaubed with ominous dark blotches, at her gloveless hands, scratched from pushing back the underbrush and stained with blood, at her disheveled black hair, trailing untidily from beneath her once spruce riding hat. "Here, let me help you."

Anthea pulled away from his hand. "I'm quite all right, Phillip. Please don't fuss over me," she said wearily.

"Of course you're not all right—you've obviously been thrown from your horse." He caught sight of Matt Corby, peering anxiously from around the door of the stable. "Corby. Come here. Why wasn't I informed that Her Serene Highness had been thrown?" An even more outrageous thought struck him. "And why is she returning to the stables alone? I'll have your hide for this, lad."

"Indeed, sir, Her Serene Highness *wasn't* thrown," stammered Matt. "That is to say, if she was thrown, I knew nothing of it. She wanted to ride by herself this morning, do you see . . ." Completely befuddled, unable to think in the face of Phillip's mounting outrage, Matt's voice trailed away.

"Don't badger the boy, Phillip," Anthea intervened. She glanced pointedly at several of the other stablemen, pursuing their tasks with studiously blank faces and obviously attentive ears. "You must see how unbecoming it is of you to discuss our affairs in front of your servants. I'll talk to you later, if you like, after I've rid myself of some of this dirt."

In her bedchamber, Anthea resigned herself to the inevitable scolding and interrogation from Hannah, cheerfully declining to give any explanation for her ruined riding habit and her scratched hands, while the elderly abigail helped her bathe and change into a figured muslin morning dress. She went down to lunch, ravenously hungry now that her dangerous adventure was behind her, to find that Julian, Fanny, Rob Sinclair and Harriet could talk of nothing but the great poaching battle.

"One of Lord Ingleside's keepers is dying," reported Fanny, "or very close to it, and they think that one of the poachers was injured, too, only they haven't caught any of them yet."

"Yes, we hear that the area is swarming with militia," Rob Sinclair chimed in. "Did you encounter any soldiers when you were out on your ride this morning, Your Highness?"

"No," replied Anthea hastily. "I ride very early, you know. The militia would scarcely have been out yet." The fib increased the discomfort that she already felt, as she was obliged to pretend ignorance of the exciting events of the early morning.

"Well, all I hope is that they'll catch these poachers and send them all to the gallows," grumbled Julian. "Perhaps then the autumn hunting won't be entirely ruined."

Harriet shivered. "I wonder that we can rest easily in our beds, with folk shooting at each other practically on our doorsteps." Her eye fell on Anthea's hands. "What on earth have you been doing to yourself, child?" she demanded.

"Oh, it's nothing, Aunt," replied Anthea, mentally cursing herself for not having invented some explanation for her scratched hands beforehand. "I—I was petting some kittens in the stables this morning, and the mother cat took exception," she extemporized, feeling moderately certain that she would not be found out. Stable cats, in her experience, were perpetually expecting! She caught Phillip's narrowed glance as she spoke, and realized that he had taken no part in the luncheon table conversation. Normally he was the authoritative center of any discussion among his family, so she was not at all surprised, at the conclusion of the meal, to have him request a meeting with her in the library.

Phillip seated her with his usual formal courtesy, but his face was grim as he stared down at her. "I must apologise for our stable cats," he said with heavy sarcasm. "I had no idea they were so ferocious."

"What did you want to see me about, Phillip?" Anthea said composedly.

Phillip's gaze sharpened. "I've been making some inquiries since we met at the stables this morning. My curiosity was aroused by Matt Corby's state of confusion—I'm tempted to call it a state of near imbecility. And then I discovered that his brother Aaron has been missing since last evening. Now, adding these observations to the news of the poaching incident on Lord Ingleside's estate, together with the curious incident of your arrival at Ashby House, minus your groom and with a stained riding habit—blood is rather unmistakable, my dear Anthea—I am forced to the conclusion that in some way you've been attempting to assist a felon, who, having been wounded by keepers legitimately trying to safeguard Lord Ingleside's property, is now fleeing for his life."

Anthea straightened her shoulders. "You may think whatever you like, Phillip. I'm not obliged to tell you anything."

"I don't need your admission," snapped Phillip. "I've checked, and I find that your horse was brought back to my stables early this morning by Matt Corby. So, if you've been helping a badly wounded man to escape the law it wasn't on horseback and it wasn't with the use of any vehicle in my stables. May I suggest that you enlisted the aid and sympathy of your almost fiancé? Recall, it won't be difficult for me to find out where Lyndock spent his morning."

Anthea rose, reflecting ruefully that, whatever virtues Phillip lacked, a swift intelligence was not among them. She said coolly, "It won't be necessary to spy on Lord Lyndock. We can leave him out of this discussion. I freely acknowledge that I helped Aaron Corby get safely away. What are you going to do about it?"

Phillip's voice was shrill with rage. "I'll tell you what I'm going to do about it. I'll have Lyndock prosecuted for being an accessory to a felony. Or, if I can't make that stick, I'll have him blackballed from every London club, and I'll see to it that he'll never again be received by any decent member of society."

Anthea stared at him in great distaste. "I doubt very much that you'll do anything of the kind. It's all pure surmise on your part. You can't prove that Aaron Corby was a member of the poaching gang, or that he was wounded and assisted to escape, except by my admission to you, which I can simply deny that I ever made. But I do tell you this, Phillip: If you publicly accuse Lord Lyndock of being involved in this incident, I will come forward myself and take full responsibility for it. I fancy that you won't enjoy having your betrothed enveloped in such notoriety."

As Phillip glared at her in angry frustration, aware that his hands were tied, Anthea felt sorry for him. She rose, saying sadly, "Of course, after all this, I can scarcely be your fiancée any longer. And I think perhaps that you'll agree with me that our engagement was always a mistake. We're just not well suited, Phillip. I don't think that we could be happy together under the best of circumstances, and now—" She shrugged. "I'll leave Ashby House as soon as I can pack up my belongings. I don't want to upset Aunt Harriet or your brothers and sisters—as I've certainly not wanted to cause you any pain—so possibly we can agree to some unexceptionable explanation for our broken engagement."

=14=

"I REALLY DON'T know, Miss Anthea. Do you think that it might be too severe?"

"It's fine, Hannah. It will do very well."

"You haven't even looked at it," accused Hannah. "Here I've been working on your new coiffure for the past half hour, and I'll wager that you couldn't tell me the first thing about it."

Anthea gazed into the dressing table mirror. Hannah had arranged her hair in a thick plait, wound around the crown of her head like a coronet and caught fast with a tortoiseshell comb. "I like it," she decided. "It looks vaguely Spanish. Perhaps we could soften it just a bit by pulling out some loose curls, just here at the temple. Yes, that's perfect. Hannah dear, I'm sorry that I've been so absentminded. I've—I've had a great deal to think about."

"Yes, so I've noticed. You've done a deal too much thinking of late, in my opinion. You ought not to sit in these rooms, brooding. Why don't you go for a drive this afternoon?"

Anthea sighed. "Perhaps I will. I *am* beginning to feel a bit cooped up." She rose, picking up the letter that she had been reading while Hannah worked on her hair, and moved to the balcony of her room, overlooking a fine view of Green Park. She had been staying here at the Pulteney Hotel in Piccadilly for almost two weeks now. She recalled with a smile her arrival at the hotel, when her host, Jean Escudier—who was also the renowned chef for his establishment—had ushered her out on the balcony, informing her with triumphant pride that Her Imperial Highness, the Grand Duchess Charlotte, sister to Czar Alexander I, had stood on this very spot in April of 1814, to watch the new French king, Louis XVIII, enter London in state. "I hope that you won't let Monsieur charge *you* over two hundred pounds a week the way he did the grand duchess," Hannah, always attuned to backstairs gossip, had exclaimed indignantly.

Reluctantly, Anthea tore her eyes away from the lively street scene below and returned her attention to her letter. She had spent the entire previous evening composing it, and now that she was reading it again for perhaps the 20th time, she was no more satisfied with it than she had been in the beginning.

She had wanted her departure from Ashby House to be as civilised and serene as possible, so she had asked Phillip to postpone telling his family about his broken engagement until after she had left the county. He had agreed to this, but in return had requested a favour. She cringed mentally when she recalled the uncomfortable scene in which Phillip had begged her in near anguish to reconsider her decision not to marry him. She had been surprised at the depth of his feeling for her, a passion that apparently made him overlook those qualities of independence and lightheartedness in Anthea that would, she could see now, have made the marriage impossible, even if her affection had been as great as his. No amount of gentle argument on Anthea's part would dissuade Phillip from his desire to reinstate their betrothal, but in the end he was obliged to settle for Anthea's promise that she would observe a two-week waiting period while she reconsidered her decision. She had never had any serious thought of changing her mind—nor, probably, did Phillip believe that she would—but writing the letter informing him of this had nevertheless been a very painful task. She had ended the letter by telling him that she was simultaneously writing to Harriet with the news. This, too, had been a difficult letter to write, but it would relieve Phillip of the necessity to discuss his broken engagement with his stepmother while the wound to his self-esteem was still fresh.

After she had despatched Hannah to the hotel porter with the letters, Anthea went to her desk, where she reached for another letter that she had also been rereading, a letter that would go unanswered. Lyndock had written very briefly and very formally. "Your Serene Highness: Lady Montville has kindly promised to send this note on to you. I thought that you might like to know that a certain friend of ours is now feeling much better and will shortly leave the area. Your most obedient servant, Lyndock."

Anthea pursed her lips as her eyes skimmed again over Lyndock's sprawling handwriting, wondering why he had bothered to keep her informed of young Aaron Corby's welfare when she had indicated so clearly at their last meeting that she had not relented in her attitude toward him. Should she give him the benefit of the doubt, admit the possibility that there was a streak of social conscience in Lyndock's otherwise lightweight character? Or had he been prompted merely by male vanity, unwilling to lose face by having it appear that his efforts on behalf of the Corbys had been prompted by a wish to ingratiate himself anew with Anthea? Not that it mattered. No matter what Lyndock's motives may have been, she was glad to know of Aaron's recovery.

Anthea sighed, suddenly conscious of a great feeling of lassitude. The finality of her decision not to marry Phillip left her at loose ends. What was she to do with her life now? She had come up to London with no definite plans, having told Harriet simply that she would like to do a spot of shopping, which Harriet had promptly interpreted to mean shopping for a trousseau. Should she lease or buy a house in London? If she were not to be Lady Montville, might she still build herself a satisfying life here in England? She might face a barrage of spiteful gossip, of course. Most of London society had expected her to marry Lyndock, and then, when that did not happen, had anticipated her engagement to Phillip. And it would be decidedly uncomfortable, at least in the beginning, to encounter constantly both Lyndock and Phillip in the course of her social engagements. But what alternatives did she have? She could wander rootlessly around the capitals of Europe, as she had done with her father for so many years, or she could return to Vienna, to an existence that she had already found rather empty. She could not look forward to either way of life with much enthusiasm.

All that day and the next she was so restless, prowling around her suite of rooms like a caged animal, that Hannah became very upset, accusing her of coming down with some unspecified ailment, until, in self-defense, Anthea sent a message to Karl von Westendorf, though she was not at all sure that he was still in London. His address during the spring had been Stephen's Hotel in New Bond Street, a favourite resort of the sporting crowd. He arrived at the Pulteney that same afternoon, charming and debonair as always.

"What a pleasure to get your note, chêrie. I was on the verge of leaving my hotel to pay a call on the Duchess of Devonshire, but of course, your wish being my command, I changed my plans immediately to answer your summons."

"More likely you were off to a cockfight or a boxing match," replied Anthea skeptically.

"My dear girl, you have no romance at all in your soul. What does it matter what my plans may really have been? I would much rather be with you than any duchess or even the prince regent. Much rather," Karl added feelingly. "Do you know, I've come to the conclusion that Prinny is a dead bore. God help English society when he becomes king."

Anthea laughed. "You have enough romance for both of us. And speaking of being bored, that's why I sent a note around to you. I was feeling just a bit in the dismals. I wasn't at all sure, though, that you were still in London. I thought that you had very probably returned to Vienna."

"I must confess that I very nearly decamped to Paris to drown my sorrows when you went to the country to spend the summer. Without you, London was very flat."

"I'm sure that you found sufficient consolation to alleviate your sorrows," said Anthea drily, to which Karl replied, grinning, "Well, I have made several very interesting stays in the country.

Why didn't you warn me that your English aristocrat gives you no peace when you accept an invitation to his country estate? It's riding, fishing, shooting, racing every day, with, in between, calls on all the neighbours and sightseeing expeditions to view every beautiful spot for miles around. Then you dance attendance on the ladies all afternoon, and in the evening you can scarcely draw a quiet breath as you're called upon to play at billiards or whist or charades or to take part in an impromptu ball.''

"You look remarkably unharmed by your ordeal.''

"Heartless female.'' Cocking an interrogative eyebrow, Karl asked, "And so, what are you doing here in London? I was surprised to see that you were staying at a hotel rather than at the Montville house in Grosvenor Square.''

Anthea hesitated. "I might as well tell you. My cousin Phillip and I were briefly—and unofficially—betrothed. Now we've changed our minds. But there's bound to be a great deal of gossip, because the betrothal was so widely anticipated. You could help there, Karl, as an old friend of mine. You might cut off some of the speculation by dropping hints that you never considered the relationship to be anything but cousinly.''

An expression of pure triumph swept over Karl's face. "I knew it. Something told me that I shouldn't lose hope, shouldn't leave England. An inner voice told me that you would never actually marry Montville. Such a stiff, solemn fellow. No sense of humour, no *joie de vivre*. You two were completely mismatched. Lord Lyndock, now,'' he added thoughtfully. "Yes, I do think that you might have gone through with a marriage to him. But Sir Phillip—never!''

Stung by Karl's reference to Lyndock, Anthea retorted, "Really, Karl, you may be an old friend, but that doesn't give you the right to say such rude things.''

"You're quite right. My most abject apologies,'' said Karl instantly. "And so, my love. What are your plans? Will you return to Vienna?''

"Oh, I don't know.'' Sounding depressed, Anthea said, "Is

Vienna really my home? I still feel something of a stranger there, you know, despite having lived there for so long. Perhaps— perhaps I have no roots anywhere."

Sitting down beside her, Karl grasped her hands in his. "But *naturellement*, Vienna is your home. It's where your oldest friends, your estates, all your property are. My darling girl, let me take you back there to show you how much you're loved, how much you've been missed." He pressed her hands to his lips, and Anthea smiled down at his bowed head, half amused, half touched by his avowals. She was thinking that perhaps Karl was right, that whatever real ties she had were in Vienna rather than in England, when Hannah came into the room. Gazing in prim disapproval at Karl, she said, "Master Julian is here to see you, Miss Anthea."

"Julian? I wonder what . . . Show him in, Hannah."

Julian came bounding in, obviously in irrepressibly high spirits, bearing no resemblance to the brooding, morose youth of the past summer. "Hullo, Cousin Anthea—oh, and good afternoon to you, Herr Graf."

Karl, who had somewhat hastily disengaged himself from Anthea, did not seem especially pleased to see Julian. He bowed politely.

"I'm delighted to see you, Julian, of course, but what brings you to London?" inquired Anthea.

"Oh, I have the most tremendous news, Cousin. I knew that you would wish to hear about it straightaway." Julian looked pointedly at Karl, who laughed suddenly and said to Anthea, "I must go. That boxing match you mentioned, remember? But I'll return this evening. We have *very* important matters to discuss."

After Karl had left, Julian stared at the door, saying, "Don't know if I like that fellow above half, Cousin. A touch too familiar, don't you think? I mean to say, I know that he's an old friend of yours from Vienna, but dash it, you *are* betrothed to my brother."

Feeling a pang of discomfort, Anthea hastened to turn Julian's attention away from the subject of her betrothal to Phillip. "Oh, you must just ignore Karl," she said lightly. "He's the world's most accomplished flirt, but he doesn't mean a thing by it. I could just as well be an old lady of eighty, for all his gallantries mean." At Julian's skeptical look, she added, "But what's this great news that you mentioned? I left the name of my hotel with your mother, of course, but I never expected to see any of the family quite so soon."

"But Cousin, you must have forgotten—my birthday is next week. My eighteenth."

"Oh, Julian, I'm truly sorry, I *had* forgotten. What would you like as a birthday gift? Something really impressive—eighteenth birthdays don't happen every day of the week!" Anthea gazed expectantly at Julian, whose lively expression became distinctly deflated.

"I thought that you, of all people, would remember, Cousin Anthea. I'm disappointed in you," he burst out.

"But Julian, what have I said?" asked Anthea, aghast. "What world-shaking thing have I forgotten?"

Julian appeared even more injured. "How could you fail to recall that, back in the summer, Lord Lyndock persuaded me not to run away to enlist in the Dragoons? He promised me that on my eighteenth birthday, if I hadn't changed my mind about wanting to enlist, he would buy me a commission."

"Oh, now of course I remember. But I did tell you then, Julian, that I thought it might be unwise for you to accept such help from Lord Lyndock. Phillip would dislike it intensely."

"Bother Phillip," said Julian defiantly. "Several days after you left Ashby House for London I received a note from Lord Lyndock recalling that my birthday would occur shortly and telling me that he had instructed his lawyers in London to pay me the money to buy my commission if I was still of a mind to join the cavalry. So here I am," he finished.

"I see. I suppose—was Phillip very upset?"

"By George, yes. I really thought at first that he would burst a blood vessel, or strike me down on the spot, or some such dreadful thing! But do you know, Cousin, after a bit, when I simply refused to back down, he declared that he would not have me beholden to Lord Lyndock. If I was absolutely determined not to take holy orders, he said, he would buy my commission himself.''

''I'm so happy for you,'' said Anthea, wondering with a hollow feeling if Phillip's dislike—and yes, jealousy—of Lyndock had had anything to do with his renewed offer—so soon after his last bitter meeting with Anthea—to frank Julian's commission. ''But I hope that there hasn't been any difficulty between Phillip and Lord Lyndock about this.''

''Oh, well, you know that they haven't been hitting it off lately, anyway,'' said Julian carelessly, with a great show of adult poise. ''But no, they haven't had a direct quarrel over it. The fact is, they haven't even seen each other since this happened. Phillip did ask me to go over to Stretton Priory to inform Lord Lyndock personally that I wouldn't be requiring his help, and his lordship was very understanding. He asked after you, by the by. I told him that you had gone off to London to select your trousseau.'' Julian creased his brow thoughtfully. ''Funny thing, for a while there, during the season—while you and I and Lord Lyndock were going on all those early morning rides in Hyde Park and racketing about seeing those old buildings and monuments and museums that you seem to dote upon—I really did think that Lord Lyndock had a case on you. But even if he did, *you* didn't, and a jolly good thing, too. I'm very happy that you're going to be my sister, Cousin Anthea.''

Looking at Julian's radiant young face, Anthea simply did not have the heart to tell him of her broken engagement and thus cast a shadow over the joy of his day. He would learn soon enough that she and Phillip would not be getting married after all. She said merely, ''Let me offer you my heartiest congratulations on your commission. I'm sure that you'll be the most bruising rider and the handsomest officer in your entire regiment, and that you'll break every heart in London!''

After Julian, blushing in disclaimer at her compliments, had left the suite, Anthea found her low spirits returning again, and welcomed Karl von Westendorf's arrival that evening with more enthusiasm than she normally allowed herself to show to Karl, who encroached a foot if you allowed him so much as an inch.

"Well, I presume that you won't be seeing any more of that young cub, Julian Montville," he observed, holding his glass of wine appreciatively to the light. "I didn't think he seemed aware that you weren't going to be his sister-in-law. Did you tell him this afternoon?"

"No. He'll find out soon enough from his mother or Phillip. Oh, I hate myself for being such a coward," Anthea burst out. "I should have told them all in person—Aunt Harriet and Julian and Fanny and the children—before I left Ashby House. I at least owed them that. But instead I wrote them a letter."

"You were very fond of the Montville family, weren't you, Anthea? And they of you."

"Yes, of course. They were all so warm and loving, they made me feel at home with them from the start. They *are* the only family that I have now, Karl."

"But you've really only known them for a very short time. And you've lived in England only a few months. Anthea, you mustn't let your fondness for your cousins blind you to the fact that you belong in Vienna." Karl rose, setting down his wineglass, and, pulling Anthea to her feet, folded her into his arms. "My dearest, loveliest girl," he murmured against her hair. "Let me take you home. And when we get there, marry me. I'll make you happy, Anthea. I'll devote my whole life to keeping every sorrow away from you."

For a few moments Anthea allowed herself to be cradled in Karl's arms. She had always recognized the pull of his sensuality. She knew, too, that while there was nothing very deep in his character, his lively charm, his amused tolerance for the foibles of mankind would make him a perfect partner if she chose to reign over the ranks of imperial Viennese society. In effect—and to put it grossly—he would be trading his charm for her money. But then, she had far more than enough money for both of them.

She pulled herself away from him. "No, Karl. Do you remember my telling you once that I didn't intend to marry again? I changed my mind when I became betrothed to Phillip Montville, and it didn't work out, because I just didn't love him. Or not enough, at any rate. And I'm sorry, Karl, but I don't love you, either." She lifted her hand with a smile. "And before you deluge me with protests of undying devotion, please do be honest and admit that, while you may indeed be very fond of me, you're even fonder of my fortune!"

Shrugging, Karl returned to his chair and reached for his wineglass. "I could assure you that your money means nothing to me," he observed with a philosophical grin. "But of course you wouldn't believe me, and rightly so. And I really am very fond of you. If it isn't love, it's the very best that I can muster up. But what you want is the grand passion you felt for that fellow Lyndock, and between the two of us, my dear, beautiful love, that isn't in the cards."

Anthea rose abruptly and walked to the window. "You're being impertinent again, Karl, and not very kind. But you are right about one thing: I really don't belong here in England. I'll be very happy to have your escort back to Vienna. It will take me a few days to get packed up and to make arrangements with my bankers."

Karl glanced out the window at the curricle being driven at breakneck speed past Anthea's berlin. "I do hope that the driver's errand is a life and death matter," he observed. "Otherwise, that fellow is risking his life for nothing."

From her seat beside Hannah, Anthea looked up without much interest. She had sat for most of the long day's journey—it was over 70 miles from London to Dover—in sombre silence, paying little attention to her surroundings. They had just passed over the Medway, going through the twin towns of Rochester and Chatham, and were climbing the higher ground toward Sittingbourne.

"Look at that," exclaimed Karl suddenly. "The fellow is deliberately blocking our way. Could he be a highwayman?"

194

Anthea craned her neck toward the window. "Oh, I'm sure that highway robbery is a thing of the past. And I certainly never heard of a highwayman operating out of a curricle," she was saying nervously, when the door of the berlin was wrenched open. "Lord Lyndock!" she gasped.

"What's the meaning of this outrage, my lord?" demanded Karl angrily.

Lyndock's jaw was set firmly and his usually laughing eyes were hard as flint as he said, "Anthea, I must talk to you."

Speaking rather more calmly than she felt, Anthea said, "I'm sorry, but we can have nothing to say to each other. Please move your curricle, my lord. You're delaying us from reaching Dover in good time before darkness."

"With respect, I must insist."

"Her Serene Highness has already indicated that she doesn't wish to speak to you," snapped Karl.

Throwing Karl the merest flick of a glance, Lyndock looked into Anthea's eyes. "I have something very important to say to you. I hardly think that you will be so unfair as to refuse me a hearing. After that—" He shrugged. "I will, naturally, do nothing more to impede your journey."

Anthea bit her lip. "Very well," she said at last. "Karl, Hannah, would you leave us, please? It won't be for long. Whatever Lord Lyndock has to say, it can't be of any great importance."

"Very well, my dear," said Karl unwillingly. "Mind, I don't think this is at all wise. I insist that you leave the door of the berlin open, so that you can call if you need me."

When Karl had left with Hannah, Lyndock took their place. He gave Anthea a strained smile, saying, "I see that you've already arrived at a verdict. But never mind, I've never shied away from an uphill fight. I wasn't at all sure, you know, that I would catch up with you before you arrived in Dover. Yesterday, when I heard that you and Phillip Montville were not going to be married after all"—he nodded at her startled expression—"Oh, yes, your Aunt Harriet broke the news in strictest confidence to several of her closest cronies, and it was common knowledge all over the county in a matter of hours. Anyway, minutes after I heard the news—well, not much more than half an hour later—I started for London. This morning I enquired at every leading hotel in the city, only to be told at the Pulteney that you had just left for the Continent. I had to guess whether you were making for Dover, Brighton or Southampton. Luckily, I chose Dover. But I don't think that any of the teams I used will ever be the same again. I drove my horses unmercifully."

Anthea raised an eyebrow. "I see. I'm sure that you'll tell me what impelled you to behave so very oddly."

Catching her shoulder, Lyndock shook her roughly. "Because, my darling, adorable, stubborn Serene Highness, I was determined that, since you had come to your senses and decided not to marry Phillip, you were jolly well going to marry me."

Struggling to free herself, Anthea said scornfully, "I fail to see by what twisted logic, my lord, you could ever imagine that I would consent to be your wife."

"Imagination has nothing to do with it. I knew that you once loved me as passionately, as completely as I loved you and that you've never stopped loving me, even though you jilted me practically at the altar."

"And for a very good reason," Anthea flashed. "You were a professional heartbreaker. You had already driven one young girl to attempted suicide, you nearly ruined my cousin Fanny's life and I made up my mind that you weren't going to add me to your victims."

Lyndock shook her again. "Will you listen to me, Anthea? I was never a 'professional heartbreaker.' I *was* a flirt, I admit it. In the days before I succeeded to my uncle's title—and recall, no one would have given a fig for my chances of inheriting: My uncle was in the prime of life and his son was a great, strapping, healthy specimen—well, as I say, in those days when I was plain Major Stretton, I was a very poor matrimonial prospect. No careful mother would have allowed me anywhere near her eligible daughter. So flirting was my only romantic outlet. And I enjoyed it, I thought of it as a delightful game, but I never intended to hurt anyone. I see now that I shouldn't have paid my attentions to Lady Henrietta, but I had no idea how unstable the girl was, or how seriously she was interpreting my advances. As for Fanny, I swear that I thought of her only as the appealing neighbourhood youngster that I used to meet out riding of a morning back in Rutland. The moment that I became aware that Fanny's feelings were seriously involved, I dropped all contact with her."

Lyndock put out his hand to her. "I may have been unthinking, or careless, even selfish, Anthea, but surely you aren't going to keep punishing me for what amounts to a few mistakes of judgement, for what almost every young blade does before he finally settles down?"

"A few mistakes in judgement?" snapped Anthea. To her horror, she found herself adding, "Your mistress, Lady Fenwick, describes your behaviour rather differently."

Lyndock looked taken aback. "But she isn't my—it's true that I once had an affair with Sarah Fenwick, and I'm sorry that you've found out about it. But surely you wouldn't have expected me to tell you about her? I don't know what the custom is in Vienna, but here in England it's just not done, discussing your former mistress with the woman you intend to marry."

At this mixture of wounded innocence and sarcasm, Anthea's long pent-up anger exploded. "I don't care a fig about your relationship with Lady Fenwick, past or present. But why did you feel it necessary to discuss all your love affairs with your mistress? To make fun of poor little Fanny's pathetic attachment to you? To laugh with Sarah Fenwick about every detail of our encounter in the Ligurian Alps? To scheme to restore your family fortunes by marrying a wealthy widow without bothering to tell her that you were fonder of her money than of her person?"

Lyndock shot out a hand to grasp her shoulder in a grip that bit into her flesh. "Explain yourself, Anthea."

Regretting her angry outburst even before the words were out of her mouth, Anthea turned her head away. "It doesn't matter, Lord Lyndock. Just go away, please."

"Not until I get to the bottom of this. What did Sarah Fenwick say to you, Anthea? I'll get it out of you if we have to spend the night together in this carriage."

Turning to face him, Anthea removed his hand from her shoulder. "I would much rather not discuss such a distasteful subject, but if doing so will persuade you to leave me to continue my journey . . ." She shrugged. Briefly, in a cold, dry monotone, she outlined the details of her encounter with Lady Fenwick.

"My God, Anthea," exclaimed Lyndock in a choked voice when she had finished. "If that's that you thought of me, no wonder you broke off our engagement. But how could you believe such appalling lies?"

"Lies?" Anthea stared at him. "Do you deny that you talked to Sarah Fenwick about both Fanny and myself? How else could she have known that you once told Fanny that you would wait for her to grow up? How else could she know that you rescued me from bandits and that we had supper together in that wretched little inn?"

Lyndock set his chin. "I still say that Lady Fenwick lied. I can explain it all to you if you'll just listen. And you will listen," he added grimly, as Anthea, shaking her head, reached for the carriage door. "Just hear me out," he said, his harsh tones softening. "If then you don't believe me, I'll leave, and never bother you again."

"Very well. I'll listen."

Speaking rapidly, as though he feared that Anthea might cut him off before he finished, Lyndock began, "It's true that I had a brief affair with Sarah Fenwick. It was nothing serious, She's— forgive me for sounding common—she's a very available woman. I've not had anything to do with her since you arrived in London. Frankly, she seemed like very damaged goods once I'd met you again. But Sarah didn't like being dropped. She prefers to do the jilting herself. She kept sending me messages to come see her.

Finally I did meet with her, hoping to end the affair gracefully. She went into hysterics when I told her that I couldn't see her again. She accused me of dropping her for the opportunity to marry a wealthy wife. Anthea, I felt that I had to tell her the truth about us, to prevent her from spreading it all over London that I was marrying you for your fortune. Yes, I did describe our meeting in the Alps, but only to convince Sarah Fenwick that I had fallen head over heels in love with you long before I knew who you really were. But I swear to you that I never talked with her about any of my relations with other women. I vaguely remember telling Fanny Montville, just in fun, that I would wait for her to grow up, but I certainly never mentioned the remark to Sarah. And as for 'restoring my family fortunes' by marrying you—well, I'm glad that you're wealthy, my girl, but you and I could live comfortably on my estate for the rest of our lives even if you didn't have a penny.''

''Lady Fenwick said that your cousin had nearly bankrupted the Lyndock estate—and Aunt Harriet agreed that he was a fearful wastrel,'' said Anthea almost absentmindedly as she cast her mind back over her conversation with Sarah Fenwick. Her first instinct had been to disbelieve the woman. It was only Fenwick's seemingly intimate knowledge of Lyndock's relations with both Anthea and Fanny that had caused Anthea to waver in her skepticism. However, building on the foundation of Lyndock's brief account, Fenwick could easily have amplified the details of Anthea's adventure in the Ligurian Alps to make it seem that she had far greater knowledge of the episode than she in fact possessed. As for Fanny, she had informed Anthea of Lyndock's laughing promise to ''wait for her,'' and it was probable that the talkative youngster had also revealed the details of her presumed romance with Lyndock to all her young friends. In a gossipy and self-contained London society, it would not have been difficult for Sarah Fenwick to learn all about Fanny's infatuation with Lyndock.

She had always had difficulty in seeing Lyndock as he really was, Anthea thought suddenly. His extraordinary good looks, his beguiling charm, had prejudiced her against him from the very beginning of their acquaintance, when she had viewed him through the distortion of her painful memories of her irresponsible, selfish father. Later, as she had begun to fall helplessly in love with Lyndock, she had pushed these first impressions to the back of her mind. But then came Lady Fenwick's spiteful innuendos, so soon after Anthea's disturbing meeting with poor Henrietta Orwell. Anthea's belief in Lyndock's love for her, her very confidence in herself as a woman, had been shattered.

"Anthea, did you hear me? I said that my cousin Harry did his very best to consume the family fortune, but he didn't live quite long enough to accomplish it. The estate will need careful management for a few years, but it's basically sound. Here's proof, if you like."

Anthea stared at the document that Lyndock had thrust into her hands.

"It's the deed to the Hampton estate, including the village of Upton," Lyndock explained. "I'd thought of giving it to you as a wedding present, but then I realized that Montville wouldn't like that above half."

"But I tried to buy the property," Anthea exclaimed. "Under an assumed name, of course. Phillip told my lawyer that he wouldn't even discuss the offer."

"Phillip always was closemouthed. He was already negotiating the sale with my lawyer—not that he knew that he was selling to me. I used an assumed name, too. Phillip thinks that the new owner is one Artemus Smith of Lancastershire. But that's not important. I think that you'll agree that I'm by no means a pauper."

Anthea looked at him with a faint smile. "I really don't care about that, my lord. As I remarked to myself the other day—in connection with Karl, actually!—I have enough money for both of us!"

"Anthea! Do you mean . . . ?"

"Yes, I will marry you, Geoffrey. But I give you fair notice: I have no intention of allowing you to become a domestic tyrant of the first water. I expect our marriage to be more like a partnership—'' But whatever else Anthea had intended to say was speedily forgotten as Lyndock's hungry lips descended on hers.

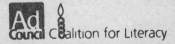